I0738336

# BOOKS BY JOHN SANFORD

## NOVELS AND STORIES

1933: *The Water Wheel*, Dragon (reissued 2020 by Tough Poets)

1935: *The Old Man's Place*, Albert & Charles Boni (reissued 1953 by Permabooks; 1957 as *The Hard Guys by Signet*; 2021 by Brash)

1939: *Seventy Times Seven*, Knopf (reissued 1954 & 1957 as *Make My Bed in Hell* by Avon; 2021 by Brash as *Make My Bed in Hell*)

1943: *The People from Heaven*, Harcourt, Brace (reissued 1995 by University of Illinois)

1951: *A Man Without Shoes*, Plantin (reissued 1982 by Black Sparrow; 2013 by Bloomsbury Reader [e-book])

1953: *The Land that Touches Mine*, Doubleday & Jonathan Cape (reissued 2021 by Tough Poets)

1964: *Every Island Fled Away*, Norton

1967: *The $300 Man*, Prentice-Hall

1976: *Adirondack Stories*, Capra

## CREATIVE INTERPRETATIONS OF HISTORY

1975: *A More Goodly Country*, Horizon

1977: *View from this Wilderness*, Capra

1980: *To Feed Their Hopes*, University of Illinois (reissued 1995 as *A Book of American Women* by University of Illinois)

1984: *The Winters of that Country*, Black Sparrow

1997: *Intruders in Paradise*, University of Illinois

## AUTOBIOGRAPHY AND MEMOIR

1984: *William Carlos Williams/John Sanford: A Correspondence*, Oyster

1985: *The Color of the Air*, Black Sparrow

1986: *The Waters of Darkness*, Black Sparrow

1987: *A Very Good Land to Fall With*, Black Sparrow

1989: *A Walk in the Fire*, Black Sparrow

1991: *The Season, It Was Winter*, Black Sparrow

1993: *Maggie: A Love Story*, Barricade (reissued 2013 by Bloomsbury Reader [e-book])

1994: *The View from Mt. Morris*, Barricade

1995: *We Have a Little Sister*, Capra

2003: *A Palace of Silver*, Capra (reissued 2013 by Bloomsbury Reader [e-book])

2021: *Speaking in an Empty Room: The Selected Letters of John Sanford*, Tough Poets

MR. LINCOLN: ". . . I undertook
to rebuke a man for foreclosing
a mortgage on a neighbor in distress.
I fear I was rather blunt, for the
man was far from new to the fault,
and unless my memory serves me ill,
I named him by his rightful name,
a ground-hog. He said, 'I ain't so
grabby, Abe. I only want the land that
touches mine . . .'"

# THE LAND THAT TOUCHES MINE

## A NOVEL BY JOHN SANFORD

Tough Poets Press
Arlington, Massachusetts

The characters and the incidents in this book
are entirely the product of the author's imagination
and have no relation to any person or event in real life.

Copyright © 1953 by John Sanford
Copyright © renewed 1981 by John Sanford
Introduction copyright © 2021 by Jack Mearns

Cover photo circa 1938 by Rondal Partridge (1917–2015),
National Archives and Records Administration,
Washington, DC.

All rights reserved, including the right to reproduce
this book or portions thereof in any form.

ISBN 978-0-578-93795-3

This edition published with permission from
the Estate of John Sanford in 2021 by:

Tough Poets Press
Arlington, Massachusetts 02476
U.S.A.

www.toughpoets.com

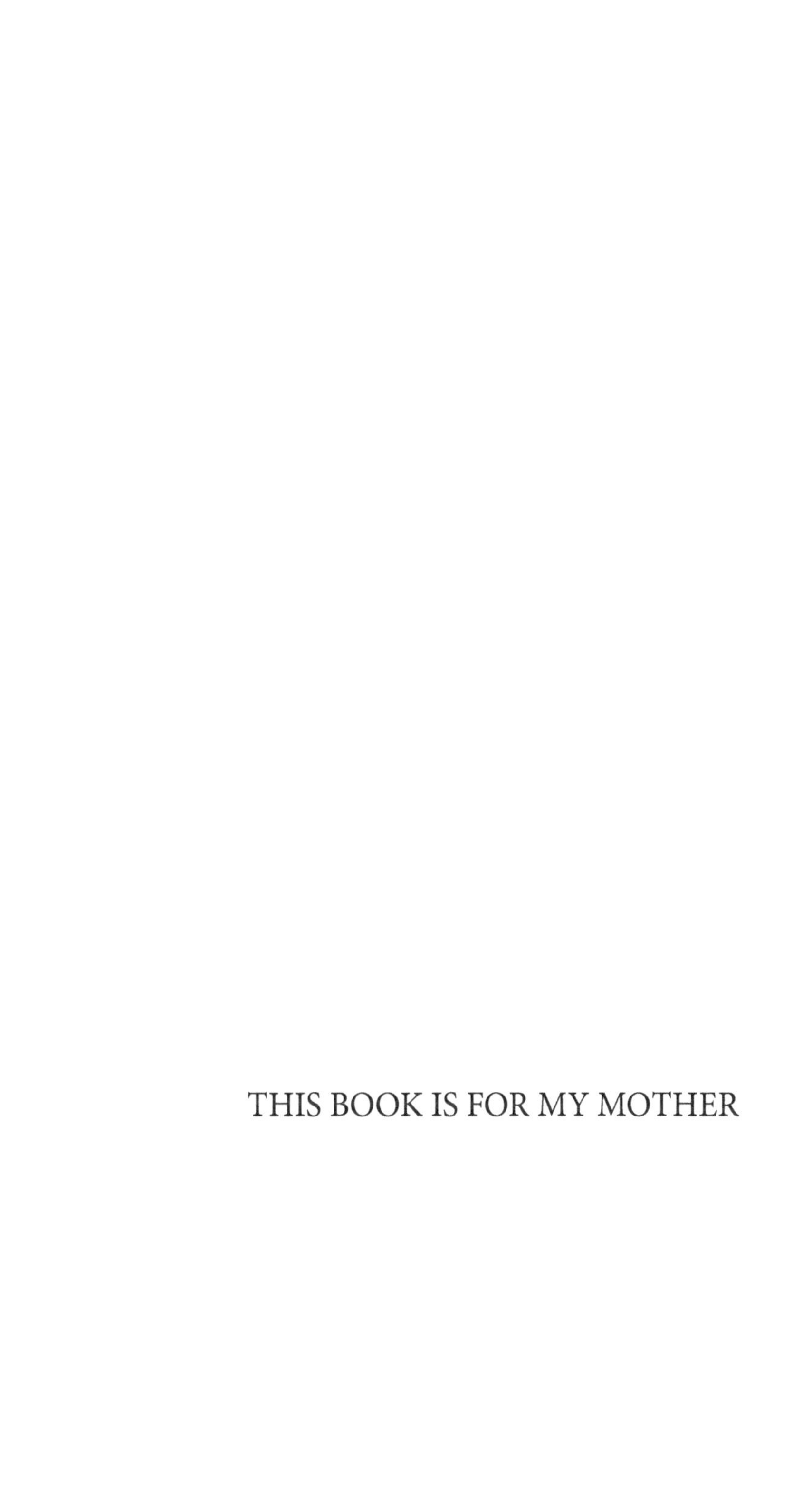

THIS BOOK IS FOR MY MOTHER

# INTRODUCTION

Americans today are perhaps as deeply divided as they have ever been. People across the political spectrum have lost trust in the nation—"America" no longer represents a unifying credo. For some, the disillusionment is so severe that they yearn to abandon or to secede from the country. For Americans racked by such bitter alienation—whether they are literally or only figuratively eyeing the exits—John Sanford's 1953 novel *The Land that Touches Mine* may provide a surprisingly incisive touchstone in these troubled times.

Surprising because, on the surface, *The Land that Touches Mine* could be discounted as an artifact. It is a proletarian novel, written—well past the days when such novels were in vogue—in the wake of World War Two and published under the cloud of the McCarthy era Blacklist. Its author remained an unrepentant Communist, whose vision of a Soviet-style egalitarian society was undimmed by revelations of Stalinist purges that led many contemporaries to renounce the Party. Even until his death at age 98 in 2003, Sanford held fast to his lament that America's ascendancy has been tarnished by the inequities between rich and poor, between the ruling class and the ruled. But only one who genuinely subscribed to the promise of America could deplore so deeply the country's failure to fulfill its covenant with its citizenry.

In *The Land that Touches Mine*, Stan Clarke—an Army deserter—grapples with profound ambivalence about America. On the one hand, Clarke embraces the ideal of America. On the other hand, he feels abashed by how far America has fallen short of its founding principles, and by the weight of cruelty America has unleashed on the unfortunate in the name of progress. In Clarke's eyes, America's moral failure has diminished the nation of his birth:

The wonder of the world, they called us, the blazing blinding wonder, but are we the wonder now or only a photograph of the sun? No square mile we began with is missing, no river, no plain, no inch of coast-line, no fine word we spoke kneeling alone or standing before all, and what we had was fruitful, and it multiplied—the square miles, the rivers, the words, the riches—and in time we came to own the earth and all that the earth contained, and still hungering much, we lost much more, for what are we profited if we gain the whole world and lose its people? Vaster now than ever, stronger, flashier, louder, even so we've dwindled in their eyes, and they say, "Beware of those who started with slogans and ended with ads. Beware of those conceived in liberty and dedicated to dividends. Beware of Christers bearing merchandise."

Clarke is caught in a dilemma: he cannot surrender himself to serving an America he has no faith in; yet neither can he abandon it.

*The Land that Touches Mine*—initially titled *The Bandage*—had its origin during World War Two, when Sanford gave a lift to a hitchhiking soldier whose hand was swaddled in gauze. Afterward, Sanford wondered: what if the bandage was a sham; what if the soldier was a deserter? This brief encounter seeded *Land*, which follows Clarke's journey, on the run from both the law and his own conscience. The second source of the novel was a newspaper story Sanford had come across about orphaned brothers who were pitted against each other in a footrace, the winner of which would be adopted. By giving Clarke this backstory, Sanford made *The Land that Touches Mine* a tale about a deserter who had been deserted, himself—by his family and, on a broader level, by his homeland.

The choice of an orphan protagonist echoes Sanford's own childhood. As the first-born, he was doted on by his mother. However, following an extended illness his mother died when Sanford was ten years old. Afterward, his mother's relatives battled his father for the boy's loyalty and affection. This family conflict left Sanford feeling estranged and homeless. It is also telling that Sanford made Clarke a defrocked teacher of history, as Sanford had a lifelong fascination with the subject. One of the few possessions he retained from his youth was a gift from his mother—R. S. Ewing's 1903 children's book, *Patriotic America*. Sanford would grow up to be an author consumed with history. Starting with his first, 1933's *The Water Wheel*, Sanford wove historical interludes into his novels. Over time, these historical elements dominated his writing.

*The Land that Touches Mine* begins with a free verse passage about the Pilgrims' spilling "savage blood" on the beach during their first hour ashore. That fundamental, internecine competition adumbrates Clarke's being pitted against his brother in their race for adoption. Sanford roots this brother-versus-brother contest in the American grain. As the adoptive father—who will take just one boy home—puts it,

> So when I say I'm leaving the choice to you, I mean you both want what only one of you can have, a situation that this life specializes in, and to put it as plain as I can, one of you simply has to beat the other out of it. It's brother against brother for real this time, but what's the history of all the world if not brother against brother under different names? The strong ones win from the weak, the smart from the foolish, the losers are always brothers. I hate to teach you such a terrible lesson, but it's only what I found out myself through bitter experience. . . . Here's how another winner and another loser will be added to the list.

Clarke is haunted by the disappearance of his brother, who never stopped running after losing the race. And since that day, Stan

Clarke also has never stopped running.

In *The Land that Touches Mine*, we find Clarke on the run from the war. Is he running out of fear—exemplified by his bandaged hand, a white badge of cowardice—or based on principle? He yearns to break free from the burden of a shameful history—both his own and the nation's. Clarke hates what America has come to represent:

> This country is heavy laden with its own ruination. . . . It's sick and sore all over, it's dead in some spots and dying in the rest, and it ought to be wheezing its last in some ditch instead of bellowing about a liberty it gives only to the rich and the son of a bitch.

Will Clarke ultimately permit himself to slip across the border to freedom in Mexico? Or will he remain, even if remaining costs him his liberty? Sanford writes: "The harpoons of history were in him to stay. No place on earth, neither here nor at a distance, offered escape, and to seek it further, by a mile or by miles in the thousands, would be to flee fire only to freeze."

Expatriation was a preoccupation in Sanford's writing from the beginning. In *The Water Wheel*, the protagonist flees New York for England, vowing never to come back. He thinks, *"Christ, how I hate this country. Im going to leave it some day. Im sick of it, the people, the ways, the noise. I hate it. I mean the cities. Ill blow one of these days. I feel it coming on. Ive felt it for months."* He envies Philip Nolan, the Man without a Country, whose expulsion for cursing America Sanford dramatized in a lengthy pastiche. But *The Water Wheel*'s protagonist finds he cannot renounce his motherland; he returns. Sanford makes the link between *The Water Wheel*'s and *The Land That Touches Mine*'s obsessions explicit when he has Clarke think: "Gettysburg: Lincoln: Everett: Hale: *Philip Nolan!*—and the soldier shook his head in bone-deep despair as he tried hopelessly to deny that soon he too would be a man without a country."

In addition to the precedents *The Land that Touches Mine* builds on in its author's youth, it is fascinating how the novel, written in the late 1940s, before the Blacklist, would so accurately presage the author's own crisis over whether to repudiate the America that banished him. Just as Stan Clarke is fired from his teaching job for propounding a version of history that questions the benign national myth extolled by the mainstream—"the same lies that other liars taught me"—Sanford found himself shunned for his vehement dissent from American orthodoxy. But, like *The Water Wheel*'s protagonist, Sanford could not turn his back on America despite its pernicious legacy. If Sanford was to better this country, he would have to do so from within it.

In addition to history, landscape and climate dominate *The Land that Touches Mine.* Sanford imprisons Clarke's psychic stasis in a straitjacket of environment, which paralyzes him. Clarke finds himself in the purgatorial desert town of El Centro, California, "where God gets His spare parts for hell." He arrives during its Hundred Days, the months-long summer stretch when the thermometer daily tops one hundred degrees. The oppressive heat is like a malign figure of authority, as described by the war widow whose life becomes entwined with Clarke's, Eugenia Bell:

> We get ready to fry by shedding our clothes. First your slip goes, then your brassiere, then your drawers and stockings, then your jewelry, the junk and the wedding-ring, and finally even your hairpins and your make-up, and you go about in sandals and the sheerest dress you own, and nothing else. For a couple of days, you try and remember not to stand between a man and the sun, but with your blood thinned out to a kind of gas, you're light in the head, and it's just too much work to worry, and then you don't care any more where you stand, and you stand where you happen to be standing,

> and if any bastard's horny enough to look through you,
> you let him look and cook to an ash. It's a free show for a
> hundred days, but that's all it is, is a show, because if any
> hot-ike ever laid a hand on you, you'd ram a nail-file in
> his eye. You sweat when you move, you sweat when you
> sit still, you sweat when you sleep, when you eat, when
> you only breathe in and breathe out, and to have a man
> put himself against you, to have him kiss you and lay
> with you, even only to *think* about it, it's enough to make
> you think you ran out of sweat, and you were starting to
> sweat blood.

The palpable heat is an inescapable hand that restrains and torments the characters.

Though Sanford had never been to El Centro, himself, he absorbed the town's climate from tales told him by his wife, the screenwriter Marguerite Roberts, who lived there briefly after leaving her native Colorado. In fact, many aspects of Eugenia's backstory were adapted from Roberts's life, which Sanford would later dramatize in his unjustly overlooked *We Have a Little Sister*. Sanford had met Roberts at Paramount Studios in 1936—both of them having made exceptional journeys to arrive in the glamorous oasis of Depression-era Hollywood. Paramount brought Sanford from New York on the basis of his second novel, *The Old Man's Place*—a gritty, violent tale that drew favorable comparisons to Ernest Hemingway, Erskine Caldwell and James M. Cain.

Sanford's tenure as a scriptwriter at Paramount was undistinguished. He received no screen credits and was let go after his contract year was up. However, his union with "Maggie" Roberts, whom he would marry in 1938, lasted over fifty years. Roberts would soon become one of the industry's highest paid screenwriters at Metro-Goldwyn-Mayer, penning scripts for the studio's A-list stars. She was also Sanford's staunchest supporter. Through Roberts' patronage, Sanford was freed from the constraint most authors face: having to sell books to make a living. He was able to write whatever he pleased without concern for sales.

During the late '30s, Sanford was recruited to join the Hollywood wing of the Communist Party. Soon, the Sanfords' social life was dominated by this affiliation—gatherings at members' houses, trips to the beach. But Party officials told Sanford that his wife, as an outsider, was a threat: she would either have to join or else be excluded from Party events. Though apolitical, Roberts chose to join. "I want to be with you," Sanford recalled her saying. Sanford did not stop her—much to his later regret—because, if he truly believed in the Cause, shouldn't he risk everything for it, including his own wife? Even though Roberts shortly broke with the Party—disenchanted with the petty greed and squabbles of the comrades—her brief membership would cost her dearly when the Blacklist was imposed.

For his C.P. membership card, Sanford picked the *nom de guerre* Starry Vere, the captain from Herman Melville's *Billy Budd*. The choice reveals Sanford's affinity for a Vere-like intransigence. Vere says of his duty to condemn the beloved sailor Billy: "However pitilessly that law may operate, we nevertheless adhere to it and administer it . . . let not warm hearts betray heads that should be cool . . . private conscience should . . . yield to that imperial one." When world events led many members to break ranks—like Stalin's purges or the Hitler-Stalin pact—Sanford redoubled his dedication to the Party. Through personal humiliations—like being demoted to the Party's housewives group, because he was not a working screenwriter—Sanford remained loyal. Decades later, even the break-up of the Soviet Union would not dim his devotion to his communist ideals.

Sanford's third novel, *Seventy Times Seven*, was already underway by the time he joined the Party. As a consequence, its themes are more ethical than political. In this novel, one winter morn-

14

ing Aaron Platt finds that the rival of his youth, Tom Paulhan, has crawled into his barn for shelter and is now freezing to death. Platt lets Paulhan die. The book plumbs the question of how much responsibility one has for one's fellow man, and it roots the protagonist's willful neglect not only in the personal history shared by the two men but also in the history of the United States. For it is in the brutal national legacy that Sanford finds the ultimate source of Americans' individual cruelty.

A central theme in *Seventy Times Seven* that is repeated in *The Land that Touches Mine* is a pairing of men—a have juxtaposed with a have-not. Platt's youth was ravaged by an abusive father, and his adulthood is a Sisyphean struggle to eke a living out of the rocky fields that are his meager legacy. Paulhan's life, on the other hand, is one of a carefree vagabond. Platt is the town pariah, whereas Paulhan is embraced by all. Platt endures a loveless marriage, while Paulhan abandons his own wife—the woman of Platt's dreams—leaving her only one way to support herself . . . to become the town whore. To explain his letting Paulhan die, Platt decries that his rival "had everything I ever wanted, and look what he went and done with it." In *Land*, Stan Clarke is the have, who has beaten out his own brother to win the greatest prize: a home and family.

Another parallel between *The Land that Touches Mine* and *Seventy Times Seven* is a character who is compelled to roam by his inability to bear the weight of the nation's violent and bloody past. Tom Paulhan explains the impetus for his wanderlust:

> *I want this—I want only to know that I shall hear no voices, that I shall see no movement, that I shall fear no invasion of my mobile space in the void. Cut me off from the long tradition of trespass. Dismiss me from history. . . .*

But Paulhan cannot outrun history—his own or the nation's—and his return home leads to a solitary death.

There are stylistic parallels between the two books, as well. Sanford's signature was interspersing amidst his fiction episodes from American history. *Seventy Times Seven* contains, mid-narrative, a blank verse poem twenty pages in length. Sanford would later refer to these historical pieces as giving the color of the air, the context in which current events play out. After *Seventy Times Seven*, Sanford's preoccupation with history blended more explicitly with his politics, with incendiary results. Even the Communist Party found 1943's *The People from Heaven* too revolutionary. They tried to suppress the novel, fearing it would incite a premature racial revolt. And 1951's *A Man Without Shoes* was so radical that Sanford was forced to print it himself. It was only by a stroke of luck that *The Land that Touches Mine* found a publisher.

The search for a publisher for *The Land that Touches Mine* is intimately tied to Sanford's star-crossed quest to place *A Man Without Shoes*. *Shoes* had initially been accepted by Reynal and Hitchcock. However, following World War Two, the book no longer fit the house's conservative drift. Sanford shopped *Land* and *Shoes* around New York until they were both accepted by Appleton-Century in 1950 on his second submission there. But his rejoicing would be short-lived when, days later, the Korean War broke out and the publisher could no longer expect a readership for one book that espoused Marxist economics and another about a turncoat. Appleton voided the contract.

In 1951, Sanford and Roberts were subpoenaed to testify before the House Committee on Un-American Activities in Los Angeles. In this U.S. incarnation of the Moscow show-trial, political apostates were compelled to admit to holding beliefs the Constitution guaranteed their right to profess, and to divulge their compatriots. Sanford took the Fifth Amendment when asked about his affiliations. Roberts asserted that she was not currently a member of the Communist Party but took the Fifth when asked if she had ever been. Both refused to name names; both were blacklisted. For Sanford, the Blacklist had no practical effect. But for Roberts the consequences were immense. She had just signed a five-year deal with M-G-M; reluctantly, the studio let her go. After more than a decade as a contract writer at Metro, she was no longer employable in Hollywood. Roberts would spend the next ten years unable to ply her craft, until she was hired by Columbia in 1961.

Following the Sanfords' blacklisting, they immediately left for Europe, fearing their passports would be confiscated if they delayed. The couple joylessly toured the Continent and then took an apartment in London, where Maggie attempted to find film work through expatriated Party members from the U.S. However, soon it became clear that, while other American screenwriters got assignments, Roberts was being blackballed. Dejected, the Sanfords returned to the States, where they endured a protracted internal exile, in what Sanford has described as a three-thousand-mile prison without walls.

There was one positive result of the Europe trip, though. Sanford had brought with him the manuscript of *The Land that Touches Mine*, which he submitted to Jonathan Cape. Sanford recalled Mr. Cape, himself, telling him, "We'll do your book, my boy!" The critic Tom Dardis reports that Cape believed *Land* "rivaled Hemingway and Faulkner in its command of narrative technique and beauty of language." Later, the head of Doubleday saw the manuscript of *The Land that Touches Mine* on Cape's desk, and Cape dared him to issue the novel in America. *Land* remains the only Sanford title published outside the U.S., as well as the only one to go into a second printing.

When *Land* came out in May of 1953, reviews were somewhat mixed. In general, reviewers praised Sanford's writing and his evocation of the brutal natural environment. In the U.S., the *New York Times* lauded the book's "muscular and economic prose," stating that "John Sanford makes a powerful bid for top billing in current fiction [with this] poetic, tragically intense tale." *Kirkus Reviews* noted its "style marked by both understatement and violence," concluding, "still hero (and the author) refuse to give up the patina of what used to be called the American Dream."

In the U.K., the *New Statesman* compared Sanford's use of language to William Faulkner's *Soldier's Pay* and Malcolm Lowry's *Under the Volcano*, highlighting "the italicized flashbacks that Mr. Sanford uses with such skill." The *Manchester Guardian* wrote that "the combination of the tough and the tender in the texture of the book is curiously real and satisfying." The London *Observer* called the book "as smooth and purposeful as a torpedo," while the *Literary Supplement* of the *London Times* deemed Sanford "a novelist with power, a vivid feel for language, and a wholly praiseworthy desire to avoid the well-worn ruts of the novel." The *Irish Times* wrote: "one is swept away by the emotional and imaginative accuracy of [the] prose. . . . Mr. Sanford writes very well indeed. His dialogue has a cutting edge and a flash of poetry's gunpowder. What a pleasure it is to encounter a writer who is born to his trade and handles words as though they are fresh and new!"

Although the Blacklist did not prohibit Sanford from writing, it nonetheless cast a heavy pall over his life and work. In his autobiography, Sanford recounts witnessing how sorely Maggie suffered while barred from Hollywood. Though he made efforts to write, he found he could not devote himself fully to his craft while Maggie was silenced. During the mid-'50s, Sanford started and abandoned a sequel to *A Man Without Shoes* called *The Big Train*. Even reprinting pulp paperback editions of the non-political *The Old Man's Place* and *Seventy Times Seven* was a tenuous venture, because—as Dardis writes—"the name Sanford was so unacceptable to" publishers during the Blacklist period.

The themes and characters of *The Land that Touches Mine* would repeat in Sanford's next two novels. In 1964's *Every Island Fled Away,* Sanford anticipated the political turmoil that would engulf the country in the next few years. Its plot revolves around a small Northern California town that is split by a young man's refusal to register for the draft. The moral center of the book, who sits in judgment over the townspeople, is a minister who happens to be the race-losing brother from *Land*. And in 1967's *The $300 Man*, the protagonist is a returned soldier, who seeks to make amends to the man drafted in his place, after he had initially received a fraudulent medical deferment.

Along with *The Water Wheel*—an overtly autobiographical book—*The Land that Touches Mine* is Sanford's most personal novel. Both books' protagonists are grappling with who they are. In *Land*, Sanford trenchantly describes this process of extreme self-examination: "You have to pick away at yourself till you find the thread that unravels you." He symbolizes abrading the superficial layers of the self in the soldier's removing the bandage that conceals his true identity: "He stripped [it] away quickly, dropping whorling yards of it on the floor before his hand came wholly exposed."

Both novels teem with self-loathing: their protagonists verbally flay themselves before love interests, trying to convince the women they are fundamentally tainted. In *The Water Wheel*, Sanford the character states: "You couldn't think me lower than I know I am." In *Land*, Sanford the author seems to acknowledge that his motivation to create works that foment radical political reform arises from self-detestation: "That's the big trouble in this world . . . people hating themselves. They can't stand being like they are, so they try and change somebody else."

One of the most intimate elements of *The Land that Touches Mine* is Eugenia's confession to Stan about an exchange in which she had lashed out unjustly and deeply wounded her father:

> 'You killed my mother,' I said, and he said, 'Is that
> what you think?' I said, 'You're God damn right I do!
> You froze her to death!' He didn't say any more. He
> simply got up and walked out of the room. . . . and I

> knew . . . that I'd have to live a long life to find out how
> to hurt a man worse than I'd done already.'

After Sanford's mother's death, his mother's vindictive sister, Aunt Rae, alienated son from father by accusing the father of killing the mother with coldness. Years later, in a moment of pique, Sanford castigated his father with Rae's words, exactly as he recounts in *Land*. Sanford sought expiation by including that incident in this excoriating novel. When Sanford's father read *Land*, he pointed to this passage in the book and said, "I know what you're trying to say, Julian. I know what you're trying to say," making the filial act of contrition via novel complete.

It is also noteworthy that *The Land that Touches Mine* is Sanford's first book set in his adopted home state. During the prior decade, Sanford had gone from a feckless lawyer wishing to be a writer, who lived with his father and pilfered coins from the father's change pocket, to an author whose most recent novels were published by Knopf and Harcourt, Brace—the writing of which was enabled by the patronage of one of the ablest screenwriters in Hollywood. While composing *Land*, Sanford resided on four lush acres in the San Fernando Valley that included a fruit orchard and stables for the racehorses Maggie adored. The couple dined frequently at one of Beverly Hills's ritziest restaurants, Chasen's, where their favorite waiter always bid Maggie adieu with "Dream of little fat angels." The distance between Julian Shapiro's and John Sanford's lives is astounding.

Ultimately, *The Land that Touches Mine* examines the fictional selves that people create. In his peeling away Stan Clarke to reveal Steve Pierce underneath, one can also imagine the author's plumbing how valid was his transformation from New York Jew Shapiro into California suburbanite Sanford. If the persona of "John Sanford" was sheared away, would anything of substance be left beneath the fabrication? Clarke expresses this uncertainty when he removes his bandage:

> He felt as if he were being dismantled. His hand, he
> thought, so long hidden by the bandage, had been
> absorbed by it and become part of the fabric, which,
> unwound, would be found hollow, and what once had
> been flesh, bone, and blood would lie in kinks and curls,
> like used yarn, on the floor.

Heightening *Land*'s meditation on identity, Sanford split the narrative voice between the dominant third-person depiction of Clarke's present and portraying his past as Pierce with italicized flashbacks, set off by brackets, in the second person—you. Sanford would later use the second person to great effect as the narrative voice of his autobiography, evoking the sense that beneath the self we present to the world is another we conceal—perhaps even from ourselves— who is not I but you.

Over eight decades, John Sanford wrote books he hoped would spur America to become a more perfect union. Along the way, he exhausted the novel as a medium. More and more had his fiction turned to teachers and preachers as surrogates to hector readers with lectures and sermons. Finally in 1967, at the age of 63, Sanford embarked on his second career, as a writer of non-fiction. It was in this work that he arrived at his consummate voice, or rather voices—an explosion of creativity in which Sanford brought to life scores of famous and lesser-known historical folk, in verse, vignette and parable. These personal interpretations of American history span from 1975's *A More Goodly Country* to 1997's *Intruders in Paradise*. Along the way, Sanford also wrote a superb five-volume autobiography, *Scenes from the Life of an American Jew*. In these non-fiction books, Sanford wove himself into the fabric of the country.

Beyond its obsession with history and politics, Sanford's oeuvre is noteworthy because of its evocative and dynamic prose. *The Land that Touches Mine* showcases Sanford as a master of his craft:

> *It was an early-winter Sunday in Easton during your senior year, and you were standing at your window on Third Street, watching lines of <u>rain</u> fall to <u>grain</u> the air like a reel of old film. Below, you remembered, the slates of the sidewalk seemed to be <u>glassed</u>, and now and then, when a trolley <u>passed</u>, it struck blue sparks from the suspended wire. You heard slipper-heels in the hallway now, and then you heard the sibilance of paper, and on the <u>floor</u>, in a gas-lit crack under the <u>door</u>, lay a letter.*

Even if the reader is not consciously aware of the three sets of interior rhymes (underlined in the above for emphasis), the mind's ear hears them—subtly infusing Sanford's prose with lithesome musicality. No wonder Jonathan Cape and reviewers classed Sanford among Nobel Prize winners and other novelists of the first order.

John Sanford's *The Land that Touches Mine* captures both a specific place and time in mid-twentieth century California and the broader scope of American history. It shows how the present, personal moment can inextricably entwine with the nation's past. In our current deeply divided times, *Land* should reverberate with those who believe in the prospects of America but find themselves disenchanted with the nation that is their home.

The foment and uncertainty that the United States grapples with today are not new. Rather they are the fruition of a savage past. *The Land that Touches Mine* engages America's unsavory history with the dilemma: do I abandon the country, or do I persevere in an attempt to make it a better place to live? *Land* wrestles with these themes beautifully, powerfully. Ultimately Sanford—the harsh critic who defied efforts by both right and left to muzzle him—harbors hope that America's promise can be fulfilled . . . "for what it could be, not for what it is." In this way, *The Land that Touches Mine* remains relevant nearly seventy years after its publication; it deserves to be read again.

*Jack Mearns*
*May 2021*

Jack Mearns is a professor of psychology at California State University, Fullerton. He is the author of *John Sanford: An Annotated Bibliography* (Oak Knoll Press, 2008).

## BARTOLOMEO VANZETTI

". . . All that they say to you, all
that they have promised to you,
it was a lie, it was an illusion,
it was a cheat, it was a fraud,
it was a crime. They promised
you liberty? Where is liberty?
They promised you prosperity.
Where is prosperity? They have
promised you elevation. Where
is the elevation . . . ?"

THE LAND THAT TOUCHES MINE

## THE ONLY GOOD INDIAN

They put a landing-party on Cape Cod beach,
Sixteen men under Standish (Captain Shrimp),
And from their knees on now suburban sand,
They spoke Early American to an English God,
Giving hunchback thanks for His lightnings,
His horseplay with wind, the leaks He sprang,
And His blowing hot and cold from the Old World
Until they'd walked on His water to the New,
And they looked up then, their Lord to adore,
And saw, looking down with awe, barbarians
(Knickknacked devils, the Christers thought;
The people from heaven, thought the heathen),
And forgetting the rapture fresh-engraved
By their thirty-odd shinbones on the strand,
These bow-downers, these squatter sovereigns
Come only for the sake of a Jesus unadorned,
These carpetbaggers freighted with prayer
(And booze and guns and case-knife hearts),
They drew savage blood in their first hour.

# LAND'S END

[ . . . *They drew your blood too, not much, hardly the thimbleful a small bird would contain, but the drops stain the sand there yet, and no rain or tide will ever wash them away. A minor injury, you'd thought it was. What you hadn't known was that you'd begun to bleed to death. . . .* ]

On the steep instep of the Santa Lucia Range, between California 1 and the Pacific, lay an abandoned farm, of which all that remained was a wracked and rotten hay-barn, a swaybacked cave-in long peeled bare by chloride fog and the wind: whatever else had once been wood nailed foursquare with the world stood knee-high now in mounds of gangrened punk. The fields had been redeemed by sage, and the volunteer grain still grown by the rains yielded to the meadowmouse and the vole and such other vermin as had survived the stalks of sparrow-hawks and Swainsons. Always the iodine savor of kelp rose and rolled in from the swashbuckling surf, and with it often came the thin dim cry (pinwheel! pinwheel!) of gulls.

From a skiff of mildewed straw in a corner of the barn, a soldier watched the far-off Piedras Blancas flash brighten and blacken a crack in a wall. A moment before, he had been brought to the surface of sleep by a sound—a started plank, a dog-bark, a word heard and contained in a dream—but, fancied or real, the sound was not repeated, and what he listened to in the punctured dark was pulse-pound and the gunfire of breakers. The beacon made another sweep and struck silver, the bracelet on the soldier's wrist, and, passing, it left an after-image that was slow to fade: the oval tag, naming and numbering him, glowed on his mind as if wrought in neon.

[ . . . *How would you describe yourself? At what point would you begin? Would the color of your eyes come first, or the color of your liver? Or would you set out from your hair and descend, through neckband and chest-expansion, to the size of your shoes? Or would you bound yourself by inch, ounce, and year, and reveal such secret data as your sex and race and the middle initial and last-known address of your*

*God? Or would it be better to open with your place of birth (the town, the house, the floor, the room, the bed, the one particular womb) and list the marks by which your corpse might be distinguished from other corpses in a catastrophe—wens, say, or webbed feet? Or would your best approach be by way of family annals and characteristics (ever incarcerated in a mental institution?), schooling, occupation, political affiliation, and/or bank (commercial or savings?)? Or would you simply state your salary per second, make mention of your favorite sport (play a musical instrument?), list three persons acquainted with you since the Crucifixion, and fill in the blanks necessary to establish you finally as an irredeemable son of a bitch . . . ? ]*

When the soldier left the barn, the sky was still dark, and, climbing a scarp to the highway, he headed south toward Piedras Blancas. If there were houses at either hand, all were empty or blindfolded, and none reflected the flare-ups of the turning light. In the hollows of the road, a milk of mist flowed across the asphalt, but above the drifts of vapor, the stars were dazzling smithereens. A bird in the brush played a woodwind as the soldier approached, was silent while he passed, and played again when he had gone.

Behind him, he heard the drumming of a motor, and he moved aside and continued along the gravel shoulder, watching an infinite shadow that grew now from his feet. The car stopped abreast of him, and the driver leaned across the seat to say, "Which way to San Luis Obispo?"

"The way you're pointed," the soldier said.

"Give you a lift, if you want."

The soldier looked at the disembodied face afloat in the doorframe. "Why not?" he said.

The road bridged a deep draw in the downs, a fissure like the cleft of a hoof, and shelved itself on a sheer headland. From a cornice of crumbling granite, a pour of pebbles now and then bounced off the bonnet of the car, and on the fall side, far below, breakers broke as in a silent film, commotion without sound.

"You know this God damn pike?" the driver said.

"Only from a map," the soldier said.

"It looks good on a map—but what road don't?"

"I've seen worse."

"You ask me, it's a bastard," the driver said. "I say to some gas-cranker in Monterey, 'How is this Route 1?' and he says, 'It's paved.' It's paved, he tells me! Ain't that a dandy? Why, Christ, there's black-top clear to hell, if that's all you're looking for! It's paved, he says! Honest to God, them greaseballs don't care if they kill you."

"Killing is the best thing people do," the soldier said. "I'm in my work-clothes."

"That's different," the driver said. "A soldier is supposed to kill. But where's the percentage in knocking off a customer?"

"Everybody's a customer."

"The Japs, maybe? Shoot, all they ever buy is a lawnmower. Kill as many as you like. You got my permission."

"I gather you don't sell lawn-mowers."

The driver said, "Where you bound for, unless it's a military secret?"

"Home," the soldier said.

"And where would home be at?"

The soldier made a vague gesture. "Back East," he said.

"What've you got—a leave?"

"No," the soldier said, and he looked away beyond the outskirts of the lamp-line. There were few trees on the narrow piedmont, an arthritic cypress, a break of cedars, a solo oak: the rest was stock-range, rock, and a night-time merge of sea and sky. "I'm out of the service."

"Account of the hand?" the driver said, and the soldier nodded, still staring away out of the dimly lighted cube of the car. "I know you fellers hate to talk, but if you'll excuse me asking, what hap-pened?"

"I got hit," the soldier said. "A tracer caught me in the palm."

The driver squirmed, saying, "That gives me a curl. Where were you wounded—what battle, I mean?"

"Gettysburg," the soldier said.

"Well, there's no law says you have to answer."

"Gettysburg, the afternoon of the third day," the soldier said. "We bit cartridges in the Angle till our faces were as black as the stone fence. [ . . . *Pickett's fifteen thousand moved out of the Spangler Woods like lava. They had seven-eighths of a mile to go, and open ground all the way ('It isn't so hard to get there as it looks,' a Reb general said. 'I nearly made it with my brigade yesterday. The trouble is to stay. The whole Yankee army is there in a bunch.'), and the butternuts, with nothing but ripe wheat to shield them for a quarter of an hour, took a plunging fire from every fieldpiece and carbine on Cemetery Ridge, and then they were diving over the piled-up stones onto what's known as cold steel, and it wasn't long before Union blades ran a temperature of ninety-eight and some change, the exact same heat as Rebel meat on the hoof. They were there now: the trouble was to stay. . . .* ] They stayed till we flood-irrigated the wheat with their blood, and then Pickett called off the living, and they backed away still loading and firing, and there were some (I saw them) who couldn't see their sights because they were crying."

The driver said nothing for a time, occasionally glancing at the soldier and once wearing a trial smile that quickly sagged. At length, he ventured to speak, saying, "I guess guys under fire get pretty keyed up." The car was directly inland of the lighthouse now, and the vast sweeps of the reflector turned weeds and grass into momentary forests of shadow on the slopes of the range. "How many candlepower is that light, I wonder?"

"On a clear night, they can see it in Japan," the soldier said. "I was wounded at Pearl, by the way."

"You don't often meet anybody was at Pearl," the driver said. "It must've been kind of a queer feeling—to be in and out of a war in an hour."

The soldier stared down at the sea's endless siege of the earth. "Many a man was in and out in less than that," he said. "Out of the war and out of this life."

"Just how many Joes did them monkeys knock off in that massacre? Or ain't you supposed to say?"

"Thousands, I guess. Nobody's ever been told."

"The sneaky yellow apes! I bet it burned you, not to be able to get hunks with 'em."

The soldier watched the light blue-pencil the dark blue night. "They weren't apes to me," he said.

"They'll do till apes come along."

The soldier said, "I don't think you understand."

"What's to understand?" the driver said. "They sure as hell ain't human."

Anger creamed up in the soldier, collared him, and brimmed over, and, turning on the man, he said, "You don't understand, God damn you! You don't understand!"

The man bug-eyed him for an instant, and then, facing the road again, he said, "Right you are, Joe. You had to be there to understand."

The soldier moved his arm, and into the lower part of his vision came the blur of a bandage, a faint white flaw in the gloom. He covered it with his other hand, and as he did so, his fingers touched the links of his bracelet. Once more, then, the lettering and numerals of the tag became incandescent on his mind.

[ ... *How would you describe yourself? At what point would you begin ... ?* ]


[ ... *Would the color of your eyes come first, or the color of your liver ... ?* ]

Near the head of Gaviota Pass, a roadside eat-stand stood endwise to the pavement. The shack was of clapboard and plywood painted Paris green, with eaves of palm-leaves baked brown, like the shaved-down walls of the canyon. On the floor of the cut, along a twisting rut of seepage from the hills, a grove of sycamores grew, and through the morning sun and shade, a jay flew, blue and gray, and disappeared.

In the shack, a woman behind the counter dropped two slices of bread into a machine, and then, drawing a mug of coffee from an urn, she served it with a miniature milk-bottle of cream. When the toast untrapped itself, she set it before the soldier and gazed past him, saying, "Going to be a hot day, looks like." The soldier tried to butter one of the pieces of toast, but it slipped from under his bandaged hand and skated off the plate. "Why didn't you sing out?" the woman said.

"I didn't know you were a music-lover," the soldier said.

"You keep your hand under the counter, how am I supposed to know you can't use it?"

"I can catch flies with it," the soldier said. "I can shuffle cards and fix a watch with it. I can even split hairs."

The woman took the knife from him. "Sure, you can," she said. "It comes natural."

"I don't want anybody to help me."

"What should people do—sit around and watch you struggle?"

"I don't mind the sitting around," the soldier said. "But why in hell do they have to watch? [ . . . *They want the cold clench of the sphincter, the sensation of fear without danger, a dry rape. They want the shock, the mincemeat, and the shattered bone to be in you, so that you can wound them safely and only with words, and they long to say (and some say it), 'How did it happen, Joe? Where were you standing, and was it night or day, and did you bleed a lot, a little, or not at all? What did it feel like, Joe? Did you fall down, did you think you were going to die, did your whole life unreel before you, like they write about? Did you rave, did you curse, did you soil your pants? Did you call for your mother, God, or a coffin-nail? And excuse me mentioning it, Joe, but I hear that when a man's shot, he has an . . .*

*You know what I mean, don't you, Joe? Now, get undressed and show me the scar. . . .'*] Will you tell me that? Why in hell do they have to watch?"

"Where's the disgrace?" the woman said. "You lose a couple of fingers, it's the same as getting bald. We all fall apart. Nobody dies looking too sightly."

"What would you do if I came in here without teeth—chew for me?"

"If you wanted, sure," the woman said. "But I got a feeling you'd sooner eat crackers and slurp. You couldn't stand the shame of a person acting human to you. I don't know what's got into the boys this war. The last one, they done something brave, they'd talk about it. Now, you'd think being brave and getting wounded was some kind of a crime."

"I'm not brave," the soldier said. "Mighty few men are."

"This war, they hide things," the woman said. "They win a medal, and if you didn't happen to read it in the paper, you'd never know till it accidently fell out of their pocket. They win a medal, the bravest thing you can do, and they shut up. They go down in the ocean in a hunk of tin, and they fly in the air in a cardboard box, and they go out and lay in the mud and snow, and they shoot and kill and get shot and killed themselves, and finally they win a medal and come home—and what do they tell you? Nothing. Not a word. Silence. Then you say they're brave, and they get sore. What're they sore about?"

"The word 'brave,'" the soldier said. "It's a hard one to listen to when you know you're something else."

"Fighting and killing all the time, how could a soldier not be brave?"

"No uniform ever made a man immortal."

The woman seemed not to have heard. "Or could he do a brave thing without being brave himself?" she said. "Maybe only the thing has to be brave, not the person." She nodded at nothing. "I never thought of it like that before."

The soldier spun a quarter on the counter: it waltzed into a dish, curtsied, and began to die. [ . . . *The town, the house, the floor, the room, the bed, the one particular womb. . . . The pattern of the rug was worn, but a few dim lines of its border remained, and you were using them as a track for a toy engine, tin-wheeled and bent, its paint peeling and its cowcatcher gone. When you wanted it to be, though, it was still an engine, as real in your mind as any on the rails beyond the back-yard fence, and you could watch it breathe and time its heart. You made a bell-sound that only you could hear, and phantom rods began to move: the toy rattled over a yard of rug and turned turtle in a ramp of sunlight slanting from the window. You pretended to look at the dust dancing down on the wreck, but your mother was dressing herself (hiding from you), and you were looking at her, not the dust. . . .* ] As the coin went into its final flutters, he rose from the stool and walked to the door. He paused there, waiting briefly for a sensed event to happen: it failed before flowering, and he started southward down the pass.

[ . . . *Your mother said, 'Little boy, what're you thinking about . . . ?'* ]

[ . . . *You said, 'I am not thinking.'*

*'People're always thinking,' she said, 'whether they know it or not.'*

*'Well, I am thinking now,' you said. 'I am thinking about how old will I get to be when I grow up.'*

*'You know the answer to that,' she said. 'If you're good, you'll live to be a hundred.'*

*'That is a long time to be good. I am now only five years of old.'*

*'It isn't very long. It isn't very long at all.'*

*She turned away then, you remembered, and for a moment you didn't have to make believe you were trying to catch the slow but slippery dust; in the mirror, you could see the things you really wanted to touch.*

*She spoke to you over her shoulder, saying, 'Five from a hundred leaves what, little boy?'*

*All at once you felt ashamed, and, looking down so that not even your eyes could know her, you said, 'A hundred.'*

*She said, 'You know better than that, little boy.'*

*'Yes,' you said, 'but I only just started to be good.'*

*You heard her laugh, and you did your best to keep your eyes down, but it was like forcing yourself to stay under water, and you had to come up. She wasn't looking at you. She was looking at the living picture of herself that the mirror held, and she was palming her body, ironing it with her hands, and you remembered what she said to a face in the glass that you'd never before seen. 'I think I just stopped,' she said.*

*The town, the house, the floor, the room, the bed, the one particular womb. . . . ]*

The soldier sat on the sand, looking out across the channel toward Catalina. The going-down sun flung small change into the water and blazed on the long low chines of the sea's marcel. The road ran close to the beach here, but between the two rose a file of oil-derricks, each skeleton of angle-iron bones housing the walking-beam of a pump, a beating heart, and from the sump of the earth, a sewage-smell of crude came on the air. The soldier lay back, and his eyes overturned.

It was evening when a tap on his shoulder awakened him. He peered up at a man's shape against the not-yet navy sky: a club dangled from a wrist-thong, and above it, a device on a sleeve, a triangle within a circle, was dim in the near dark. "I'm the air warden for this stretch of beach," the man said. "I'm afraid you'll have to move on."

The soldier stood up, slapping himself free of sand-grains. "I was having a good dream," he said.

"It's rules: Nobody on shore after sundown."

"I dreamt that I was dreaming, and in the second dream there was a third, and in the third a fourth. I was in deep."

"I ain't out to bother people," the warden said. "But it's account of the wells. I guess they think the Japs don't know there's wells at Huntington Beach."

"I hate to give up a sweet dream," the soldier said. "Maybe I'll have it again, though."

"Things don't always add up," the warden said. "There's nothing so out of the way in a soldier being down here—not when he's got what you have." They were at the roadside now, and the derricks behind them were black on the last pastel above the horizon. "But like it says in the saying: Rules is rules."

"Well, I'll remember you," the soldier said, and, cutting the leave-taking to a gesture, he moved away.

The warden let him cover several yards before reining him in. "Wait a minute, son," he said, and he closed the gap between them. "Where you going?"

"San Diego," the soldier said.

"Expect to make it tonight?"

"It's only eighty-odd miles. Why not?"

"There ain't much traffic between here and Dago, not like in the old days."

"I don't have to be there on the dot."

"What'll you do if you get stuck?"

"Stop over wherever I'm dropped."

"You could stay here. There's no rush, you say."

"A man doesn't have to be in a rush to feel like traveling, does he?"

"The older I get, the more I think so."

"Look," the soldier said. "Are you trying to tell me I *have* to stay?"

"Why would I do that?" the warden said. "All I'm out for is to get you bedded down. No harm in that, is there?"

"None. It's a good thought."

"Then what makes you so jumpy—the hand?"

The soldier shook his head. "Not the hand so much," he said. "The bandage."

"I come home from the last war wearing a mile of it."

"Were you jumpy?"

"Christ, I was a kangaroo," the warden said. "But they calmed me down, and that's all I wanted to do for you. Come on over the station, and I'll rustle you up a cot. Don't be fooled by the club."

"I'm slept out," the soldier said.

"Another thing, its gets cold from here on south."

"If it's all the same . . . ," the soldier said.

The warden nodded, but only once up and once down. "It's all the same," he said, and this time, when the soldier moved off, he made no effort to stop him.

[ . . . *She went away one night—you'd never known where to or with whom—and when she came back, she came in a box. Your father let Carlo look at her, because Carlo was older, but you were told to think of her as you'd seen her last, and you tried, remembering two faces, her own and the one in the glass, but you knew that they were both her own, and each blurred the other, and the composite gave you nothing that you could ever recognize.*

*From the next room, you heard your father laugh and say, 'There will be no columns, no fallen crosses, no hooded urns. Our stone will be a book, a marble book, so carved that it lies open, and on facing pages, it will tell our histories, my wife's and mine: a name for each and a pair of dates—that and only that,' and again you heard his high and heartbroken laughter.*

*Your mother was buried the following day. There were two carriages—one for your father, riding alone, and one for you and Carlo. . . .*]


[ . . . *The next time, there was only one carriage, for you and*

*Carlo, and at the edge of town, it took the river-road, slicing the first grooves in a new fall of snow. The fence-rails wore ruffs of it, you remembered, and the rocks were wigged, and snowsnakes sunned themselves away on the tops of branches and the spars of power-poles. The cemetery was on a low hill a mile upstream, and the iron arch of the gate seemed to be embroidered on the Zion-blue sky.*

*Up the slope, near a mound of earth, two men were waiting. They stood bareheaded in the winter wind, their caps slung on the handles of their spades. From somewhere (the next room? the next world?), you heard a voice say, 'There will be no columns, no fallen crosses, no hooded urns,' and then clods began to make a hollow sound on the sunken box, and the voice became fainter. . . . ]*

In the front booth of a bar-and-grill, the soldier sat leaning against the painted plate-glass window. The coating had been picked at and chipped—by nails, knives, keys, coins, and cocktail sticks—until there were peepholes at eye-level framing sections of the street. Through one of these, the soldier saw a car pass, and, leaning closer, he watched it approach a barrier lowered across the road. As it came to a stop, the driver's hand, tanned dark, presented a paper to a white hand extended from a sentry-box, and then both hands disappeared. After a moment, the white hand emerged with the paper, and the brown hand accepted its return: the latter waved and withdrew; the former merely fell out of sight. The barrier then rose, and the car moved toward Mexico.

Still squinting through the hole in the paint, the soldier groped for his beer-glass. It seemed of its own accord to come within reach, and he turned to find a man seated opposite him in the booth. The man was nudging the glass with his finger, and he said, "You looked like you could use company."

The soldier drained the last spittle of his beer. "Yours?" he said.

With the edge of a match-book, the man dislodged a shred of food from between two teeth. He examined it, saying, "I'll do."

"I can find a cat-house with a sack over my head."

"I can too, and I keep it on when I go inside," the man said. "But if you have me down as a pimp, you miss by a mile. A pimp couldn't make coffee—and in wartime, not with every housewife giving it away free. You'd think it was part of the war effort." He broke a match from the book and swabbed the underside of a thumbnail. "So I'm not pimping, and now's your chance to say, 'What *have* you been doing lately?'" He struck the match and studied the flame for a moment: from its blue and yellow chalice, a glowing stamen grew. He shook the fire dead. "Don't look at me like something you blew out of your nose. Make a remark."

"The quick brown fox jumped over the lazy dogs."

"Guys like you I read like a book," the man said. "For a hundred bucks, you're past that gate out there, uniform and all."

With a fingertip, the soldier drew spokes from an axle of beer-sweat on the table-top. "You think I want over the hill?" he said.

The man rocked his head, saying, "And out."

"For what ails you, they give shots now."

"A hundred bucks, and you're in Mexico."

"What would I be doing in Mexico?"

"The same as here, minus the loose bowels."

"What happens when you tackle a patriot?"

The man laughed. "I have to chop the price," he said. "Any time a guy gives three cheers for the Red, White, and Blue, he means the national colors of Panama."

"Lucky for you I'm different, no?"

"Guys like you I read like a book."

"Panama, right or wrong!" the soldier said, and he unbuttoned one of the breast-pockets of his blouse and ejected a wallet. Flipping it open, he shoved it across the table. "You read, you say?"

"Without even moving my lips," the man said, and he delicately tipped the wallet into making a half-spin on its crease. "Army of the United States,'" he read from a small photostat under celluloid. "'Honorable Discharge. . . .'"

"Go on," the soldier said. "'This is to certify that. . . .'"

The man shut the wallet. Keeping his hand on it, he looked at a point just above the soldier's eyes, and he said, "Odd how I could be so far out. I never been that far out before." He rose now, saying, "Nice to met you, though," and he grinned. He was still grinning when he walked away.

[ . . . *The open book had been snowed under, but with a stalk of frozen grass, you reprinted its scanty legend, complete except for the final date, and two lives that now would always seem to have been birth and death only were ended—and then you and Carlo walked back to the carriage, not waiting for the last of the dirt to fall on your past. . . .* ]

I ONLY WANT THE LAND THAT TOUCHES MINE

Brothers, by these signs were we to know Him
When He returned from His journey to the sun:
He would wear a white gown, He said, a cloud
Chosen from those in the blue wigwam overhead,
And a flight of birds would bear Him company,
And rare perfumes would mull the morning airs,
And blooms would spring from sand, He said,
And cotton flourish in vivid hues, and maize
That men in pairs must portage like canoes. . . .

They came, they said, to spread the word of God,
And knowing none but Him that dwelt in the dawn,
We thought them God-sent to fathom our hearts:
They plumbed us first with beads and other trash,
And then with lead from the sticks-that-speak
A dead language, a tongue we were slow to understand;
We learned it on the long retreat from the beach
That we gave them for their knees and Jesus;
We learned it on the run to the world's end,
Where the night swims, and the day drowns,
And tides drain all they left us of the earth.

. . . A gown from the wardrobe of the sky, He said,
And spice on the wind, and flying minstrels. . . .

# LAS PALMAS DE DIOS

*[ . . . The driver went back to Red Bank along the same frozen mile of the Navesink, and, standing before the house, you and Carlo, you watched the carriage dwindle away down the leafless arbor of lindens that overreached the road. When it had turned a corner and disappeared, you started up the path toward the porch, noticing for the first time that the steps sagged a little, like a slack jaw, and you knew that you were seeing the place now as it was in fact, as you would always see it whenever it came to mind: it had grown old in hours, and, aging, it had shrunk. The ship-lap siding, white once, was gray flesh, loose and graven, and the door and upstairs eyes, compressed, expressed a fagged and mild surprise. The house had withered in a single winter afternoon, you thought, and you found yourself feeling pity for it, as if it were a living thing nearing the end of its life.*

*A man was waiting for you in the parlor, a smaller room on a smaller floor. You had never seen him before, but you knew suddenly, as if long forewarned, that something more than the house was about to end, and that as soon as the man spoke it would die.*

*He said, 'I come from the County Home. . . .'* ]

From the shade of a rock at the roadside, the soldier sat staring down east at the Salton Sink. It was late in the day, and a heat-haze, smoked out of the earth since morning, hung over the valley and paled its bolder colors, those of the sea and the vegetation, to smears of chalk. A hot wind, silt-laden, lumbered up to the summit, and in the cinder air, the baked road seemed wet and mobile, as if newly paved. Towed by its gaunt silhouette, an old Ford crawled up the last rise of asphalt from the west. The soldier climbed to his feet, but when he saw a woman at the wheel, he made no move to flag the car.

It came to a stop, however, and above its motor the sky milled as if molten. The woman opened the door, saying, "You want a ride, or do you like it here?"

"Christ in the mountains, I'm got!" the soldier said as he slid into the seat. "My blood is carbonated. I'm sweating fizz."

The woman shifted to low gear and let the car roll downgrade. "This is nothing," she said. "Wait till you're in the Sink. The hollow of God's hand, they call it. Ought to be, the hollow of His heart."

"You live down there?"

"You live where you make a living."

"What do you do about breathing?"

"People get used to anything, I guess."

"Except dying," the soldier said.

"That too. Living is good practice for it."

"What do you work at?"

"Ever hear of car-hopping? I'm a waitress at a roadhouse."

"Where—in El Centro?"

"Between there and Brawley, on the main pike. The Rancho Canada, the name is."

"What were you doing in San Diego, if that's where you're coming from?"

"Minding my own business," the woman said. "You ask a lot of questions for a person hasn't said a thing about himself. Not that I care. It just struck me."

"If there's anything you want to know, you'll ask."

"And you'll answer?"

"It all depends," the soldier said.

"That's what I thought. That's why I don't ask."

"Most people expect a story about the medal. Do you?"

"The story's always the same: somebody got hurt."

A snail of sweat crept down the soldier's chest. "You take a good attitude," he said.

"Where's the attitude? Millions of guys go crazy and start killing each other. What am I supposed to do—cheer?"

"I take it you're not in favor of this war."

"This or any," the woman said. "There's nothing in all this fighting. You lose even if you win. The country maybe can win, but not me, not since the day my husband got killed. Shot in the head, a friend of his wrote. He was sitting on the ground, leaning against a tree and smoking a cigarette, and the next minute, the next puff, he was dead—still sitting there, I suppose, and still with the cigarette in his mouth. Is that what people're born and live thirty years for—to leave their brains on a tree in some swamp? Is that what life is—dying like a swatted fly? Christ, if that's all, there better be a heaven!"

"There is," the soldier said, "but it's posted. 'No peddlers,' it says on the gate. 'No hunting or fishing.' 'No people,' it says."

All but the far rim of the Sink was now in lilac shade. On the flat floor, clustered lights rippled as if under water. "El Centro," the woman said, indicating one of the glittering shoals of shattered glass, "where God gets His spare parts for hell. Every time I see this hole from up here, I tell myself: 'Turn around! Turn around and never look back!' And then you know what I do? I keep straight smack on, like I ran on rails. What's the matter with people? Why do they stay put?"

"Some do. Some don't."

The woman said, "I tell myself: 'Jump the track and see what it's like in the ditch!'" She switched on the brights, and in the white spray, spinning sand flashed. "But I'd settle for a dime on the dollar. Things don't have to get better; they only have to get different. That's all I ask: let it be different. Or is that too God damn much too?"

The soldier said, "Even less is too much if you only ask. You have to take." He let his hand trail from the window, and, stung by pins and needles of flying grit, it felt as if it were asleep. "And for that, a lot of people need a lot of guns."

"A lot of people have them," the woman said. "What're they taking?"

"Soldiers still kill what's in front of them. Some day, though, they'll learn to look around. When that happens, you'll have your wish."

"I'm afraid I'll have to wait a long time."

"It gets better for you with every shot."

"They do enough shooting, and we'll all be dead," the woman said. She disengaged the motor, and the car coasted, whistling for the wind. "It might be a good thing. Who wants to live in a world where people'll kill you for blueberry pie, or tile toilets, or God any style, like eggs, or the right to vote for the burglar of their own choosing?"

With the remnants of the sun gone, the evening was star-salted, but the heat remained, and through a filter of silt, towns danced on the prostrate earth. "Where could a person stay in El Centro?" the soldier said. "If he wanted to lay over, I mean."

"You'd lay over about one day," the woman said. "Unless you dropped dead before dark. That happens all the time at a hundred and twenty degrees."

"A job ought to pay like a gold-mine."

The woman glanced at him. "You've got a job," she said.

"Not any more," the soldier said. "They retired me."

"Then why don't you go home?"

"Home is where you hang yourself."

"El Centro's no place for a human being to work, or even an animal," the woman said. "There ought to be only machines, especially now, when we're getting on towards the Hundred Days. That's a part of the year don't show on the calendar. It begins when the first rag-head is found laying face-down in some culvert. A heat-suicide, the paper'll say, but likely the poor slob only walked down the street in a squeaky pair of shoes. At a hundred and twenty, he could even been knocked off for not squeaking. But what's all this got to do with the price of buckwheat?"

"You were telling me why I shouldn't stay."

"Was I?" the woman said. "What the hell is it to me if you stay or go? I mightn't even stay myself." She made the sound of laughter with a straight face. "Now's the time the women start clearing out for Coronado and La Jolla—the ones with money. The others, the ones like me, we get ready to fry by shedding our clothes. First your slip goes, then your brassiere, then your drawers and stockings, then your jewelry, the junk and the wedding-ring, and finally even your hairpins and your make-up, and you go about in sandals and the sheerest dress you own, and nothing else. For a couple of days, you try and remember not to stand between a man and the sun, but with your blood thinned out to a kind of gas, you're light in the head, and it's just too much work to worry, and then you don't care any more where you stand, and you stand where you happen to be standing, and if any bastard's horny enough to look through you, you let him look and cook to an ash. It's a free show for a hundred days, but that's all it is, is a show, because if any hot-ike ever laid a hand on you, you'd ram a nail-file in his eye. You sweat when you move, you sweat when you sit still, you sweat when you sleep, when you eat, when you only breathe in and breathe out, and to have a man put himself against you, to have him kiss you and lay with you, even only to think about it, it's enough to make you think you ran out of sweat, and you were starting to sweat blood. . . . But all the same, you sometimes at night get to imagining . . . I mean, you remember times when you. . . ."

The car went a long way down the road while the soldier awaited the missing parts of speech. They were still missing when he said, "Times when you what?"

The woman said nothing in answer to the prompt, and she said little else for the many miles of descent to the flat of the Sink. The car was running through the ravelings of El Centro when she looked briefly at the soldier, saying, "Made up your mind where you want to get dropped?"

"Anywhere," he said. "I don't know the town."

The woman made a turn into a eucalyptus-lined lane, dark except for the drill of the lamps, and the tires mashed peels of bark and fallen pods, sweeping up a cough-drop flavor for the air. The lane dead-ended at the butt of a five-foot euc. A warning-eye was nailed to the stump, its glass glowing until the woman cut the lights. "It's a half a mile to the main part of town," she said.

"Well, thanks for the ride," the soldier said, and he opened the door and stepped out. "It was nice talking to you."

"Likewise. See you some more, maybe."

"Sure," he said, and he went back toward the street, his shoes sliding on skids of bark, and once, when pods rolled him away like casters, he stumbled and stopped, breathing the liniment locker-room odor of the dark. He was nearly at the road when he heard footsteps, and behind him dry leaves crackered. He turned, waiting.

"I forgot to ask," the woman said. "How's the money-situation?"

"A good thought," the soldier said. "But I happen to be loaded."

"You wouldn't be too proud, would you?"

"That kind of pride no longer wears me out."

"Well, no harm done," the woman said. "What about if you can't find a room in town? It's pretty late."

"I'll sleep somewhere. What difference does it make to you?"

"What am I supposed to say to that?"

"You're supposed to say why you take such an interest."

"I'm only trying to give you a good steer. Is that what you call an interest?"

"A couple of minutes ago, you were willing to let me walk away. Why did you change your mind?"

"You make it tough," the woman said.

"You pick me up along the road, and we talk for thirty-forty miles, and we say good-bye, and then all of a sudden you don't like the idea that the trip is over and that we're only a couple of strangers standing around somewhere in the dark."

"I hardly ever talk about my husband any more," the woman said, "and when I do, I always come to regret it. People think I'm looking for sympathy, like it wasn't Paul that died, but me. That's a pretty cruel way to make you feel when all you're after is to understand a man doing a little harmless thing like smoking a cigarette and dying in the act. I can't seem to get it out of my mind, how the cigarette and the dying went together, as if one was a punishment for the other, and I get to believing it must be the brain of an idiot running all this if you can get killed so easy out of a clear blue sky." She reached for a pendent euc-leaf and snapped its spine. "I forget what I was out to prove. Nothing, I guess, except that I hate to see you go. We can say good-bye, if you like—I'll live—only why do we have to say it here and now?"

"When would we say it—tomorrow?"

"Tomorrow. The next day. Whenever you want."

"What would we do in the meantime? Or is that making it tough too?"

The woman studied him for a moment and shook her head. "You don't ask for much," she said. "In fact, you don't actually ask for anything. But you really want a great deal, don't you? You really want it all."

"I don't want any more than you do," the soldier said. "Or any less."

"But, for Christ's sake, I *ask* for it!"

"I haven't heard you do any asking."

"You're not the type to let a word get past you," the woman said. "Or a meaning, either. You know full well what I almost told you back there in the car, but you want me to finish it. You want me to say the whole thing, and the cruder the better. If you were some big dumb hunk—a trucker, a mechanic—I maybe would understand, but you're a long chalk from that, so all I can figure is you're hard, and you want to see me crawl. I'm not the best to look at, I suppose, but even if I was the worst, you'd wait a long time for me to beg."

The soldier watched her walk away and listened to the diminishing sound of scuffed-up trash, and then he heard a screen-door gnash its springs, and afterward it was quiet again in the lane. He stood where he was for an interval, waiting for some last fraction of force to upset the balance, and in the end, rustling fronds of blue-gum leaves, he followed the path taken by the woman. The house was dark, but on the porch the coal of a cigarette wrote an orange arc. It flared into a hand of light holding the woman's face.

"Mind if I sit?" the soldier said.

"Sit. Stand. Suit yourself."

"You had me right about being broke. I'm worth around three bucks."

"Is that what you came back to say?"

"That and this: I'm glad you didn't crawl. You don't have to."

"This isn't a hotel," the woman said. "There's no charge for a room."

"You think I'm buttering you up?"

"I'm not thinking. I'm played out, and if you're getting set for a passionate speech, save your sweat."

"Now you're the one who's making it tough."

"This is no kind of weather to battle in," the woman said, "especially if it's only about words. Let's just sit still and keep our salt. Which reminds me, for no reason: there might be a beer inside. I forget what I left when I went away. You want to take a look?" When the soldier returned, he was carrying two glasses wearing jabots of foam. "I was expecting you to bring the bottle."

"You like it in the jug?" the soldier said. "I'll pour it back for you."

"I meant, having only one hand to do with, how did you work the opener?"

"I held the bottle between my knees. I'm getting skillful. I'll be shaving with my feet some day."

"You aren't ever going to have the use of that hand?"

"I was joshing. I do fine with it right now."

"Why not take off the bandage, then?"

"The skin is still too tender."

"Seems like the air and sun would do it good. Toughen it up."

"Some people think I'm too tough as it is," the soldier said. "But tell me about this job of yours. The Rancho Canada, was it?"

"What's there to tell?" the woman said. "It's a job. All jobs are jobs. Show me one that isn't, and I'll grab it."

"I'll be on the lookout for two."

"I don't have any special kick, I guess. I make good-enough money, and the guy that owns the joint, so far he's only made passes over his till, and for out in the desert like this, the hours are hard to beat, six to around midnight. The food is fierce, though, and the what-do-you-call-it atmosphere is worse. You get riffraff at a road-house—the help and the trade, both—and with cabins handy out back, you could turn into a first-class bum without any trouble."

"Even a second-class," the soldier said, and in the pause now, he sat listening to his rocker stutter the start of an uncertain speech.

"Why don't you say what you're thinking?" the woman said.

"I would, if I knew what it was."

"Do I work the cars or the cabins?"

"Is that what I'm thinking?"

"Well, a person would naturally wonder."

"Some other person," the soldier said. "What was running through my mind had nothing to do with that drive-in jump-joint. I happened to be trying to guess your age. My mind zigzags. I wander with it."

"I'm thirty-one," the woman said.

"Twenty-five, I'd've thought."

"I wish you were right. I'd do a lot of things different. Or the same things worse. Who knows?"

"Where do you come from?"

"Up in the San Joaquin. I was born in Bakersfield."

"How long did you live there?"

"Till a while after I got married—four-five years ago."

"Did you come here after that?"

"We were all over," the woman said. "We had a little business that kept us on the move, and when it blew up, Paul got into hauling oil out of San Pedro. But the company was always shifting him, so you might say we wandered too, only not with our mind: Mojave, Barstow, Taft, San Berdoo, and here. Anything else?"

"My mind is footsore," the soldier said.

"It don't bother me to give out information," the woman said, "but I ought to have the right to sign my name to it."

"Odd thing for me to omit," the soldier said.

"It was odd this afternoon," the woman said, "but it stopped being. If you didn't want to tell your own name, you could've made up a fake one. Who'd've known?"

"My name is Clarke," the soldier said. "With an *e*. Stanley Clarke."

"Mine is Jean Bell. It's really Eugenia."

"Why do people insist on knowing names? Why does it matter so much? What does Stan Clarke mean, or Jean Bell?"

"Nothing," the woman said. "But it's a good way to call out to somebody in a crowd. Or in the dark."

"A number would do as well," the soldier said. "But even a number is a name. Maybe what I object to is the claim people seem to get by being able to identify a thing."

"Do you think we have any claim?"

"A better one than we had before."

"We had none before," the woman said. "We have none now."

"When we've said Stan and Jean a few times, we'll forget that yesterday we didn't even know each other."

"Saying our names, how does that give us a claim?"

"Eugenia Bell," the soldier said. "A pleasant arrangement of vowels and consonants."

"Play around with it," the woman said. "I'm going to bed. If you feel like, you can use the couch in the parlor."

For a time, the soldier remained on the porch, attending the night-borne sounds: the wind-up and pitch of beetles against the screen, the taffeta rasp of leaves, a distant auto-horn, and a distant backfire. In the house, a shower began to run, and when the rain was over, a drain drank, and then, after a while, a bed-rail rang. No lamps were burning when the soldier entered the front room, and what light found its way in from without was contained in stifled stars on picture-panes, pottery, and facets of metal. The air seemed thin and sapped, as if lacking an element.

The soldier felt his way along a hall toward the bathroom, a faint gleam on tile. Locking the door, he flipped a switch on the wall and began to remove the bandage. The tape binding it down was soiled and furling, and for an inch or two its gum was gone. Tugging at the rolled-back tab, he tore the last lap loose, exposing a white track on gray, and then he ripped round after round away, until he reached the gauze. This he stripped quickly, dropping whorling yards of it on the floor before his hand came wholly exposed.

The nails were clean and pale, and the flesh was pale too as high as the wristbone, its pores open and distinct, as if long soaked, but the hand was entire, and there was no scar on it to show that it had not always been so. The soldier made a fist and stared at the red-dened grooves across his knuckles, and then he let the fingers open and watched the redness fade. He looked up at his image in the mirror, and he said, "You son of a bitch." [ ... *Who should know it better than you? Who, in fact, should know it at all, for who else has occupied your skin? In all these years, who else has lived in his partic-ular sack of organs, bone, nerves, fat, cartilage, liquid, and such alien odds and ends as splinters, food in passage, and tattoo-ink (but not shrapnel)? Who else has sailed this endless serpentine . . . ?* ] "You son of a bitch," he said again. [ ... *But why mourn like the only Judas in a world of Christs? What are the rest but turncoats too? What have you sold that they left unsold in the eighteen-hundreds, and where is the silver evidence of sale—among their plunder or yours? Were you the first to begin with emblems and end with trade-marks, or did you learn to fink from masters of the art? And the virus of history, did you catch it from the Holy Ghost, or was its host your handed-down blood and your brain? Put the blame where it belongs, on your time and place of birth, and shame not to sing 'Halleluiah!' with the flock, nor to bawl 'Amen, brother!' and 'God be praised!' while you rock in adoration at Bethlehem, Penna., and wash the feet and lick the scabs of Pinkertons. . . .* ] Finding tape and bandage in the medicine-chest, the soldier rebound his hand. Then, after disposing of the old dressing, he started back toward the front room.

The woman called to him as he passed her door, and he went to the bedside and looked down at her, saying, "What is it, Jean?"

"Would you please kiss me good-night?" she said.

He stooped to put his mouth on hers, but he did not otherwise touch her, and the contact was brief. "Is there anything else?" he said.

"That's all I wanted," she said. "Is there something you want?"

When he spoke, he was eying the blue floor, the navy and near-navy stripes laid down by the slats and slits of the bamboo blinds. "You give me the advantage, Jean," he said. "You always give me the advantage."

"Somebody has to give it to somebody."

"But why should it be you? Why not make me give it?"

"What would I do with it when I had it?" the woman said. "What good is it?"

"None," the soldier said, and he left the room.

[ *. . . The man said, 'I come from the County Home. I'd like to take you back there with me.'*

*Carlo said, 'This is our home.'*

*The man said, 'It doesn't belong to you, son.'*

*Carlo said, 'It has to. We live here.'*

*The man said, 'I'm sorry, but it belongs to a man called the landlord.'*

*Carlo said, 'But we always lived here, and he never said anything.'*

*The man said, 'Your father, while he was alive, paid him rent, that's why.'*

*Carlo said, 'What's rent?'*

*The man said, 'Rent is money that you pay to the owner of a house, the landlord. In return, he lets you live in the house.'*

*Carlo said, 'Suppose you don't have any money—only a couple of nickels, maybe, or a quarter.'*

*The man said, 'Well, sometimes if the landlord's a bad man, he puts you out of the house.'*

*Carlo said, 'Would you put us out of your house?'*

*The man shook his head. 'My house is free,' he said. 'Will you come there and live with me? I'd like very much to have you. . . .' ]*

THE UNSPOTTYD LAMBS OF THE LORD

"Whereas interrogatory hath been made whether
Indean or Negroe, manumittyd or otherhow free,
Be qualifyed to purchass a Christyan servant
And hold him to bondage and accompt as Master,
Be it enactyd that noe such Indean or Negroe,
Though he be himself baptyzed and at liberty,
Shall have lycence to traffick in Christyans,
But naught herein contayned shall debarr him
From the like adventure with his owne kynde."

If you want my opinion, it ought to be banned,
This immersion of niggers and crimson imps:
They're dyed-in-the-wool and guaranteed fast,
And if the day arrives when their color runs,
They'll have to run like hell to keep up with it.
But over and above the danger of fading them,
There's the little matter of giving them ideas,
Like, if all men are equal kneeling in a brook,
They're just as equal, maybe equaler, on land,
And, mister, that'd sure play hob with my ease.

They'll never be equal except they're white,
And white all over, top to toe and inside-out,
White from A to izzard and halfway back to A,
White in the bloodstream and white in the bone,
White, understand, white clean to the marrow,
White, mister, by a white sire on a white dam,
White as God's laundry, the clouds in the sky,
White like His beard on the brow of His bride,
White like her milk in the mouth of her son:
That's the one kind of Christian—the only one.

*They have promised you elevation.*
*Where is the elevation . . . ?*

# A DAY ON
# THE TOWN

[ *. . . And then time was like a train: the separate days were separate cars, alike but alone, and coupled one with the next by sleep. Each began somewhere in the dark, and in the dark each somewhere ended, and you remembered many a night when you had tried to stay awake to see an end and a beginning, but always your eyes had closed before they came, and you had dreamed through them, walking from car to car—and then it was morning.*

*When you went to the Home, Carlo was nine, and you were eight—and one day you realized that miles and miles of cars were gone (had you ever lived them, you wondered, had they ever been part of the train?): five years had passed. Five years, you thought, and what did you remember of them?: a single day in each, the day of the Picnic. . . .* ]

The soldier slept until noon, and, awaking supine, he lay for a moment in a wet print of himself on the sheet. He was wet too wherever skin touched skin—in his armpits, in the creases of his neck, and between his thighs—and here and there, where sweat seeped from some slant of his body, it balled and ran, cutting a channel in the sediment that had settled on him during the night. Above him, a green buzzer stunted around a dusty light-bulb, flying loops and slow figure-eights and finally landing upside-down on the fuzzed plaster. His thin interest petering out, the soldier shored himself up on his elbows and inspected the room.

It held little to detain the eye: a table, a rocker, a straightback chair, a bookrack, a few sepia prints, some Mexican ware, a reed rug, and a lamp. A fine powder furred all top surfaces, and a powder was in the air, sidling and tumbling in planes of light made by the blinds. The soldier sat up, and new sweat sprang, a flow of it starting colorless from his chest and reaching the belt of his shorts black, like a tadpole. The inside of the bandage was damp, the outside already overcast and shopworn.

On the wall near the couch hung several photographs. One, of a man in uniform, had been taken out of focus, and the features, the shade of the hair, even the nature of the expression, were blurred, leaving little more than a shape before a background. The woman appeared in the other three pictures, and at her feet in each lay the shadow of the camera-holder. In the first, she stood on a sand-dune, her summer dress hard against her in the wind; in the next, she was seated on the running-board of a tank-truck; and in the third, she was caught coming from the surf, with sharp light and shade showing on the rounds of her body.

The woman entered the room, and the soldier, indicating the last snapshot, said, "I like that one best."

"Why?" the woman said.

"It took you alive. In the others, you're stuffed."

"Is that the only reason?"

"It gives me an idea of what you're probably like when you're alone."

"Does it? What am I like, probably?"

"Quiet. I think you know how to wait it out."

The woman laughed. "You ought to be with me when I'm alone," she said. "I stall-walk, that's what I do, and I'd drive you crazy, like I drive myself." She went to the door. "If you want some grub, come in the kitchen. With pants or like you are. It cuts no ice."

When the soldier rejoined her, she was at a card-table in front of the open refrigerator. Trained on the box, an electric-fan force-fed air into the cool cave. "My own invention," she said. "I see you got formal."

"All I want is hot coffee," the soldier said, "but don't ask me why."

"There's fruit in that sack there."

"Coffee is all. I want to sweat coffee steam."

"Learn how to wait it out—was that what you said?—and you'll quit oozing. There's tricks you have to catch onto, though. For instance, when you take a shower, you don't use a towel after: you let the air dry you. Otherwise, you only have to take another shower."

"I still don't understand why anybody lives here," the soldier said. "Why go to so much trouble to die?"

The woman broke a rod of ash from her cigarette and mashed it with the coal. "What were you like before, Stan?" she said.

"Before what—the war?"

"The war didn't make you like this. You're sour, and I think you've been sour a long time. The war only brought it out."

"People don't change?"

"They change," she said, "but not like magic, where you do a pass, and a punkin turns into a Packard. You had the makings of what you are from way back."

"'Don't shoot, Mr. Crockett. I'll come down.'"

"And the queer part is, I think what you're sour about is yourself. You try to make it look like the war, or your hand, or the way the world is, but you don't really believe it."

"Where does all this lead to, Jean?"

The woman put her cigarette out, making a cloven hoof of it in the tray. "No place," she said, and she backed her chair away from the table. "Anyhow, not for me. I go to work again tonight, and there's still some shopping I should've done in Dago. I was having a time, though, and I said the hell with it. You going to be here later, or you taking off?"

"Which do you want?" the soldier said.

"I only want to know."

"You're not giving me the advantage."

"Let's not slug it out," the woman said. "If you feel like staying, stay. If you feel like going, good-bye."

"But you have no preference?"

"Last night, maybe. Today, no. So which'll it be, Stan?"

He let her reach the hallway before saying, "I'll stick around."

She glanced back. "What decided you?" she said.

"I like the way you say 'Stan.'"

She paused on the walk outside, and he saw her through the

dark converge of the hall as if it were a finder. Framed by the screen-door, she was bright in the sun—her hair, her face, her light dress, and the broad-brim straw hat that she held in her hand. "See you, then," she said, and she went away.

For a long while after the woman had gone, the soldier remained where he was, staring at the solid circle of the fan-vanes and listening to the monotone of the motor. He switched off the current, and the blades spun for a time and slowly died, and then drowned-out sound returned: a kitchen-clock clucked, and, denying its springs, it seemed to say *electric-electric;* drops of water fell punctually from a faucet into a pan; and again and again a fly revved up and rammed a windowpane.

[ *. . . For Christ's sake, what're you waiting for? For the water to stop dripping, or, better, to become wine? For the fly to crack its trunk and die? Or are you waiting for death yourself, and if so, why are you waiting here, in this particular cubic yard of space? Why wait any-where at all? Why let death choose the time and place for the knife to fall? Why not make it run for your life . . . ?* ]

It was mid-afternoon before the soldier left the house, crossed a scorched lawn, and headed up the lane of dappled blue-gums toward the main street of El Centro. The back of his blouse was a blot of sweat when he entered the first arcade, and a spot near the base of his skull was pulsing. For a moment, in the shade, his eyes saw black, and then the black began to fade, and there were peo-ple, many of them, along the length of the perforated tunnel, some sitting on benches at the building-line or leaning against the brick arches, some going into shops or emerging, and some simply pass-ing him by, and he heard greetings, laughter, and scraps of speech, but all motion seemed retarded and all sound subdued, as if the heat had measurable weight and density. A cold exhaust came from a closing door: there was beer on the bar's breath. The soldier went inside and sat a stool halfway down the mahogany.

"Name it," the bartender said.

"Beer," the soldier said. "Got anything good?"

"I'm supposed to push the domestic."

"I can scrape that off any phone-pole."

"Just between you and I," the bartender said, "dog-wet has more age on it."

"What do *you* take when you're taking?"

"You like it light and mild, the Mex can't be beat."

"Draw two," the soldier said, and when his glass was before him, he took a mouthful and let it go down a little at a time.

"Yes or no," the bartender said.

"Yes."

The bartender brought his own glass from under the drain and drank the treat in one lift. "I wish I had to do that for my health," he said. "I'd hope to never get well. How can Mexican beer be so good if ours is so lousy? Tell me that."

"If you want the answer," the soldier said, "I'll give it to you. I happen to know it."

"We're better than the Mexicans. That only stands to reason. So how come we don't make better beer? I ast a question. I'm always out to learn."

"Here you go, then: we're *not* better than the Mexicans, at beer-making or anything else."

With a folded towel, the bartender made a few palmer-method swirls over the woodwork. "That's an odd saying for a white man," he said.

"Who's white?" the soldier said. "I'm not, and neither are you. We're the color of canned salmon."

"Everybody in the world knows an American is better than a Mexican," the bartender said. "Even the Mexicans."

"They never voted that way."

"They don't have to vote it. It's a thing you can see with half an eye."

"Why not use the other eye and a half?" the soldier said. "You might see something different."

"Listen, a man only has to use his smeller. Them greasers'd whiff a buzzard off a dead snake."

"There ought to be a law against that," the soldier said. "What the hell is this country coming to—letting the Mexicans get all the snakes? Why, God damn it, they ought to be forced to eat in a restaurant!"

"*In!*" the bartender said. "They're forced to stay *out!*"

"That's what I mean," the soldier said. "If you know what I mean."

"Odd sayings run out of your ears."

"I'm one odd Joe," the soldier said, and the bartender, after studying him for a moment, walked away.

At intervals, glass rang on glass to chime like distant bell-buoys, and coins rang as they danced on the bar, and the till rang too and stuck out its tongue. All sound seemed remote, and it was a pleasant place to be, the soldier thought, a pleasant place, and slowly its lines and shapes and colors began to melt in his drowsy view. He blinked sleep away, and, sucking in the processed air, he inflated himself against cold spots in his uniform. It was a pleasant place, he thought, so pleasant that he wondered why so few people frequented it. Many were outside, he noticed, loafing in the dimmer parts of the gallery. Now and then a woman passed, and eyes dogged her while her skirt was in the sun.

"Anything else?" the bartender said, and the soldier shook his head. "Two Mex comes to sixty cents." The soldier put three quarters on the counter and slid off the stool. "You know good brew," the bartender said, "but that's about all."

The soldier turned. "Meaning . . . ?" he said.

"No meaning," the bartender said.

The heat had been waiting for him, the soldier thought, for him in particular. In the street, a crowd of it, a crush of air, closed about him and bore in, as if a vacuum that he was at the core of had burst. The chill in his clothes wore off almost at once, and, warm again, they felt moist where he had supposed them dry. Fresh sweat bled from him as if by concussion, and thumbs behind his eyeballs pressed them outward like dents in a hat. The pavement sideslipped a little, and with it cars, buildings, and people walking or standing still—everything but himself—and then by a trick of sight, some objects began to grow, some to shrink, and some, as if reflected in the latitudes of a rippling mirror, to do both.

Wrenched and ruined, the figure of a man approached, dragging a tortured boy away from a distorted window far uphill. The boy was saying, "But you promised! You promised!" They went by, and again the soldier heard the boy say, "You promised!" and again, and yet again, and each time the words were fainter, and it was only when he could no longer hear them that he saw the man slap the boy's face.

For some reason, the soldier felt compelled to say, "But you promised!" and then he looked about, but no one seemed to have been listening. At any instant now, the soldier thought, he would shoot-the-chutes and slide off the listing earth. He reached for a capsizing door-frame, but his hand closed into a fist holding nothing, and he started to fall the long distance the street appeared to be from his face. An arm stayed him, and then he was steered toward a chair in the doorway. The arm brought him water, and he drank, and little by little the slanting world righted itself.

A voice said, "What're you trying to do—die young?"

The soldier's gaze followed the arm to a body and the body to a face. "Didn't I die?" he said.

"Not yet," the man said, "but phrig around in this heat, and you will. This is El Centro."

"El Centro of what?"

"See if you can stand without rocking the boat," the man said.

The soldier steadied himself against a table set lengthwise in the aisle of the shop. Trays on top and bins below were loaded with metal castings: sprinkler-heads, valves, nozzles, faucets, rainbirds, and assorted pipe-joints. "What do you do with all this iron?" he said.

"Sell it," the man said. "Need some?"

"Don't tell me you *live* off this heat."

"K-rect. Any kick?"

"I've always wondered about people that sell people what their tongues are hanging out for."

"Economics. Supply and demand. Ever heard of economics?"

"It's when you have the supply, and somebody else has the demand, isn't it?"

"Never heard it better put," the man said.

"If a lot of people need a thing, it ought to be free. That'd be real economics."

"Sure, but you couldn't make a profit off it."

"Think how the people would love you, though."

"Screw the people," the man said. "Let 'em hate me, just so they plank down the dough." He followed the soldier to the door. "Before you go, take some of those." He indicated a box hung from the jamb; it was filled with white buttons. "Salt," the man said. "For free, so the people'll love me."

As the soldier cruised the street, putting in at a window here and there, he thought of the woman and said her name in his head (*Eugenia Bell*, he heard himself say), and the name seemed to summon her face, and her face brought her voice, remembered as quelled by fatigue and lenient, and now other things about her were remembered—her pliant but not double-jointed hands, her high instep, and the way her nails were set in her fingers, countersunk like watch-crystals (*Eugenia Bell*, he imagined saying)—and suddenly he started back toward the house.

[ ... *The Home, you thought, the Home—and you tried to make yourself stop thinking (Let it stay where it is, buried under a twenty-year fall of time!), but the remembrance was in being, and scenes were looming through the mists of the mind.*

*The day of the Picnic.*

*Once each summer, a man from Red Bank (he was no one in the public eye, and neither rich nor poor nor seeking praise: he was a man with a single and infrequent passion, and not until your fifth year at the Home did you know more about him than his name), once each summer, he came with a truckload of food and a few chartered jitneys, and all of you—the little ones, the middle ones, the big ones, and the teachers, sometimes even the superintendent—went off on a spree to Pleasure Bay.*

*You remembered the birches at the riverside, the old inn near the iron bridge, the boat-landing for side-wheelers from the Battery, and the end of the trolley-lines, where the open yellow cars waited for the Mary Patten. And you remembered the scows you used for crabbing, and you remembered the feast in the birch-park, and the rest-period, and the games, and the swim, and the last treat at the pavilion (all the ice-cream and cake you could hold), and then you climbed into the jitneys again, and, cheering (What? The end of one year or the beginning of another?), you were driven back to the Home—and the Picnic was over.*

*You wondered whether anyone there, no matter how rich he struck it later or how long he lived, would forget the faintest taste, the briefest breath, the least detail of such a day. Very few crabs were ever brought to net, and the Shrewsbury was only a shallow tidal marsh, and the food was neither better nor worse than you had at the Home, but for some reason (because all things were big to the small?), the two or three soft-shells you caught seemed monstrous yet, and the stream that low tide would drain to a channel in the mud was still a deep broad roadstead, and always would the banquet among the hacked and bleeding birches be incomparable. . . . ]*

By the time the soldier reached the lane, the sun had gone down behind the trees, and their flirting leaves appeared to be aflame. The lawn, even in the block of dusk cast by the house, still spoke of the fervor of day, its dry grass drier and crisping underfoot like excelsior. The woman lay in a deckchair near the porch. She was staring at the sky when the soldier first saw her, and she continued to stare at the sky.

He sat down alongside her on the cured turf, saying, "What would you do if I died?"

A mile above them, a plane trespassed on a chain of privacies. Watching it, the woman said, "Get somebody to roll you away."

"I went into an air-cooled bar, and it damn near killed me. Why didn't you tell me about air-cooling—and about salt-pills?"

"I meant to. It slipped my mind."

"When I got outside, the pavement rose up and said, 'This is El Centro.' Or was that the plumbing-man? I forget. Anyway, I fell into his store. He gives away salt. Everything else, he sells. Out to make a profit, he said. Screw the people."

"Gus Walsh, it must've been. A dirty-talking old goat."

"Salty, I'd say. Eats his own pills."

"He ought to get his mouth cleaned out with one of his toilet-plungers. A steamer-up, he is."

"What words does he use?" the soldier said. "And are they technical or colloquial?"

"Words never made me throw up. It's how people work with them."

"How does Walsh?"

"Like they're hands. To give you a feel with."

"I talked to another guy in town. He was a shitepoke too. Some bartender with a beef about the Mexicans. I rubbed some language on him."

The woman said, "You a fire-eater, Stan?"

"I burn once in a while. Who doesn't?"

"There's better places for it than El Centro. You'll likely be leaving soon, so it don't matter too much. But while you're still around, don't put anybody out with your mouth. I should've told you—that and the air-cooling."

"What makes you think I'll be leaving?"

"This, that, and the other."

"Did you think about me today?"

"Yes," the woman said.

"And what did you think?"

"I thought, 'I'll be sorry when he goes.'"

"Did you wonder why?"

"I like you, that's why," the woman said. "I didn't have to wonder." She sat up and swung her feet to the ground. "One of the car-hops is calling for me in a little while."

"Don't you want to know whether I'll be here when you get back?"

"I'll know soon enough—when I get back."

"Wouldn't you like to know in advance?"

"What for? I'm ready for the worst."

"You think I'm an irritating bastard, don't you?"

"It never occurred to me," the woman said.

"You can take my word for it."

"That's about all I *do* have your word for."

"Here's something else," the soldier said. "You say you thought about me today? Well, I thought about you."

"Did you? What am I supposed to do now?"

"You're supposed to inquire into the nature and quality of the thoughts."

"And then lay back and soak up a speech?"

"But inquire casually, you understand, as if you were merely being polite, as if you really didn't care."

"I've got the feeling that you're just waiting for me to ask my first solid question," the woman said. "No matter what it is, you're going to climb a stump to answer it. You're all primed to bull me." She started to rise, but the soldier reached for her hand. "I'm late now, so let's forget it. Also, let's stop holding hands."

"We never seem to get very far with a conversation," the soldier said. "It's no sooner born than you strangle it. What's the matter with you?"

"Ah, please," the woman said. "You're not going to sit there sucking your thumb, are you?"

"I've got to do something with my face. I'm not allowed to talk with it."

"Talk is good, and I enjoy it," the woman said. "But you don't want to talk. You want to bull me."

"Mention one thing that I've bulled you about."

"I only said you wanted to. You've been wanting to right along."

"How do you know all this—by instinct?"

"How else?" the woman said. "What do *you* go on?"

"I hate to bring this up, but people have been known to think."

"That takes a classy brain, like yours. I have to gimp along on hunches."

"You ought to have more than hunches by this time. We've been together for over a day."

"*What* more? Your name is Stan Clarke, and you come from where-did-you-say?"

"I'll tell you whatever you want to know about me. Ask."

"Ask!" the woman said, and now she stood up. "What bull you get when you ask!"

She moved away from him and went toward the porch, and he heard her footsteps on the hollow stoop and the sound of a spring being sprung as the screen-door opened, and in a pause that seemed to palpitate, he heard the baying of a distant locomotive, and then the door closed.

[ . . . *Pick yourself up and go! But go now, not after you've said good-bye, not after more talk and more silence under forced draught, not tomorrow or the next day, and not presently, or in the course of time, or as soon as, or even forthwith, but this very instant of now . . . !* ]

At the street-end of the lane, an auto-horn spoke twice. The woman came from the house, and, without looking at the soldier, she went off over the friable grass. She was carrying a small valise of cardboard pressed and stained to resemble leather, but the dye had worn away in some places or run in some rain, and the sharp corner of something had punched a triangle out of one of the flanks, and the valise looked like what it was: cardboard pressed and stained to resemble leather. The soldier felt the stir of pity start, and he knew that the time to go had come and gone.

A car-door slammed, and wheels spun for traction in sand, and the soldier listened to a motor moving away until its sound had shriveled to nothing. He entered the house, and, knowing his way now, he let it stay dark as he passed through the parlor and the hall to a curtain of odor blooming from the woman's room. He tried to identify it, but it was a blend, and it seemed to grow fainter in the attempt. He went into the room and stood for a moment looking down at a head and body poorly written on the rumpled bedding, and then he lay down near them, and their flavors were beginning to unravel when he fell asleep.

*[ . . . The superintendent was a human being, and in all the time that you were at the Home, you never saw a boy beaten or sent to bed hungry or punished in any way that gave pleasure to the punisher. Good enough years, they were, you remembered, but still they were years in an orphan-asylum, and all who lived there yearned for someone on the outside to become attached to, even to belong to, because, within, you seemed to belong to nothing, not even to yourself. Now and then, some boy was lucky enough to be adopted (only the superintendent used that word; among yourselves, it was 'taken'), and every year a few of you reached the legal age for leaving on your own, and you never saw each other again. But you and Carlo had a long time to wait for legal age, and if there was little chance of being 'taken' separately, there was almost none of going together—and you stayed on and on through five years, through five of the Great Days*

*called the Picnic.*

*It was on the last of them, you remembered, that you and Carlo spoke to the Picnic-man for the first time. He had driven the food-truck himself that day, and you had had the job of stowing trash in the hampers and rinsing out the milk-cans, and when the bugler blew retreat, the man waved you and Carlo into the cab with him, and all the way back to the Home, he asked questions, and you answered them. A few weeks later, when you reported for your last class on a Friday afternoon, you were told that the superintendent wanted both of you on the carpet at once. It wasn't for any rule you had broken, though: the Picnic-man was in the office, and he had asked for permission to take you home for the week-end, just Carlo and you. You were happy, you remembered, so happy that you hardly let yourselves dwell on what the invitation could mean—but there were moments when you and Carlo merely looked at each other, and the look alone was language.*

*You made many such trips before the summer was over, but that first one you always recalled as the best. It had to be: all you touched or used, all you walked on or passed between, all you saw, including the man and his wife—all of it and the two of you were going to belong to each other some day, and you liked everything, the people, the house, the smell of the place, the sounds in the road, and the color of the particular piece of sky you could see from the bed you slept in, and it was a new kind of sleep that you had, both nights of that first weekend, a sleep where for once you were free of the day before and certain of the day to come.*

*All the rest of the summer, the man called for you every Friday and brought you back to the Home every Sunday evening, and while neither he nor his wife had ever mentioned the one thing you wanted to hear, both you and Carlo were always certain that next time would be the time, always next time—and over Labor Day week-end, the time finally came. A week-end so many years ago, you thought, but so often resurrected and so often re-endured that it presented itself now set and constant, and you heard the words and saw the scenes not as years and distance might have translated them, but as they once and actually had been spoken and played. . . . ]*

He awoke, again with the sense of having been awakened. A cough, a scraped match, a footfall, a tap on the screen, a name called—some sound seemed to have sunk into the cocaine of sleep and struck bottom. He waited, and, hearing the word "Eugenia" muted, he went along the hall to the door, and then there were more words, spoken aloud now. "I dropped by to see if you got back all right," the voice said. "I didn't mean to disturb you."

"Didn't you?" the soldier said from the black passage to the blue porch. "What *did* you mean to do?"

The conversation stopped short and marked time. It stumbled forward again as the voice, a man's, maundered, "I thought you—I though Mrs. Bell—I beg your," and then the thicket of speech thinned, and the voice came into the clear: "I'm a friend of Mrs. Bell's," it said.

"So I gathered." the soldier said.

"As a shepherd of the Lord, one has a multitude of friends."

The soldier laughed. "Especially among the sheep," he said. He pushed the screen open, forcing the man to step back, and took a seat at the far end of the porch. "Would you care to state your name, or do you think Mrs. Bell will recognize you from my description?"

The man let a few seconds pass before saying, "That would depend on the description."

"A man of the cloth called, I'll say."

"I think that would serve."

"I'd better be more specific: there are many denominations. This one was working the graveyard-shift, I'll tell her."

Again the man hesitated. "I'm sure you mean no mockery of my calling," he said.

"About forty-five, I ought to add. Medium height, medium weight—in fact, medium all around, except for the voice. I'll describe it as a trained voice, trained for whispering down a hall in the dead of night."

"You do lack respect, I see. I'm the pastor of a flock, my son."

"In the dead of night," the soldier said. "Shall we synchronize our watches?"

"The Lord's work knows no hours."

"Are you here on the Lord's work? I could've sworn you were in business for yourself."

"Mrs. Bell was in a run-down condition when she left last week. I came to inquire whether her trip had proved beneficial."

"You came without cymbals."

"'Take heed that ye do not your alms before men, to be seen of them,'" the man said. He turned away now and descended the steps of the porch. At the bottom, he paused to say, "My name is Pryor, Earl Pryor, and I suggest that you mention it to Mrs. Bell. She might not know me from the rest of your account."

After the man had gone, the soldier began to rock himself, as if to dull by motion an awareness of a faster-pumping heart, but the piston of his blood remained dominant, and at length he was driven to motion of a different kind—flight—and its schedule took him first into the house to hunt for whatever traces of his presence he could find. He turned up only an empty packet of matches bearing the name of a San Francisco hotel, and this, along with the bandage he had been wearing he flushed down the toilet-bowl. Making a fresh wrap with the last of the materials in the medicine-chest, he looked carefully about once more, and then he left the house and walked rapidly up the lane toward the street. Halfway there, he thought of the woman's car and returned to search it. There was nothing on the seat or the shelf behind it, and all that he found on the floor was a few hairpins, some scraps of tin-foil, and a dry and fractured stick of gum. Withdrawing his arm from under the wheel, he grazed a key-chain and plinked its beads against the dash.

At that moment, the schedule, the sense of plan and rehearsal, failed, and he stood still, as if waiting to remind himself of what he had been about to do. He recalled only its essence—motion—and climbing into the car, he drove out of the lane and headed in the direction of the town. He had no idea of his destination until he reached the main intersection. There a legend in electricity ran on and off the sky: RANCHO CANADA—9 MILES NORTH ON 99.

Although it was near midnight, neon still glowed everywhere, framing windows, coursing cornices, and winking down from the air. Red or blue gas throbbed in dozens of arteries, but here and there an occlusion in the circulatory system of a display deadened a word or part of a word, or maimed some figure designed to jig and jerk without end. Many people were about, and almost all seemed aimless, even those emerging from an emptying picture-house: they joined the slow eddying on the pavement, or stopped to watch a man on a ladder garbling the title of a film, or simply stopped. From a cross-street came the sound of a church-bell, the word *bronze* at a full gallop.

Stores and showrooms gave way to gas-stations and diners, and these to used-car parks and lumberyards, and then there were grain-elevators, packing-sheds, and fenced-in mounds of rusting junk and wreckage. Few homes were left along the highway, and those surviving the onslaught of the expanding town seemed drawn back in indignation at the all-night glare of motels. Beyond this sector, the concrete was a groove in a green plain. Now and then, at some junction, the car passed through a bar of music, and where flumes ran parallel to the pike, the soldier saw the lamps strike water, and once, far off, a train, a chain of lights, went by.

[ ... *There was something unusual about that week-end from the start, and Carlo knew it, and you knew it, but it was something you'd have missed if you hadn't been tight-wound, waiting for a sign. The man talked about himself more than he ever had before, and his wife was quieter, even a little ill at ease, and at times they both seemed remote from you in their minds, and yet as near to what you wanted them to say as opening their mouths and saying it: it was almost in the air. The three days went, though, and again you were wondering how you'd manage to live till the next time, but as you were leaving for the Home, all of a sudden the woman began to cry. It was a helpless kind of crying, as if it were only a flow of water seeking its own level, but it was more than the man could bear to watch, and be went outside to the car. The woman kissed Carlo and you, and then she turned away and ran upstairs.*

*The man had very little to say during the drive out of Red Bank, and Carlo and you, still disturbed by the strange holiday, were quiet too. It was a good hour of the day for silence, you remembered: the sun was behind the trees, and the world seemed to be running down. There were no other cars on the road, a dirt track through the woods along a reed-bound brook, and on the punk-sticks of cattail, you saw chevroned blackbirds sway. Some distance from the Home, the man stopped the car, and for a while the three of you sat there saying nothing: you watched branches fly the fall wind, and you counted the colors in a turning maple, but you said nothing. The man worked the steering-wheel as if he were still driving, and finally he climbed out of the car into the road, where he walked about, kicking at stones or dust, or just kicking, and once he picked something up and threw it away, and then he broke a twig from a bush and stripped its leaves, making a green rose of them in his fist —and now, as he began to peel the bark, he spoke, saying . . . ]*

The roadside edge of the grounds was lined with white-washed pepper trees from two of which hung lanterns marking the entrance. Toward the rear of a gravel parking stood the ranch-house, long, low, tile-roofed, and made of adobe, a mission from which floated the wheedling of clarinets and a saxophone drone. In an open-front kitchen, countermen stacked food on trays, and girls in uniform skimmed away under them to darkened cars. The soldier nosed the Ford into a gap in the rank.

A car-hop waded through his lights, pantomiming blindness,

and he threw the switch. She plastered a bill of fare on the windshield, and, aiming a pencil at an order-pad, she said, "What'll you be having, brother?"

The soldier itemized her with his eyes. She was wearing a bolero of red satin, a white blouse, trunks to match the jacket, and white cowboy-boots inset with red butterflies. He said, "I'm looking for Jean."

"Jean who—Bell? She don't work this end."

"Would you mind calling her over?"

"She works the other end, I told you. Tool up there if you want her."

"I'd hate to deprive you," the soldier said.

"No depravity."

"That's still a good one. I never fail to laugh."

"What's a good what?" the car-hop said.

"A good play on words."

"Look. I don't have time to gum-beat. What're you eating?"

"Make it a hamburger and a malt."

"Burg and malt," the car-hop said, crossing two boxes on the pad. "What flavor?"

"Plain."

At the counter, the woman clipped the order to a plastic drum and spun it away to the chef. While she was preparing a tray with water and cutlery, Jean joined her, and the two spoke. Jean shook her head and went away without looking at the Ford.

When the food was brought, the soldier said, "What did she say?"

"Just about what I would," the car-hop said.

"You mean, 'No depravity'?" he said, and, taking up his straw, he broke one end of the wrapper and blew the tissue tube into the air. The woman considered him briefly and walked off.

By the time the soldier had finished eating, the last car left in the section served by Jean was flashing its brights for the check. He watched her make change and take the tray away, and he continued watching as she returned to the car-hop bench and smoked a cigarette. She used it until it was no more than a pinch of burning paper, and then she dropped it and stared out across the parking, the pepper trees, and the dished-in champaign of the Sink. On the road, cars passed from time to time, and the razz of Diesels rose to drown the dance-hall jazz and then fell, but no other patrons came to toe the line, and the few at different stations were silent, a head at a window, a red spark in the dark.

At length, the woman left the bench and strolled over to the Ford. "Kind of a surprise," she said.

"I was beginning to think you'd never get over it," the soldier said.

"Don't be sore. I'm too tired for anybody to get sore."

"Why were you surprised?"

"I expected you to be on your way."

"You're always expecting that. Where would I be on my way to?"

"Wherever you're going. I don't know."

"I like it here," he said. "I like the people."

"It was good of you to come after me. You didn't have to."

"What time will you be through?"

"If it keeps slow like this, any time."

The other car-hop came to the window. "Anything else?" she said.

The soldier's eyes made a round-trip from hers to her boots. "If there is," he said, "it fails to come to mind."

The woman sailed a check in across the tray. "Collecting," she said.

Creasing a dollar-bill into the check, he sailed it back, and the woman unclamped the tray and left. He turned to Jean, saying, "She acts like she's still on, but what the hell's she playing?"

"Herself. Charlsie Oliver."

"She works mighty hard to say it can be had for a deuce."

"Ten."

"For ten, she'd throw in the boots."

"Twenty, sometimes," Jean said, "and once, fifty. I heard it offered, so I know. A guy from up the Sink, it was. Ran a gas-station over by the Sea. A popular hunk too, not the kind generally has to pay. Fifty, he wanted to give her." A counterman came from the kitchen, flagged the car-hops, and began to lower screens over the service-front. "Be back when I change."

[ . . . *'I honestly don't know how to tell you this. I've thought and thought, and time and again I've talked it over with the missis, but I've got the feeling that no matter what I say or how I say it, it'll be the wrong thing in the wrong words. I don't blame anybody for getting me in a fix like this. I got in it myself, and now that I'm in, I don't see any way out except saying what I have to say and hoping for the best—but I know in my heart that even the best will be bad for all of us.*

*'I took to you boys from the start, both of you, and so did the missis—there never was any question about that, and I want you to believe it. We studied you as carefully as we knew how, as carefully as people have to when they're thinking of taking someone into their home, and by the time we got to know you well enough to form an opinion (this is the hardest thing I ever had to say, the hardest and the meanest, I guess), we realized that it was going to be almost impossible to choose between you.'*

*He stopped there for a moment or two (a little nubbin on the twig seemed to require all his attention), and then he rolled on over your lives.*

*'We never spoke of adoption, but you understood all along that that's what we had in mind. Not till this past week, though, did it dawn on us that the two at you might be expecting to go together. How we could've been so blind—call it cruel, even—well, that's something we'll have to answer for if there's anything to answer to. But the fact remains, we never gave it a thought: we were too busy all summer*

*trying to pick one of you over the other, and to this very day we simply haven't been able to. You're good boys, fine boys, the kind we would've been proud to have as our own flesh and blood, but after all this time, watching you, talking to you, sounding you out, testing you in ways you never knew you were being tested, we're no further towards making a choice than we were at the beginning.*

*'If it was possible, if I was a man of means instead of only a small-town merchant, I give you my solemn word of honor I'd take the two at you and be glad of the chance to provide you a home and a decent future. If I was even in the class of people that could give one of you the best of everything, I'd take you both and divide it, share and share alike, because the right kind of people don't need the best to be happy, only something solid they can depend on, something that has dignity. That's all I ever had, and that's all I can give to just one of you, but as God is my judge, I don't know which one it should be.'*

*It came to your mind to say, 'You think we're the same, but you're wrong. We never were, and we never will be, so take Carlo. Listen to me and take Carlo.' But the thought stayed in your mind and died there, and you said nothing. . . . ]*

Bus-boys had cached the spare food in iceboxes and lockers, the lights were out, and the drive-in zone, except for the Ford, was deserted. Several cars were still clustered about the dance-hall end of the building, but the band no longer moaned low and squealed high into the hot wind running down the Sink. A door in the adobe opened, making a golden oblong, and closed.

"That was quick enough," the soldier said as the woman approached the car.

"Nothing to take off, nothing to put on," she said. "I'll drive, if you want."

"I made it this far."

"You feel like going straight back?"

"You're tired, you said."

"I'm always tired, but that don't mean I can sleep. I damn near never sleep this season."

"Where would you like to go?" he said.

"Ever hear of the Dunes? They're desert. Not sage or mesquite, or with Joshua trees and cactus. Not with anything: the Sahara, if that's what the Sahara is like. It's nice there at night, though. If you care to see it, I'll show you the way."

The turnoff was a sand road flanked by ditches. On either side, beyond the starred water, the crop-green was incessant to the limit of sight. "Fifty dollars," the soldier said. "A new American record."

"She didn't take it," the woman said. "That's another American record. She didn't want the guy that went with it."

"Why not?"

"How can you know things like that? I've seen her take on trade just because it was trade: she's a spraddle-leg. Ranchers, tool-dressers, dope-peddlers, schoolboys, anybody. Anybody but this gas-station guy. Why all them and a hundred others, and not him? You answer."

"Maybe she was drawing the line," the soldier said. "Don't people like to feel there's still something that they balk at?"

"When you lay for money, you lay *anybody* for money," the woman said. "You don't get respectable by ruling out one particular and harmless slob. Or do you? Who knows?" They were passing orchards of date-palms now, squat fat-butted sprouts like giant pineapples, each underslung with shocks of fruit like swarms of bees. "He got to be a local joke, the poor bastard, but I never thought it was so terribly funny, watching him sneak out back to the cabins to see who she'd taken instead of him—some pimple-face boy, maybe, or whatever else staggered in off the road. I don't know what kind of a bang she got out of leaving this one guy loaded, but it must've been a big one, because she took to looking for him so that she could have the extra fun of seeing his tongue hang out. One night, though, he didn't show up, and she acted like she came out of her house, and the front steps were gone. He didn't show up the next night, either, or the next after, and it sank in for the rest of us that the guy was through. *He* might've been, but not Charlsie: she'd got used to him being around for her feet, and when he stayed away a couple of more nights in a row, what did she do but drive herself to his joint thirty miles up the Sink?" The car climbed the eastern slope of the basin and ran between reaches of sand as arid as the road. "Before she left, she told us what she was going to do—chafe him up with sweet talk and then give him a workout. She did, but not the way she'd had in mind. He figured she meant business, and she no sooner got the tease started than he dumped her on the ground and climbed all over her—and not for fifty dollars, either, or even for two. For nothing, he had it." The lamps were beginning to pick out arcs of an old plank road, rotted away in places and partly overblown. "Anywheres along here," the woman said.

They left the car on the highway ridge and descended the slope to what appeared, under the rent pavilion of the sky, to be a vast beach, and in the rare clear air, bold and bottomless shadows were cast by the corrugated sheers of sand. On these, as on some stylized sea, schooners of upswept dust were sailed by the wind, and they moved with a granular rustle, a sound like that of sugar being poured.

Against a drift that concealed them from the road, the soldier and the woman sat down, and, looking off across the chamfered strand of nothing, he said, "This is private enough."

"For what?" the woman said.

He made an hourglass of his hand and let sand cascade. "For me," he said.

"I kind of gathered you were a private guy."

"I think I'm something on a stick, don't I?"

"If you thought you were so good, you wouldn't want to be so private," she said. "But the hell with it. The hell with talk. This is the Dunes." She let herself rock over backward, and, outflung, she lay like a fallen dress.

"Do you know a man named Pryor?" the soldier said.

"Yes," the woman said. "Why?"

"He came to the house tonight. He was looking for someone called Eugenia."

"Why did you ask? To see if I'd deny it?"

"He was anxious about your health, he said. At eleven o'clock at night, your health preyed on his mind."

"How late would it prey on yours, Stan?"

"You were ill when you went away, he said, and from then till now he lay on thorns, no doubt refusing food and drink. At eleven o'clock tonight, he could endure no more, and he came to you whispering, 'Eugenia!' by which he meant, of course, 'How are you feeling, Mrs. Bell? Quite well, I trust.'"

"What Pryor said and did—how does it affect me?"

"'Eugenia!' he said, but pianissimo, like a drummer trying to make sure he was in the room of the right chambermaid. How *does* it affect you?"

"Women are always getting whistled at. Not all of them stop."

"What about the ones who do?" the soldier said.

"They go to hell, I guess. They sin and go plumb to hell." The woman stared at the chinked roof overhead. "You look up at all that blue stuff, but if you just turn your mind around, you're looking down, and the stuff is water, not sky, and what you're doing is the dead-man's float. Would you care very much if you were dead?"

"The only part of death that bothers me is the dying," the soldier said. "I could get used to being dead if the thing didn't have to happen inside of me. If I could watch it, the way you watch night coming on, I don't think I'd give a damn whether I lived or died."

"You're yellow, aren't you, Stan?"

"But it almost never happens like that: most of the time, death comes out of an alley and slugs you. That's one of the things that's supposed to make life bearable—you don't know when it's going to end."

"Aren't you?" the woman said.

Smoothing out a span of sand, the soldier turned up a small shell. He rubbed it free of its pepper-and-salt and fingered its fine concave and fluted convex. "Yellow is only a color," he said. "Certain flowers are yellow, and hair is a kind of yellow sometimes, and cheap paper, and the yolk of an egg, and gold. Yellow describes all those things in a way, but it doesn't describe me. The color was never mixed that does." He showed the woman the shell. "Like a little fan," he said, and he placed it in the hollow of her throat.

"What're you so afraid of, Stan?" she said.

"Does it show very plainly?"

"If a person is with you long enough, yes. It's no sign on your back, though."

"Were you ever afraid?" he said.

"I don't know. I've never thought much about it."

"If you had, you'd know it isn't the sign on your back that matters—let people think what they like. But the sign you have to look at all day long, the sign you can see with your eyes closed, because it's painted on your mind—that *does* matter."

"You care a whole lot what people think," the woman said. "You wouldn't be wearing that bandage if you didn't. You don't have to wear it: you said so. But you don't want to do without it. You want people to see it and say, 'Ah, wounded in action. Purple Heart. A brave guy.' There's a sign on you, all right, but it doesn't read, 'Yellow.' It's the bandage, and it reads, 'Brave.' I think that's the only thing I don't like about you."

"You like it that I'm yellow?" he said.

"It doesn't count worth a cent—and you could be a lion, and that wouldn't count, either."

"I always thought women liked their guys to drag the cape."

She turned to look at him, and the shell tipped over and fell to the sand. "You're not my guy," she said. "What makes you think you're my guy?"

He picked up the shell and flicked it out of sight across a mound. "I didn't mean it that way," he said.

"What way did you mean it? Do you ever mean anything?"

"Not any more," he said, and, taking up a fistful of sand, he watched its waterlike evasion. "I'm meaningless."

"When you said we never got very far talking, you were right. But you were wrong about why. I don't stop you, not when you're really going to say something. You stop yourself."

"Sometimes," he said. "When I reach a thing I don't want to say even in my head."

"You always reach a thing," she said. "No matter where you start, you stop at the same place. The thing must be the same thing all the time."

"Why don't we quit this jabbering?" he said, and, lighting a cigarette, he looked away over the arrested and motionless ocean of the Dunes. There was no wind now to trail veils of sand, and there were fewer sweeps and upshoots of light from cars on the distant road. Low down near the spine of the Chocolates, a star cut a gash, a knife-slash, in the night.

[ . . . *It was the man who spoke, and he said, 'And not knowing which of you to choose, I'm going to leave the choice, you might say, to you. But if the missis and me, after a whole summer of discussion, couldn't come to a decision, it stands to reason that you two couldn't, either, not even if you talked it over for twice as long as we did: it's something that talk just won't settle. So when I say I'm leaving the choice to you, I mean you both want what only one of you can have, a situation that this life specializes in, and to put it as plain as I can, one of you simply has to beat the other out of it. It's brother against brother for real this time, but what's the history of all the world if not brother against brother under different names? The strong ones win from the weak, the smart from the foolish, the coldhearted from the warmhearted—but the winner and the loser are always brothers. I hate to teach you such a terrible lesson, but it's only what I found out myself through bitter experience. I won't say any more. There's really nothing more to say except, God forgive me, here's how another winner and another loser will be added to the list.'*

*In the moment before he put it into words, you took one wild guess at what he had in mind, but you missed it by a realm, by all the many divisions between youth and maturity. You hadn't lived long enough to be as brutal as an adult—or had you? You'd always wondered. . . . ]*

The woman said, "How did you know you were my guy, Stan?"

"You make no secret of it," he said.

"I don't hide much, do I?"

"You don't try to."

"I'm easy to read, don't you think?" she said. "Big type, little words. But all the same, it'll take more than me to make you my guy."

He looked down at her, trying to say, "Have a heart, Jean," but the words seemed to shrink in the making, and they came out a size smaller than speech.

"I have one," the woman said. "What would I need two for?"

"One for yourself," he said, "and one for me. I'm a son of a bitch. I hope you never know how much of a son of a bitch."

The woman said, "When I was a kid, I remember, I did a mean thing. I don't know what it was any more, but it must've bothered me a good deal, because I went to my old man and told him about it. He wasn't exactly bright enough to read by, but every once in a while he'd get something off. You know what he said? He said, 'Hell, everybody sweats.'"

"Did that make you feel better? Did it ease your mind?"

"I think it did."

"A man goes blind," the soldier said, "and they put him in a home with four hundred other blind men, saying, 'Not so bad now, huh?' But, God damn it, now it's worse by four hundred! Now there are four hundred and one guys to fumble around in the dark, and none can see any better for the company he's in. What is it to me that other people sweat? I have to live in my own skin, and all by myself."

"Would it ease you any to give me a kiss?" the woman said. "I know it would ease me."

"I told you what I was. Believe it. Don't make me prove it."

"You didn't prove anything when you kissed me last night. Why would it be different now?"

"Because I like you," he said. "Last night I didn't."

"Don't you ever kiss a woman when you like her? It's good that way, Stan."

"With me, it's no good either way. I might be married, I might have a dose, I might be a fag—you only know me by sight."

"I have answers for all those things. If you were sick, you'd tell me, and if you were a fag, *I'd* tell *you*, and if you were married, well, marriage isn't made of iron."

"No," he said, "but people are."

"Not all people. Not you."

"How can I alienate you? What can I say to make you hate me? Suppose I describe you, exactly and honestly. Suppose I give you back what I see, not what you hope I see. Will you take offense, finally? Will you show me the door?"

"I know better than you what I look like."

"Hair of no special color and texture, not very dark, not very light, and not very fine. Features without distinction, run-of-the-mill, one and all. Legs and feet extremely beautiful. Hands better than average. Breasts average (a guess, of course). Posture below average. Intelligence less. Intellect none. Culture minus. Total impression: ordinary."

"I never thought I was a beaut," the woman said. "But do you really think my legs are so good?"

"It doesn't make you angry to be called ordinary?"

"Not particularly—and not at all at you."

"At whom, then—at God?"

"When I was seven-eight years old," the woman said, "somebody gave me a secondhand doll. Of all things, it was a man-doll. That is, he wore a man's clothes. Underneath, he wasn't much of anything. He had a beard, I remember, and a little silk hat came with him, and for no good reason, I sort of got to thinking of him as God, and I used to pray to him for things, whatever I happened to want. I was so wrapped up in praying and waiting, praying and waiting, that it took me a long while to realize that he wasn't delivering the goods. I kept on praying, but I left off waiting, and I put the clouts to him whenever there were no results right away quick, which was always: the little guy never did come through. That's all there is to the story, except that one day I got the idea of nailing him to a fence-picket, and when his dirty hands broke off, I threw him into the road. I went back to waiting, but there were no more prayers."

Keeled over now, as if he had run aground, the soldier stared across the woman at the sprawling city in the sky. "You seem to remember a good deal of your childhood," he said. "But can you remember where memory began—the sight, the sound, the scene, that all else came after?"

"I was never much at arranging things."

"It isn't a matter of arrangement. In fact, it's the opposite. You have to pick away at yourself till you find the thread that unravels you."

"I quit picking a long time ago," the woman said. "Probably because I know so God damn well I'll only find more of the same. There's nothing I specially look back on, just like there's nothing I specially look ahead to. It's a piece of cheese, life is, from end to end."

"But what you get at with your memory is the time when it might've been something else."

"As far as I'm concerned, it could only have been a different kind of cheese. Other people maybe had a turning-point—you, I guess, from the way you're talking—but I came straight from nowhere to no place."

"The turning-point," the soldier said. "Brother against brother."

[ *. . . He made you and Carlo decide your lives with a hundred-yard dash!*

*A race!*

*You had to run a race!*

*Jesus Christ, one of you had to run the other to death . . . !* ]

"Would you like to talk about it?" the woman said.

"I've been half my life trying to forget it," the soldier said. "I never will, but I'll always try."

"You might forget it if you told somebody about it. You might get it off your mind."

"I'd only get it deeper in. Talk is the wrong tool for this splinter. A gun would be just about perfect."

"As long as you keep the thing to yourself, you'll live backwards, a way I wouldn't wish on anybody. A person has to get his ass behind him, where it belongs."

The soldier said, "If life is cheese through and through, as you say, what's the difference how you face?"

[ *. . . You wanted to look at Carlo, but you couldn't, and you never learned whether he was looking at you. All you could do was think desperately to stop yourself from thinking.*

*You thought, 'Red Bank is a small town in New Jersey.'*

*You thought, 'There goes a meadowlark, like a fife.'*

*You thought, 'I am thirteen years old.'*

*'I'll stand here next to the car,' the man said. 'You two go back to the telephone-pole at the bridge and wait for my signal.*

*'When I blow the horn—like this—start running.' Using the twig, he scraped a line in the dirt from one side of the road to the other. 'The first one to cross that is the winner.'*

*(Had you known what you were doing at the moment, you won-*

*dered, or had the realization come later, to be grafted, with the passage of time, on the original event? Had the horror you felt whenever you thought back, as now, sprung from a horror engendered before or after the horrible act?)*

*As you and Carlo went off toward the bridge, you thought, 'I'm not going to try my hardest. I don't want to win.'*

*And then you thought, 'I wonder if Carlo does. I wonder how hard he's going to try.'*

*And then you thought, 'What difference does it make? I'm going to let him win.'*

*And then you thought, 'Red Bank is on the Navesink River. I wonder what Carlo is thinking.'*

*From down the road, the man said, 'On your marks' and you kneeled, and he said, 'Get set' and you were on your toes and fingertips, and then there was an instant when your whole body seemed to be a heart, and you felt yourself beat twice, and you thought, 'I won't run at all,' and then the horn sounded, and you were running—half a stride ahead of Carlo!*

*You thought, 'When we get to that tree-shadow, I'll slow down. I'll stop trying and let him take the lead. I could beat him if I wanted to, but I'm going to hold back, and he'll win. It isn't far to the shadow now, and that's where my brother against brother against brother against brother.'*

*But you couldn't make yourself give up! You couldn't lose, not even if it meant dying to stay in front! You couldn't lose to your own brother! He could've been God Almighty, and still you'd've tried to win—and you did win!*

*When you passed the finish-line, you stopped, but Carlo kept on running, and he ran on and on till he fell down, and you watched him pick himself up and run some more, never once looking back, and then he came to a curve in the road, and he was still running when he disappeared. . . . ]*

With her arms outspread, the woman's head and body formed

a cross on the sand. "It could change," she said. "It could change so easy that you eat your heart out wondering why it doesn't." She seemed suddenly to intensify, as if a hand had been placed upon her, and then she went slack and trembled like a spring unsprung. "If you want, Stan," she said. "Please, Stan, if you want."

Kneeling beside her, he opened her dress, and the cross of flesh came alive at a touch, and its arms embraced him, and its staff was riven.

*[ . . . You went to Carlo's dorm in the morning to say good-bye, but he wasn't there, and neither were his things: he'd run away during the night.*

*You stood there in the doorway, looking at the empty bed and the empty locker, and a roommate of Carlo's was talking to you, trying to tell you something, but the words he used had no meaning that you were able to understand, and always, afterward, they came back to you as sounds that might've been made by an animal or a machine. You turned away, and they waned.*

*You had no idea where you were going. You were merely walking through high wide halls, touching familiar objects— knobs, door-jambs, panes of glass—as you passed them by, objects that Carlo too had touched, and you knew, in a flare of recognition, that they were your last common ground. A bell rang, signifying for all but you the beginning of another year at the Home—all but you and Carlo.*

*And then, as if it had been your known destination all along, you were in the superintendent's office, and you were saying to him, 'I can't go with the Picnic-man. I want to stay here.'*

*There were some pencils on his desk, you remembered, and, before speaking, he made them lie side by side with their points all in line. 'You wanted to go as late as yesterday,' he said. 'You must've, or you'd not have tried so hard against Carlo.'*

*'I didn't know Carlo would run away,' you said. 'If I did, I would've lost the race.'*

*'Would you?' he said. 'Be truthful, son.'*

*'I didn't want to win till I won,' you said. 'All the time I was running, I thought to myself how I would try to lose.'*

*'In the end, though, you didn't lose: you won.'*

*'Why did I? If I wanted to lose, why did it all come out like this?'*

*'I don't know everything,' he said. 'I'm only the superintendent of an orphan-asylum.'*

*'But somebody has to tell me what to do!' you said. 'Somebody has to tell me how to talk to myself when I'm alone! I can't ask the Picnic-man. He'll only say what he said before—that you always win a race from your brother. Maybe he's right, but I still have to find out why I want to live yesterday all over again, but never tomorrow. I feel like all the rest of my life was in my hand, and I was looking for a place to throw it away.'*

*And now the superintendent rose from his desk, saying, 'Don't ever throw it away, son! Keep it, and if you live long enough to become human, some day you'll learn how the Picnic-man was right and wrong, both. He was right when he said that all races are won from brothers: that's the way things are. But he was wrong when he failed to say this: that the way things are is not the way they always have to be. So go with him, son, and do what you can to change them.' And then he came around the desk and gave you his hand, and he said, 'I've known so many boys that you might think there'd be some I couldn't love—but I love them all, and all I hate is to say good-bye. . . .'*]

EVER THUS TO TYRANTS

That was a big man what he come freein' the slaves,
Six-four in sock-feet, they say, but sinful thin,
Scant-chested, like he taken the gallopin' grief,
And sad, cemetery-sad, 'less if he maken a smile,
And then, great Gawd, he Christ up in the blue!—
A big tall heist-up man, a slave-lovin' buckra
From who laid the chuck, and he change things.

Overlooker Buford with the hoss-pistol he gone,
And the sonabitchin' preacher what he preach us
"Work hard, and you go to the kitchen of heaven"
And Ole Marster, white father of black bastards,
The spit dreen down the stroke-side of his mouth,
The side he smoke on when they still was a South:
That big mournful drawed-out man he change things.

We don't show permission-passes to come and go,
And we don't live and die by no blast on a horn
(None but the last), and we get to book-read some,
Which they like to wore you out for that once,
And studyin' this Gospel they set such store by,
It don't relate is the Lawd white or whatsoever,
But it promise a hell of a lot to the pore nigger
And a bigger lot of hell to the nigger-rich:
That skinny homemade man he done some changin'.

But they shoot a gun and kill him down to death,
And what he come to change with the freedom-war
They half-change it back with their K-K-Klux.
They don't fight us bucks for side-bets now,
Nor breed us like hawgs or feed us in a trough,

And they pay us cash, not cobbler on Sundays off,
And we hold more land than we need for a grave.

But in the end, half-free amount to all-slave,
And they's a sign to say it wherever we look,
On the cars and jakes and streets and schools,
On the white-meat sluts and the houses of prayer,
On the dirt that we eat and the tools we live by,
On the one door open and the twenty they shuts,
And spinnin' on many and many a turnpike tree.

If you read them signs and stay in your place,
If you stand down-wind and grin like a chimp,
If you roll your eyes and wear polka-dot ties,
If you go back on your soul to keep your balls,
They calls you a good nigra, a shinin' example
(What they mean is with shoes and toilet-seats):
The trash under sheets they change what counts.

We waitin' long now on a brother of that man,
Big or small, short or tall, sad or otherwise,
But it look like that kind don't come in pairs,
Or else he dead too, shot in the head and forgot:
Them good ones can sure soak up a lot of lead.
But the bad can die from the self-same sick
White skin ain't no harder to stick than black,
And hot blue blood ain't so blue when it cold.

Three hundred years is too damn much bowin' down!

"TURN OUT
ALL LIGHTS
BEFORE
LEAVING"

*[ . . . You spent that night alone in a room that all summer you'd believed was for you and Carlo, and from your bed in the darkness, you looked out at your particular piece of sky—and when you thought ahead to the many nights that were before you, all of them lonely and all won from someone lonelier, you wept, you wept. . . . ]*

The soldier lay asleep, but a faint scent in the air was bestirring his mind, and a dream began to shred like lifting mist. The search for a name to give the flavor went slowly, and, impatient and baffled, he shifted from his back to his side. A hand of sunlight spanned his face, and with his eyes open a little, he recorded a black-and-white first image: the staves and spaces of the blind. He sat up suddenly, saying, "You don't understand! You don't understand!" The bars on his vision were no longer vertical, as they had seemed when he was lying down, but before he could stop speech, he had spoken again. "You don't understand," he said.

From the doorway of the bedroom, the woman said, "Understand what?"

The soldier dabbed aimlessly at an outbreak of sweat. "I don't know," he said. "I must've had a dream." He looked down at his finger-streaked chest. "There's mud in my blood."

"Who doesn't understand what?" the woman said.

"Come around here," he said. "I want to see you in the light." The woman entered the room, but she paused at the bed, partly hidden by a sheet that had been flung over the footrail. "Between me and the window," he said. Her wrapper was a silk print of falling leaves: red, yellow, and brown. Those pierced by the sun were pale; the others appeared to have been transferred to the woman's body. "You're good," he said. "You're even better than I remembered."

"I want you to answer me, Stan."

"Thin, but good—and you left a good taste. I can't name it, but I'd know it through a mouthful of crow."

"I'm asking about the dream."

"You don't give up, do you? Well, there was no dream—or none that followed me. I lied, as usual."

"What were you scared of, then?"

"The window. I thought it was barred."

"Why should that scare you?"

"Why should anything scare anybody?"

"You always come back with something like that," the woman said. "It's supposed to be an answer."

"What more do I have to say? A jail has barred windows: I thought I was in jail. That's plain enough, isn't it?"

"What made you think you were in jail?"

He smeared a start of sweat from his armpit. "Symbolic," he said. "For jail, read: what I got myself into with you last night."

The woman came closer to him, and, through the printed leaves, he discerned her own leaf. "You're still lying, Stan," she said. "What we did last night only tied us while we were doing it. Where's the jail?"

"In my mind," he said, and lying back, he drew the woman with him.

"Please not, Stan," she said, "not if it's only a way to hide," but when he tried to take his hands away, she held them against her, saying, "I didn't mean you couldn't. You can, if you really want. You always can."

He shook his head. "Do you think I'll ever be worth it?" he said.

"You're worth it now," she said. "But you have a grudge against yourself—what for, God only knows—and you sit in your own light all the time, eating yourself up with hate."

"What would you do if I told you why?"

"If telling'll get rid of the thing, tell."

"It won't. It's here to stay, and there's no one to forgive me."

"Forgive yourself. Why be so hardhearted?"

"You don't understand, Jean."

"Only you understand, is that it?" the woman said, and, sitting up, she stared at the floor. Her wrapper was open, and she made a mild and absent effort to cover the reveal. "Only Stan Clarke," she said, and now she rose and went toward the door.

"I'll tell you," he said, "and then you'll understand too."

She looked back at him from the doorway, saying, "It wouldn't be so hard to guess."

"Pick a card," he said. "Any card."

"You keep inside yourself, and you think nobody knows you're there, but over and over, you give yourself away."

"Do I? How?"

"By trying to hide still further."

"'The wicked flee when no man pursueth,'" he said. "That's not original. I quote a man named Proverbs."

"Another place to hide—that's what you use me for."

"Woman: the coward's grave," he said.

"Not that I care too much. It's nothing to me what you have in your mind when you do it. The same thing can have a lot of meanings, no two alike."

"What does the thing mean to you?" he said. "Describe its significance, if any, and give dimensions. Or is the thing a thing of the spirit to you, to be apprehended but not explained?"

"You want to make me sore at you," the woman said, "but I'm only sore at what you say," and she went up the hall to the kitchen.

After dressing, the soldier joined her. "Am I too formal today, or not enough so?" he said. "I can either take off my pants or put on my *fourragère*."

"You can be a whole shitepoke without half-trying."

"Without trying at all," he said, and, sitting opposite the woman at the card-table, he drew vanishing lines in the linoleum with the tines of a fork. "But by trying very hard, I can sometimes be halfway human."

"I was only stinging you," the woman said. "You need stinging now and then."

"You know what I need?" he said. "I need to get kicked out of here on my kidneys."

"Maybe, but would that get me anything I need?"

"There's better guys anywhere and everywhere."

"Better for me?"

"In all things," he said. He took an orange from the refrigerator and looked at the rind, thinking *bitter*, and he bit it with his mind, and his mouth shrank from the imagined juice. "What good am I if I'm hardly ever here?" he said. "I'm not even here this minute. I'm talking to you from very far away."

"It's like we were in the same room," the woman said.

*[ . . . On the terrace of the fraternity-house, you remembered, there was a black rubber mat inlaid with white rubber lettering, and, before opening the door, you stomped your snow-caked galoshes, one on the Zeta and one on the Psi. In the dog-trot hall, you set your basket on the bottom step of the staircase, saying, 'Sandwiches! Fruit! Candy bars!' and then upper classmen came from the library and the billiard-room to paw your stock and flip you coins.*

*Up the stair-well, someone said, 'What ho! It's Shoeless Joe!' and a pair of wing-tip cordovans, tied together and bumping the spindles, slid down the banister and fell into the basket. There was laughter. 'Shoeless Joe! Look out below!' the voice said, and a frosh ass-skated down from the first landing. He dusted his hands and bowed (laughter), and then he helped himself to an apple and dropped a quarter into one of your galoshes (more laughter). 'They're yours,' he said, indicating the shoes. 'After tonight, Shoeless Joe is no more.'*

*You took the shoes out of the basket and put them on the floor, but you said nothing, not even when the frosh moved so close to you that he blurred. 'When you get home,' he said, 'take those God damn galoshes off and burn them, or eat them, or shove them up your bung—but don't wear them around here again. Other guys are working their way through Lafayette, but you're the only one who flaunts his shabby rags with pride, and I won't stand for it. The pov-*

*erty-racket, that's what it is, the poor-but-proud game straight out of Horatio Alger. You have no right to dress as you do; it's an insult to people who can dress better.'*

*'I'm due at the Deke house,' you said, and you picked up the basket and started for the door.*

*'Remember what I told you,' the frosh said.*

*You turned, saying, 'If there's as much wear left in your face as there is in these galoshes, come out on the terrace, you snot-nosed mother-lover.'*

*He came, but the others came with him, and they piled on you and pinned you down while somebody fiddled with your feet. When you were allowed to stand, you stood in the cordovans, one on the Zeta and one on the Psi, and the door was closing (sustained laughter). . . . ]*

"This husband of yours," the soldier said. "Were you far gone on him?"

The woman tapped the tip of a knife on the table-top, making the blade blear and chime. "You mean, did I love him?" she said.

"That's one way of putting it."

"Not your way, I gather. Far gone: what an expression!"

"It has this advantage over love," the soldier said. "You'll never see it written on a fence."

"I suppose if food was written on a fence, you'd stop eating."

"I'm a private guy. Remember?"

"When we got married," the woman said, "we were so broke that we couldn't even rent us a room. My old man let us use the sleeping-porch, and that was our home for pretty near a year—screens on the street-side and windows on the parlor-side. We were private guys too. Even in the dark, it was no good: either the springs gave the show away, or else when you got up afterwards to go to the bathroom, it was like hollering out to the family, 'We just did it! Paul and me just did it!' It got so we'd sooner do it in the bushes, and, God damn it, many's the time that's just where we went. All along, though, we were scratching pennies together. . . . But what did I start out to prove?"

"How far gone you were in public," the soldier said.

"I get to talking, and after a while I forget where I'm going. I guess that's a sign of something."

"'Scratching pennies,' you were saying."

"If you want to hear more of this crap," the woman said, "one of us finally saw an ad in the paper: a Kansas City outfit called the Mecca Gem Company that sent you phony pearls on consignment. You paid five dollars a dozen strings, and you sold them for whatever you could get. The way the ad said, you could clear a hundred a week easy, on account of people all over were crying out loud for these pearls—and we fell for it. We bought us that old wreck of a flivver, loaded it to the gills with our first consignment, and tried ourselves out on the territory around Bakersfield, towns like Visalia, Maricopa, Porterville. Well, a month went by, and we were ready to lay down and die: we only sold about two dozen strings, mostly by accident, and our total take was a handful of small change. We were lousy at the game, green as grass. Neither of us could've peddled bock beer at a salt-lick. But the worst of it was how the feeling of being ashamed came back, of doing something sneaky and dirty in the dark, only this time all we were after was trying to make a living. I remember a night in Modesto, a Saturday, usually the best of the week for selling, and we weren't even out on the street with a satchel. We were sitting in a motel room, and we were dead beat. There was cash for about three-four more days on the road, and after that, we'd either have to eat the pearls or hock the Ford, but either way, we'd be out of business and practically broke, and a whole year of saving would've gone up the flue. We were beat, and I guess it was being beat that I got the idea from, that or out of the air, but wherever, it struck me that mighty few people in the San Joaquin were going to *buy* any jewelry: the trick was to *sell* it. That's all the idea was, a teaser, and I put it to Paul that we ought to take and blow the rest of our money, fifteen-twenty bucks, on a low-cut dress, black and plain, no fiddle-faddle, and then show me off in some store-front wearing the pearls while he stood outside and sold to the gawkers. Old as the hills, the stunt was, and I knew it, but I had a body, and I didn't have to be original if it sold pearls. Paul had an objection. He wanted to know, what would people think of him, practically letting his wife do a strip in the street?" The woman scraped a scatter of crumbs into a line, and then she looked up at the soldier.

"Am I expected to speak?" he said.

"I just wanted that to sink in: what would people think of *him*."

"It sank," the soldier said.

From an adjacent house, the one next door or the one beyond, came the sound of music. The soldier tried to entitle the melody, but it reached him partly washed out by other sounds—tires on pavement, flushed water, crocked crockery, and the talk of tools—and he failed to fill in the blanks.

"So you're not my first hard-shell," the woman said, "and the chances are, you won't be my last. It's my luck to all the time get the same kind of a guy—the what-do-you-call-it educated kind."

"Maybe that's the kind you go for."

"Whichever, that's what I wind up with—some piss-proud gent that can't even get along with himself, let alone me or the world. My people were just people, not such a much, but Paul's was big stuff once, or so he used to say, and he said it often enough to make me understand what a comedown it was for him to marry me. Paul Hampton Bell, his whole name was, and he had wonderful manners. He could eat a hamburg or a roasten-ear like a duke—and me, the first meal we had together, I held my fork like a cello. When he saw that, he like to faint dead away, and I'm only sorry he didn't: I wouldn't have had to sit in a crowded restaurant taking an eating-lesson from him. He had wonderful manners, Paul Hampton Bell."

Again through the lift and fall of sound, the music surfaced. "Did you get the dress?" the soldier said.

"After a fight," the woman said. "I wore it right out of the store, and the first good corner we came to, we made a deal for window-space with a druggist, a dime on every sale, and I climbed in and started slinking. Somebody's son stepped up and bought the string straight off of my neck, and the rush was on. Modesto sure must've been hungry for a medicine-show, because we sold half a gross of pearls in a quarter of an hour. It was the same everywhere else, though. The whole Southwest we decked out in those pearls, sometimes making enough in a couple hours to knock off for a week and live like tourists. A year, more than a year, we went on that way, and then all at once Mecca Gem got ambitious and hiked the price up out of sight, and we were through. Paul landed a job hauling oil from anywhere to nowhere, and I made my first stab at keeping house. By rights, we should've got along fine and died fifty years later an hour apart, like you read in the papers, but a peculiar thing: Paul never got over the time we lived on that porch. All the rest of his life that I know about, he was still living there, and it only seemed to get worse in a place of our own. Me, I think I was cured by all that faunching around as a window-display, but Paul it made so he wouldn't even go near me in the daytime, to kiss me or to hand me a light, and when we walked in the street, there'd be room for another couple between us, and the thing you get married for, it had to be dark for him to do that, with the shades down for extra dark, and it had to stay dark afterwards too. I used to lay there next to him, I remember, wondering what under God was the expression on his face that he was trying to hide, and it came to me finally that he really wasn't hiding anything at all. The opposite, he was *showing* something: what a shame it was that a Bell had to sleep with a cheap one like me. He was either making small of me or big of himself, but one or the other, it was my head that he stood on to grow tall." The woman combed the crumbs into a cupped hand and then looked at them as if puzzled by their presence. She returned them to the table, and again she herded them with the knife-blade. "Far gone—how can you be far gone on that?" she said, and then she smiled, saying, "But I suppose 'how' has nothing to do with it, because now I'm the same about you."

"I'm just the first guy that happened down the pike."

"I won't fool you—you aren't."

"No? What number *am* I?"

Her smile foundering, the woman shook her head and said, "Nobody in the world can be as mean as you."

"But, God damn it, Jean," the soldier said, "you've got to have a reason for feeling the way you do!"

"Lots of people talk that can't spell."

"Why, Christ, you don't even know my right name!" he said. "Stan, you call me, Stan, Stan—and half the time I have to stop myself from looking around for the bastard. You don't know where I was coming from the other day, or where I'm apt to be next week, except that it certainly won't be here. If you wanted to trace me, 'A guy I picked up on the road,' is all you'd be able to say. 'A guy in uniform.' He raised his bandaged hand. 'A wounded guy,' maybe. 'A guy wearing a Purple Heart.'"

"Would I have a reason if I knew your name?" the woman said. "If I knew where you came from and where you're going, would that be a reason?"

[ . . . *It was a summer evening between your first and second years at Lafayette, and you were back in Red Bank and living at (you could only call it the Picnic-man's) home. You'd never been able to make yourself enjoy it more fully than as a right-of-way revocable at any time, for beyond such license to come and go at will, you seemed to possess nothing there, neither the people nor the personality nor the cube of space referred to as 'your room.'*

*You were walking along the river-road that evening, you remem-bered, and where sprinklers still seeded the lawns, you traversed cool and dustless caverns of air, and through a break in a bank of willows, you saw a bejeweled steamer on the bejeweled stream, and then, rounding a bend in the road, you entered an intervale filled with faint music from a house set far within a wrought-iron palisade. There were parked cars at either side of the way, and you remembered leaning against one of them while you watched long shadows rake the grass in the tempo of the tune.*

*A voice behind you spoke so calmly that it seemed to have issued from a scene in your mind. 'Give us a drag before you throw it away,' it said, and you turned, and a hand appeared in the window of the car. Offering it the stub of your cigarette, you saw the coal fan a girl's face to flame and then fade.*

*'What were you thinking about?' she said. 'When you were watching them dance in there, what was running through your mind?'*

*'So far as I know, nothing,' you said. 'Why?'*

*'Were you wishing you were in there instead of out here?' she said. 'Because I can make the wish come true: it's my house.'*

*'There was no wish,' you said. 'I was only watching and listening, and when I had enough of that, I'd have moved on.'*

*'You don't feel left out?'*

*'If I do, I think I feel it far less than you.'*

*'I'm not left out,' she said. 'How can you be left out of your own party?'*

*'I was getting ready to ask,' you said.*

*'I'm only sitting outside of myself for a while. It's like taking your shoes off.'*

*You laughed, saying, 'Would you care to put them on again?'*

*'What's so comical?'*

*'I was thinking we might take a walk.'*

*'Think again, townie,' she said. 'I don't walk with everybody.'*

*'Probably not,' you said. 'You only smoke their snipes.' You tossed her the rest of your pack. 'Try those and keep pure for Princeton,' you said, and then you went away.*

*You were well up the road when head-lamps took a fast fall out of your shadow. A car came abreast of you and stopped, and the same voice said, 'I'll walk with you, townie. I'll walk to Atlantic Highlands.'*

*'What made you change your mind?' you said.*

*'What you said about not feeling left out. It came over me that you were telling the truth.'*

*'Didn't you believe me when I said it?'*

*'No more than you believed me when I told you the house was mine.'*

*'But I did believe you,' you said.*

*'What the hell would I be doing out in the cold if I belonged inside?'*

*'The same thing I was—reading about royalty.'*

*'I mean to be royal myself. Some day, I'm going to be on the other side of that God damn fence.'*

*'What's in there that you want so much?'*

*'Oh, Jesus Christ!' she said.*

*'I didn't intend to sound so priestly. I'll recast the question.'*

*'It'll still be straight from the soul, townie,' she said, 'and I have about as much use for the soul as a third tit. All the same, I'll answer you. My father told me once, "Never worry about being rich, but always worry about being poor."'*

*'When you followed me, then, you followed the wrong guy.'*

*'I know that,' she said, 'but I'm hoping that some day you'll be able to tell me why.'*

*You looked at her for a moment, and then you went to the car and opened the door, saying, 'Right now, I can only tell you this: I think we're going to ruin each other.'*

*She stood close to you in the road. 'I know that too,' she said. . . . ]*

The soldier put his swathed hand on the table, watching it as if for a sign of life, and then he thrust at the woman the heavy weight concealed in the soiled tape and cotton. "Take it off for me, will you, Jean?" he said.

The woman sat still, saying, "You never needed help before. Why do you need it now?"

"I said take it off!"

"I'm giving you a chance to think, Stan."

"I want to stop thinking!"

"How will me taking the bandage off make you stop?"

He stared at her. "My God, don't tell me you don't know!" he said. "After all this, don't tell me you're thick!"

"Take your hand out of my face," the woman said. "You know only too well if I'm thick or not. I didn't put that bandage on. *You* did—and you know what you put it on for. All I'm asking is, how does it do you any good for me to take it off? Will that stop you being sick in the head? Will you be cured once and for all? Or will you still think you hurt, only without a bandage to tell you where?"

"*You're* standing on *my* head now," the soldier said, and suddenly a dustwhirl of anger bored up through him. "You cornfield push, even *you* have to stand on somebody else!"

The woman spoke without raising her voice, saying, "For all the books you've read, you educated fool, you have the manners of a horse. This is still my house, and don't forget it—or I might forget why I'm letting you stay. You've been on the run, like crazy and for a long time, and you're pretty damn near run out."

"Quit it, Jean," the soldier said. "For God's sake, quit it. Quit it!"

"Quit running," the woman said, and taking up his hand, she began to rip the tape away.

He felt as if he were being dismantled. His hand, he thought, so long hidden by the bandage, had been absorbed by it and become part of the fabric, which, unwound, would be found hollow, and what once had been flesh, bone, and blood would lie in kinks and curls, like used yarn, on the floor. The bandage was off now, and his hand lay exposed, huddled like something newborn and sleeping. He caused it to stir, but the joints were stiff, and it remained crabbed and clenched. The woman turned its palm upward and put her mouth to it.

The soldier felt an astringent emotion shrink his gums, and he looked at the woman, who wavered as if seen through a rained-on winpowpane, saying, "I'll never find a better time to kill myself."

He watched her move away along the hall, her robe windborne, and when the last swirl of its skirt disappeared through the door of her room, he imagined her walking out of the pattern of leaves falling and letting it fall whispering, and then he imagined her lying down, with an arm across her eyes, and waiting for him naked in her own dark. As he followed her, a thought of Paul Bell dropped into his mind, like a pebble in a pool, and a turbid cloud of scenes, a sediment, rose. He saw two people take shape in an auto-court room (at Barstow, was it, or Merced?), one of them rocking himself and the other sitting still as she read and reread a sign on the wall (Turnout all lights before leaving); and then he saw a black dress (satin, had she said, or velvet?) in the hard two-hundred-watt brilliance of a store-front, and many faces outside with swarming maggot eyes; and then the room again, dark now, and the dress was on a hanger, limp and empty, and the man and woman were seated as before, one rocking himself and the other reading words on a wall in her mind (Turn out all lights before leaving).

"Eugenia," the soldier said. "Eugenia!"

[ . . . *You thought of a name that you hadn't spoken for years ('Ann,' you thought, 'my Ann'), and you went back to an Indian-summer afternoon in the woods. The trees burned with color-turn, and as you waded through the windfalls, they rasped underfoot and powdered, and you left brown talc prints behind you on the ground. You remembered a chipmunk sitting spellbound on a stump, and you remembered an osprey on patrol in the charred and leaf-smoked air, and you remembered, finally, how a long silence was broken.*

*She said, 'How far do we have to go before you ruin me?'*

*'Is that the only reason for a turn in the woods?' you said.*

*'It's the only one I've known since I was fifteen.'*

*'I'd have supposed you started earlier. You disappoint me.'*

*'I mean to make up for lost time,' she said, and you laughed. 'You have a fatal gift for laughing in the wrong place, townie.'*

*'Listen,' you said. 'If you were laid at fifteen, it was in a dream within a dream. You're a wild enough piece—I've learned that much these last few weeks—but most of it is in your mind. Dirty pictures.'*

*'When I was fifteen,' she said, 'anybody could make money, even a frost like my father, and he stumbled across enough of it to afford a chauffeur. A mick, he was, and we called him Collins. I never did know his other name. Maybe be had none. After all, he was only a chauffeur.'*

*'But he fascinated you.'*

*'He had red hair on his wrists,' she said. 'He fascinated me.'*

*'You talk as if the main drain of your house goes through your bedroom.'*

*'Orange red, like rust.'*

*'And you were only fifteen, and inquisitive.'*

*'A bare fifteen,' she said, and then she paused, and when she spoke again, the words seemed to come from someone else.*

*'Did I help you enjoy the summer, Steve?' she said. 'Will you always remember it?'*

*You looked about you—at the fallen leaves and the leaves falling through the smoke-screened air—and you tried to reconstruct the season from the season's end (to replace the leaves, you thought), and at length you faced her to say, 'There was no summer—and no day and night, no sea and sky, no earth. There was only Ann.'*

*She moved away from you a little, and, stooping for a russet leaf, she stood twirling it for a moment, and then she said, 'You still have a couple of hours before traintime, Steve. Make them go slowly for us. Make them last. . . .'* ]

The soldier was brought up from sleep by the sound of a shower running, and, keeping his eyes closed, he thought of gargling gutters, of rain-grains dripping from eaves, of windshake sprinting away over shingles like birds, and then the shower was shut off, and through half-open lids he peered out at a brass afternoon. Weaving in on waves of heat came the same tin tune that he had heard earlier, and again he tried to recall its title, and again he failed. The woman appeared in the doorway, her body damp and glinting, and her hair slick, like a caul.

She went to her dressing-table, and, sitting before its three-paned mirror, she regarded herself without interest or emotion, as if she were independent of the image and not responsible for its actions or appearance. The soldier watched her, hoping that by some form of recognition she would relieve him of a sense of trespass, but she continued to gaze into the glass as through a window giving on a scene of small concern. After a period, she picked up a comb and idly ticked its teeth a few times, and then she drew a center-part like a scar and carded the halves of hair sideways, flinging broken strings of water-beads to the floor.

The soldier said, "What did Paul say when you did this?"

"I don't recall that he said anything."

"Didn't he ever pin a rose on you?" the soldier said as the woman wrought one of the halves into a gleaming braid. "Or was he too busy decorating Paul Hampton Bell?"

"What's so poetic about fixing hair?"

"Highborn Paul. He must've been a purebred zero, by null out of void."

"He wasn't such a bad guy, Stan. He had his good side."

"That's a hell of a sentence to have on a tombstone."

The woman completed the second braid and bound the two overhead. "What do you think you'll have on yours?" she said.

The soldier sat up, feeling empty-handed, and he stared at silt milling in a buttress of sunlight. "I was very close to something very good," he said.

The woman was beside him on the bed, saying, "I didn't mean that, Stan—not the way you think."

"Very close, I was. I almost had words to reach it with."

"You're no further account of Paul," the woman said. "He's dead. He was dead before he ever went away."

"'Sweet and seemly it is to die for your country,'" the soldier said. "That's what he ought to have on his stone. '*Dulce et decorum est pro patria mori.*'"

"What was the good of him dying for his country if he lived for himself?"

"My God, what do you think I live for?"

"That's for you to say—or not to say. It doesn't matter."

"Paul died for his country, and I'm a deserter," the soldier said. "That doesn't matter?"

"Not to me," the woman said.

"The only way I'll ever die for my country is in front of a firing-squad. Would that matter?"

"Yes, because it would mean you got caught."

"I don't know how to talk to you," the soldier said. "I don't know what words to use. I'm a deserter. *A deserter!* A tinhorn Judas! The one sweet and seemly thing for me to do would be to hang myself in some outhouse!"

"I hate it when you talk like that, because you can be good when you want, Stan—wonderfully good."

"Yes," he said. "I can speak so that people mistake me for a human being."

"More than speak."

"I regret that more than all the rest. I did enough without crawling into you with my shabby little life."

"It didn't seem so shabby. No worse than my own."

"Everybody sweats," the soldier said. "We're back on the old belt-line."

"With the kind of a mind you've got," the woman said, and the words trailed each other in fatigue and defeat, "I guess you'll always be the only Judas. Wherever a person turns, some mean bastard is putting himself out to make a rotten world rottener, but you don't see that—or if you do, you forgive it, like you were Jesus and Judas both. And maybe you are, because most of us are a mixture of good things and bad things. But you carry it too far, Stan. There's other guys on the Cross. There's other guys that sold out." She hesitated, and, contemplative, she seemed to be watching her last phrase move away beyond reach or recall. "I wish I could con you about that, but I can't. What you did was a thing only a mean bastard would do—but the point is, it's done. It's done, Stan, and it's going to stay done even if they catch you and shoot you for it. They could shoot you twice, and you could die twice, but it'll never be different. That being so, I say, Christ, why die at all?"

"I've been dying all my life," the soldier said. "Maybe I'll begin living after my death."

"There's no rule that a sinner has to go on sinning. If you think you're on the wrong train, don't just sit there. God damn it, get off!"

"I'm not on the train," the soldier said. "I'm the train itself."

"I might've known you'd have an answer that wasn't an answer. You always do."

"It's a *good* answer," the soldier said. "What do you think a sin is—something you can put down when you're tired of it, a bundle, a suitcase? It's a part of you, like your blood, and you put it down only when you die—and if there's a hell, not even then. Eternity with a suitcase—what a thought!"

"Don't worry your head," the woman said. "When you go, you're gone."

[ . . . *It was an early-winter Sunday in Easton during your senior year, and you were standing at your window on Third Street, watching lines of rain fall to grain the air like a reel of old film. Below, you remembered, the slates of the sidewalk seemed to be glassed, and now and then, when a trolley passed, it struck blue sparks from the suspended wire. You heard slipper-heels in the hallway now, and then you heard the sibilance of paper, and on the floor, in a gas-lit crack under the door, lay a letter. You took it to the window and looked at the canceled stamps, an azure Special and a purple three, and you looked at the Red Bank postmark and the hour of mailing, and you looked at your name and address slurred out on a slant across the envelope—and you tried to rewind one day of time, to be with her while she was writing, while she was walking to the mailbox, and after the letter was gone—and then you looked at her photograph in the frame of the mirror. . . .*

*'. . . Out for a drive,' she had written, 'and I saw a rock that some crank had daubed JESUS SAVES on. I thought, "Saves what? He couldn't even save Himself," and then I thought, "I wonder what He'd have turned out to be if He hadn't been crucified," and I couldn't help thinking, "One of the crucifiers, probably. . . ."*

*'. . . A house party at somebody's place on Rumson Road,' she had written. 'Nobody you'd know. Ed Porter, I think his name was. Some slob from Princeton. . . .*

*'. . . Before I forget,' she had written, 'I must tell you about a little incident on the street the other day. It was snowing, and I was in a hurry to get home, but a man and woman stopped in front of me, blocking the way. They seemed to have stopped especially to stop me, because the man took his hat off and stood there looking me over. I'd never seen the people before, and, not being in the mood for an inspection by unknowns, I tried to go around them. But the man put his hand out, saying, "Excuse me, young lady, but I'd like to have a conversation with you." I said, "I don't talk to strangers," which was a God damn lie, because that's how I met you, and he said, "In reality, decent self-respecting people aren't strangers, even if they were never formally introduced." I said, "It's hardly the day for making fine points on a street-corner, so if you don't mind," and then, as if it explained all, he came out with this piece of nonsense. "I'm the Picnic-man," he said. I knew now that he was fruity, and, saying, "Delighted to meet you," I tried once more to pass. He said, "The Picnic-man—doesn't that mean anything to you? Didn't a mutual friend*

*ever tell you about the Picnic-man?" For some reason, he looked a little hurt, but it's no use trying to fathom that kind, and I said, "No, and if you don't take your hand off my arm, I'll call for help." He let go, saying, "It will not be necessary, young lady," and then he bowed and walked away with the woman. He seemed to have forgotten about the hat, and the snow lay on his head like white hair, as if he'd suddenly grown old. And without knowing why, I began to cry. . . .*

*'. . . I miss you, Steve,' she had written. 'We're only a few hours apart, but whenever you're away, it's as if we were separated by all time, and the days and nights go by like some endless funeral. Until we see each other again, Steve my Steve, dream of little fat angels. That's what Collins used to tell me. Remember Collins . . . ?'* ]

Wearing a cotton print, a little faded, and cotton pumps of the same pattern, faded too, the woman passed the soldier on her way to the door, and a wave of her flavor came to him on the intricate air. He listened as her footfalls ebbed on the leaf-strewn walk, and he found himself shaking his head, and he heard himself say, "When you go, you're gone."

He glanced about the room, again deriving a sense of trespass, this time, and unaccountably, from the eloquent posture of the tousled bedclothes, the kickshaws in disarray, and the garments flung and spent or hung and shrunken, but the compulsion to make an even deeper invasion of the woman's preserve was irresistible, and, drawing the chair from the kneehole of the dressing-table, he sat down facing his face between a pair of lamps with their shades askew, like hats on drunks. A battery of bottles and jars was scattered over powder-frosted glass, and one of these stood close to the edge above a partly open drawer. Opening it further, the soldier exposed a tray of dime-store gimcracks—curlers, barrettes, hairpins, lipstick-cartridges, and clips—some of them new, some of them bent or sprung into trash. Behind the tray lay a beige collapse of knotted stockings.

The drawer below held paper—bills, vouchers, snapshots, circulars, blank stationery, recipes, and scribbled-on cards. Under this rummage was a packet of letters bound with a rubber band. The topmost, addressed to Miss Eugenia Hahn at Bakersfield, had been posted from Stockton; its enclosure, covering both sides of a company letterhead and typed by Paul Bell (PB/pb), bore a date in the fall of 1938. It read:

When I left you the other night, I had no way of knowing that, due to a transfer to the "upstate" plant, it might be several weeks before I saw you again. In the "normal" course of things, I'd have called on you the following evening and told you in person, and with some decorum, what I now feel obliged to commit to the hazards of a hasty note. I use the word obliged, because I feel that the "events" of the night in question give you the right to know my "intentions" without delay. Much as I'd like the opportunity of declaring myself in your actual presence, I believe that this new phase of our "relationship" imposes urgent demands on my honor.

You will not doubt my word when I say that in making our last "date," I had no conscious thought of its ending as it did. I'll not deny that I'd looked forward to those hours in your "company," nor even that I'd hoped for your usual warm embrace as I took my leave, but anything beyond that I can truthfully disclaim. Yet from the very first, when I saw you coming toward me on the street, I was aware of a change. I felt oddly formal, like a man trying to make an "impression," and I remember talking in a kind of desperation, as if at any moment you might forget that I was there and go away.

Nothing of what I said comes back to me, however, and if we walked, I'll never know how long or where to or who we met on the way. Words were all that seemed important, and I must've made many of them before I realized that we were nearing your house again, and that the evening was almost over. At the same instant, I knew where my talk had been tending all along: I had taken advantage of a certain command of language to make a "seduction-speech." In view of the differences in our background and training, what followed when I asked you to visit my room, became as inexcusable as the use of force.

A heritage of family honor impels me to make amends in the only manner open to a gentleman, and I therefore respectfully request that you accept my hand in marriage.

The soldier folded the letter and sat for a while tapping the crease against his thumbnail. He saw an empty office in (where was it?) Stockton—desks, files, hooded business-apparatus, and a going-down sun slanting in to glare on a lumberyard calendar above an open typewriter. The keys were firing in bursts, and line after line of language (a certain command of) was rolled up by the platen, but no hands were visible on the board, and no face hovered over the machine-made words.

The soldier drew the second letter from the pack:

Having no exact copy of what I wrote before me, I'm at something of a disadvantage in defending myself. I happen to have retained a few notes, however, and these have served to "refresh" my recollection at least to this extent: that nothing I can recall having written explains your refusal of me.

You state, "There wasn't one single word in the whole letter about me. It was all about you, what you did, what you felt, what you thought, what your intentions were."

I think you're being unjust, Eugenia, and I'm sure that you'll agree when you give the matter calmer consideration. Any reasonable person, any objective and disinterested "third party," would support my contention that in offering marriage, my sole interest was you, not myself. We live in strange times if what once was chivalrous has become sordid. I prefer to believe that that is no truer in Bakersfield than it was in Savannah. My honor means much to me, but your "honor" means more, and I urge you—

Christ Christ Jesus Christ save me I'm no damn good but save me forget the million words I used to build myself up with and remember how I cried when you opened your dress one of those tears meant more than all of the talk you let me live for a while you made my blood hot for once and you simply can't throw me back in my own face now have pity Jean for God's sake have pity on me. . . .

The soldier riffled the letters for the one bearing the most recent date. It was a V-mail photostat that had been sent through an army post-office from "an island in the Pacific," but he was unable to read beyond the salutation. He lifted his eyes from the small shining sheet, wondering why he balked at this stage of the encroachment, now well begun: the dead man would never know, he thought, and the living woman would little care. He tried to force himself to continue, but the disability seemed actual, and, powerless to overcome it, he was equally powerless to fathom the split that made his mind reach for what his vision had refused. Did the letter speak once more and finally of failure, he wondered, or did it relate some belated success? Did it mention people or merely call attention to their place of birth? Did it show compassion, or did it instruct a wife in the use of a knife and fork? Did it hold in its single fold a single word of love, or had its spelling been worthy of Carolina to the end?

The soldier returned the letters to the drawer, and then, rising, he wandered about the house with the sensation of being close to some discovery, but, having no knowledge of what he sought, he found nothing. The tour concluded where it had begun, in the woman's room, and, more fatigued than ever, he lay down again, his eyes closing as if weighted and axled, like those of a doll, and he foundered quickly in deep sleep and a dream. He dreamed that his heart had stopped beating, yet he had remained alive: there was no other change. He moved in the spotless spaces of thought as he had moved through septic matter: he spoke, he ate and drank, he slept and awakened, he reasoned, and he was aware of no impairment of his senses. He lived, but with a stilled heart, the only change. He knew nevertheless, within the dream and while dreaming it, that a greater change would come to him when it ended: his heart would beat again, yet he would die.

[ . . . *The night before the midwinter Prom, it was, cold, clear, made of blown glass, and you were standing, you remembered, on the platform of the Phillipsburg station, waiting for the Black Diamond to roll in from the east. You could hear it up the track, a dozen dark green Pullmans with a shortstacked Pacific on the head-end, and then you could see its lamp looming, whitening the faces and blackening the backs of the crowd, and now the rails and ties and splintered planking had the shakes, and through your feet you felt the brakeshoes grind—and the high cars began to pass, dripping snow-melt and steaming.*

*When the train stopped, there was a rush for the vestibules, and you watched the Prom-girls being singled out as they descended, and soon the platform was covered with pairs poised face to face, as if a dance had just come to an end. But after a moment, they hurried off to the cars and cabs that would take them to the Karldon, or to Seip's, or to the frat-houses on the Hill—or, best of all, to some dim warm quiet private planned-for place.*

*You were a car-length apart when you saw each other, and as you closed the gap, you tried to memorize what she wore (her colors, her trim) and how she looked (her lines, her form), because all your life you would want to summon her as she seemed to you then—a home of your own, the first, and the last you would ever deeply desire to live in—but when she stood within reach, you knew that you knew nothing more than you'd known before, her name, and as if that too were insecure, you tried to fix it by repetition, but you gave and heard the one-word recitation within your mind.*

*You had no car, and you hired no cab: you walked. You crossed the bridge, and through a new snow, already old there near the tracks, you made your way up Northampton Street past the coonskin jam around Seip's, and then, crossing the Circle, you kept on along Third to your boardinghouse at the foot of Sullivan Hill. The hallway and the stair-well were dim in a doll's-hand of gaslight, and a gas-log fire was the only illumination for your room. You indicated a card-table set for two before the iron mantel, and you said, 'I hope you're hungry, Ann. Otherwise my landlady won't believe you're my wife.'*

*She gave you a look that began as a smile and ended as a twitch. 'Am I here as your wife?' she said.*

*'You're everywhere as my wife,' you said. 'Didn't you know that?'*

*At the card-table, she raised a corner of a damp napkin, revealing a plate of sandwiches. 'An intimate little supper for your boarding-house bride,' she said. 'And how will you toast me—in celery tonic out of your toothbrush glass?'*

*You removed a lidded pot from the radiator and placed it near the sandwiches. 'I'm afraid there's only coffee, Ann,' you said.*

*'You must give me the name of your florist. How cleverly he did up these seventeen violets with twine!'*

*'A little old Italian, he is. He's always on the Circle somewhere.'*

*'And such discretion with the Boniface!' she said. 'A ruse worthy of Boccaccio, this wife-business.'*

*From alongside one of the settings, you took up a sheet of ruled note-paper, saying, 'This is for you from the landlady. It reads: "Your man have many time talk of you, and I see always your picture when I come clean up the room. I almost get to know you like that, so I glad to welcome you my house. I hope you will have a good enjoyment at the Ball."'*

*She went to the window and stared out at a gas-log suspended in the dark. 'Why did you tell her I was your wife, Steve?' she said.*

*'Because when it comes true,' you said, 'it'll be true for now as well as then.'*

*'How can that be?'*

*'I expect to marry your whole life, not just a part.'*

*'The rotten along with the good?'*

*'All of it, Ann, every damn minute of it.'*

*'What if it's all rotten?'*

*'It couldn't be. Nobody's life ever is.'*

*She came back from the window, saying, 'What do you know about me? After two and a half years, what do you really know?'*

*'I know enough to be as simple as my landlady: I glad to welcome you my house.'*

*But, shaking her head, she said, 'When you look at me, and I look in the mirror, we see different things, a different person.'*

*'I don't have to see what you see,' you said. 'Or won't you rest till I do?'*

*'You talk of marrying my whole life, but I think you're scared to death of the part you don't know. It's safer to imagine it. That way, you can tell yourself it doesn't count.'*

*'I can't, because it does. The things you did before we knew each other, the things that were done to you—that's how you got to be this.'*

*'You can get a lot of things done in twenty-one years,' she said. 'Some of them more than once.'*

*'That doesn't mean they have to be itemized. You can't add people up like a bill for plumbing.'*

*'You can't add them up at all if you only add what's in your mind. What you get is a dream.'*

*'If you aren't real, then, great Christ, neither is rain. What're you trying to tell me—that all this time I've been making love to my fist?'*

*'That's as good a way of putting it as any,' she said.*

*You remembered looking down at the landlady's note and, because you saw words, reading it through as if for the first time, and then you spoke, saying, 'I've never been sure that we'd last one another all our lives. All along I've known that some day we might meet head-on and have a finish fight. It's what I must've been afraid of the night we met, when I said I thought we'd ruin each other. This could be that fight, Ann, because we're both relentless: you want to show me the dirt under the rug, and I say it doesn't control; you say I've got to love that dirt, and I say it no longer exists. If you're very sure of yourself—and if you're surer of me than you have any right on earth to be—go ahead and roll back your rug. Start with your first dirty thought and end with your last dirty act, but blame no one if we never have a good enjoyment at the Ball.' She gazed at the blue simmer on the logs, the mobile grubs of gas, and, putting her hands out to the fire, she said, 'I told you once about a chauffeur named Collins. . . .'*

*But you stopped her to say, 'There's one thing, Ann, and you ought to know it before it's too late: I have a rug too. If you finish that story—no matter how, so long as you finish it—if you feel bound to say it and bind me to hearing it, if you finally make it a fact one way or the other, then I'm going to tell you a story about myself, and once I do, you'll not be able to tell me what I still can tell you, Collins or no Collins: I glad to welcome you my house. That's all, Ann.'*

*It took her a moment to decide, and when she did, she spoke very slowly and very quietly—she must've been very sure of herself and very sure of you. 'I haven't lied to you yet, and I never will,' she said. 'Collins was my first dirty act. . . .'*]

The room was dark, and there were stripes on the window, black and bandana-blue. The soldier rose, and, wondering how late it was, he went to the kitchen: the phosphorescent hands of the clock were almost overlapped at eleven. Forgetting this fact the moment he had learned it, again he found himself moving from room to room as if condemned to a quest with no destination. His temporary concern with time, he thought, his searches that seemed to be made for the sake of the seeking—were these the signs of loneliness only, or was his will disintegrating, was his mind unsound? Had he been reduced to sorting (buttons, stamps, stones, blocks) inanimate objects? Was the one thing he had ever yearned to arrange—his life—now beyond all arrangement?

He went to the door and looked out at the night-long neon

dawn breaking over the distant town. There were no lights in the rooms behind him, and except where a square of screen contained a star, there were no lights to be seen outside. In the next dooryard, a lawn-spray made a fine and slowly falling crepe-de-Chine, and now and then, on lunges of wind, came a bar or two of the harped-on song. Bare to the waist, the soldier crossed cremated grass to a space invaded by the settling vapor, and, stopping in it, he let it fog him over.

Beyond a wall, a voice spoke, and a voice replied, but the spray-sound drowned all but the inflection, and then metal touched metal, and a valve closed, and the withdrawing drizzle was like a curtain subsiding into a room. It was a silent and abandoned moment, the soldier thought, and he shivered until the held-back air returned to sweat him. He straddled the deck-chair, and, lying back, he stared at the sky.

Leaves cracked in the lane, and then shoes scraped on the walk and the steps, and knuckles knocked, and words went through the screen. "Earl Pryor calling, Mrs. Bell," the man said, and he waited for a reply. After a moment, he rapped again, saying, "Is anyone at home?"

"I am," the soldier said, and, as the man came toward him across the lawn, he dropped his left hand out of sight over the edge of the chair. "The name is Clarke."

"Mrs. Bell is at work, I assume," the man said. "I can't imagine where I got the impression that she'd be on vacation till the end of the week."

"I can't, either," the soldier said. "But you came to see me tonight."

"What makes you think that?"

"I get impressions too."

"Wrong ones, like mine."

"There's a good way to prove it. All you have to do is leave."

After an interval, the man said, "Why do you dislike me?"

"Do you want it with cream and sugar, or barefoot?"

"Barefoot," the man said.

"I never thought I'd get this chance," the soldier said. "I dislike you because you're a hypocrite."

"In what way?"

"You're supposed to be a man of God, and maybe you are on Sunday. The rest of the week, you have all the earmarks of a whoremaster."

"How does that distinguish me from you, except that you're a whoremaster all week long?"

"I make no pretence," the soldier said.

"That'll be a frail reed on Judgment Day."

"Whatever *you* rely on will get you about as far into heaven as the first saloon."

"You must take Christ for a fool," the man said. "I won't get into heaven at all."

"You face it with a stiff upper lip. You couldn't do better if you were an unbeliever."

"Do you believe?" the man said.

"In what you sell?"

"In heaven and hell."

"All I believe in is Baltimore," the soldier said. "I've *been* there."

"Heaven and hell are just as real."

"How come you don't mend your ways, then?"

"I do the best I can. I'm only human."

"Christ'll be a sight when He hears that."

"There's nothing magical about an ordination," the man said. "The man who comes forth is only the man who went in, purified in his intention, perhaps, but otherwise little changed."

"You're cool enough to skate on," the soldier said. "You've got enough cheek for another face."

"The Church makes the same error that you do: it expects lust to wither before the organs of lust run dry."

"Preach what you practice, and you'll have the biggest congregation in America: the First Venereal, you can call it. Or do you content yourself with such controversial topics as 'Mother,' 'Humility,' and 'Christ was a businessman'?"

"I've been in the Church for twenty years," the man said, "and the longer I remain, the emptier it gets. It had little to offer at the beginning, and now it has nothing at all. Some Sunday—not too far off now, I think—I'll shake hands with my people, as usual, and send them home to their greasy dinners, and with my wife on my arm, I'll start home for mine. A block away, though, I'll stop and look back at my ugly little House of God and say, 'My dear, we've seen enough of that corpse to know it's as dead as a dog,' and she'll say, 'I wonder why it took us so long to notice the stench.' From then on, till I come to die, I'll try to make up for being a one-day saint in a seven-day world. I'll be like you, by Christ! I'll sin without end!"

"If it's all right with your wife, it's all right with me—if it's all right with Eugenia."

"Please tell her I called," the man said, and he turned away.

The soldier did not leave until some time after midnight, and, driving through an uprising of heat to El Centro, he made a stop at a drugstore on the main street. With his left hand in his pocket, he said to the clerk, "A couple of rolls of bandage."

"What size?" the clerk said.

"Two-inch—and some inch tape."

The clerk registered the sale, counted out some change, and dropped the purchases into a paper sack, but he did not at once relinquish it. Wringing its neck, he chin-pointed at the soldier's chest and said, "There's sure a slew of them Purple Hearts floating around."

"That's no lie," the soldier said.

"Where'd you win yours?"

"You don't exactly *win* a Purple Heart. They give it to you for getting in the way of something—for your blood, you might say."

"Well, that takes a certain amount of nerve, don't it?"

"Sometimes you get in the way by trying your best to get out. You never know where the hell to hide."

"Somehow, I never think of our guys as ducking."

The soldier took the sack from the clerk, and for a moment he eyed the military arrangement of merchandise on the shelves—hair-oil on parade, cough-medicine in file, ammunition-dumps of toothpaste—receptacles filled not with blood, but flavored junk and gismo. "Nationally-advertised shit!" he said, and he left the store.

In the car, the soldier made a white muff of his hand, and then he drove northward, making for the Rancho Canada. Little but truck traffic was on the road, most of it moving with him up-valley. Where ditches cut under the pavement, they laminated the air with water-cooled partitions. Insects flew into the funnels of lamplight, sailed up at the soldier's face, and ended their flight in red and yellow punctuation marks on the windshield.

[ . . . *The Picnic-man came to Easton for Commencement Exercises. He wore a new suit for the occasion, something with a pinstripe, you remembered, and it was too long in the skirt and too short in the cuff, and the collar climbed, and the sleeves flared, but you liked it because he carried it for what it was—a rag—and both of you laughed when you found the stitching of a tag on a point of the vest, and you stopped to pick it out on the steps of Colton Chapel, with the bell tolling and the crowd going in.*

*'I only wish the missis could've been here,' he said. 'I only wish she could've lived to see this day.'*

*When the ceremonies were over, you took him for a walk around the campus, showing him Pardee ("We'll gather 'neath the twilight's glow"), South, Gayley, Van Buskirk, and the rest, but he wasn't interested in the buildings, or the traditions, or the view, or the few members of your class who troubled to pause for farewells—and although some rare flavor of the place would remain with you always, you knew that you too were an outsider now. You no longer belonged there, you thought, and if the grass and trees and the piles of brick and stone were part of your past, they were also part of the future of others: time was a continuous action in ejectment, and all, even those yet to come, were only squatters.*

*You sat on the stoop of Blair Hall (Was it really Blair, you wondered, or was Blair the one dormitory name in Poor Man's Row that came back to you?), and for a while you and the Picnic-man watched the groups of three passing by—a father, a mother, and a walking cap and gown—and finally he said, 'There's a subject that sooner or later we'll have to talk about, Steve. I hate to bring it up on a day like this, graduating and all, but maybe it's as good a time as I'll ever find.'*

*'What am I going to do with my life?' you said. 'Is that it?'*

*'I spent every dollar I had to keep her alive,' he said, 'but with the kind of sickness she had, it wouldn't have helped to been a millionaire. So what I'm trying to say is, I can't do for you like the missis and me always planned. I'm busted, Steve, and I just haven't got the heart to start all over again now, not after what I been through. I'll never have more than I got right now, which is the house and my job, but that means we'll both eat under a roof, and you can always count on me for practical business advice. . . .'*

*'I'd like to be a teacher,' you said.*

*He probed his pocket for one of his nickel cigars, and he trimmed it and lit it and grayed the air with its nickel smoke, and then he said, 'I think she would've liked that. It has dignity—not much money, maybe, but lots of dignity. . . .']*

A JUROR: "I'D HANG ALL THE DAMN BUGGERS."

Not the ones who sold the Army defective guns
And worm-eaten hulls that wouldn't hold a nail,
Nor those who made paper shoes and blue shoddy
That faded to gray and fell apart in the rain,
Nor the peddlers of tainted beef, death in cans,
Nor the ghouls who cashed in on gullible grief,
Shipping mule-bones north as the Union's slain,
Nor the dry witches walking on watered stock,
Nor their one-star shills, the brazen brigadiers,
Nor the trained animals in the act on the Bench,
Nor the pastors and the pastor-masters, the rich:
"I'd hang all the damn buggers," the juror said,
But he meant the eight framed in the Haymarket.

The ritual of the law consumed a Chicago summer
Habitually reserved for croquet at Lake Forest,
A bit of garter at one of the better beaches,
And muskellunge on light tackle off Charlevoix,
But Judge Gary (U. S. Steel) made the best of it:
He entertained ladies of fashion behind the Bar,
Executing sleights of hand for their amusement,
Feeding them bonbons, and telling droll fictions
To beguile their minds from the luminous passion
Of eight dirty radicals on trial for their lives;
In general, the fillies and mares were charmed,
But the prosecutor's wife whiled away the time
Covering sheets of paper with knots and nooses.

"I'd hang all the damn buggers," the juror said,
But he was given only five—only four, really,
Because Louis Lingg smoked a stick of dynamite

That a policeman concealed in a nickel cigar,
And you couldn't snap spines you couldn't find.

# THE WALLS
# KEEP TALKING
# TO YOU

[ . . . *The day after your graduation from Lafayette, you landed a job in a Red Bank garage, and you held it down till the day before classes started at State Teachers' in Newark. For three months, you put in seventy-two hours a week on the night-shift, and you saved almost every dollar that came your way but in the end you'd have been a hundred short of tuition-money if it hadn't been for the Picnic-man. The morning you left, you remembered, he walked you to the station, and, nodding you over behind a baggage-truck, he pulled out a roll of ones and fives, counted it, and stuffed it into your pocket, saying, 'The 8:05 is always late.'*

*'Where'd you get that money?' you said.*

*'There's no use asking, because I won't tell you.'*

*'Business stinks,' you said. 'How'd you manage to fish up a hundred bucks?'*

*'What do you care? You got it, ain't you?'*

*'If you don't tell me, I won't go.'*

*'And if I do—what then?'*

*'I'll take it as a loan,' you said, 'but I've got to know where it came from.'*

*'I hocked the car,' he said. 'Now, are you satisfied?' But you could only shake your head and look away. 'I got a question too, Steve. How long is it since you saw that girl?'*

*'Months,' you said. 'She came out to Easton for the Prom last winter.'*

*'I got another question. Why did you stop being friends?'*

*'If it's all the same, I'd sooner not say.'*

*'What I want to know is, has it anything to do with me?'*

*'It's personal, and I'd like to forget it.'*

*'I had a discussion with her once. She told you about that?'*

*'Yes,' you said.*

*'She got mad at me, but she didn't know who I was.'*

*'She was sorry afterward, if that's an excuse.'*

*'It's a good thing to be sorry,' the man said. 'It shows you have a*

heart.'

'*The time to show you have a heart is before you've been heartless.*'

'*I think you expect too much from people, Steve,*' *he said.* '*They aren't perfect yet. They make mistakes. They're human, you know, and you have to be human too. You have to overlook certain things.*'

*The train was in now, and just before you ran for it, you said,* '*For once, may I call you Pop?*'

'*For more than that, son,*' *he said.* . . . ]

At the Rancho, the soldier coasted the car past the woman's post. She saw him and nodded, and when he indicated the far edge of the parking-space, she nodded again and turned away. He ran the Ford off the gravel near the dragging gown of a pepper tree, and, finding a bench underneath, he stretched himself out and stared up the filigreed petticoats at the sky. Music came to him from the roadhouse, but distance had drained it, thinning it to thumps and soprano skids, and he heard it as if through the floor of some flat.

At the sound of footsteps, he sat up, saying, "Under here, Jean," and he watched a pair of white boots pause, change their course, and come toward him. Branches parted, framing the car-hop who had served him the night before. "I'm sorry," he said. "I thought you were Jean Bell."

"In the dark," she said, letting the branches fall behind her.

"The things that happen in the dark," he said.

She seated herself at the end of the bench, saying, "How's for a cheroot?" He offered her one, and as she leaned for a struck match, the flame buffed up a silver cross dangling from her neck. "You and Jean shacked up?" she said.

"That's a big devil-chaser you're wearing," he said. "The next size must be for steeples."

"You and Jean, we're talking about."

"Would you mind moving your snout?" he said. "You happen to be rooting in my roses."

"No need to go on the prod, Joe. What're you so touchy about?"

"The bigger the broad, the bigger the cross," he said. "Why is that?"

"If a little is pretty, a lot is prettier."

"Some guy said that one horseshoe might bring you luck, but a load of horseshoes was iron. I forget his name."

"Jean's the quiet type," she said. "The type you never know what they're doing, or with who. You have to figure."

"I remember now—Elbert Hubbard," he said. "Nobody has to figure you, only the cross. Your customers must know what it feels like to be crucified."

"The Purple-Heart boy," she said. "You know, you remind me of an egg went through here a couple or three months back. A captain, he was, and he had ribbons over his left lung till hell wouldn't have it. The Silver Star, the Service Cross, the Flying Cross, and God knows what-all, also the Purple Heart, and not just once, but three times. He was shot up like a signpost, the poor slob, and being patriotic, the least I could do was try and make him happy before he went back to war. I tried all night long, but in the morning the only scar I could see on the louse was where he mangled a finger in some coin-return."

"A shocking fraud," the soldier said, "but that wasn't what bothered you. It was his diddling you into giving it away when you could've sold it—like under that gas-pump up the Sink."

She paced him off with her eyes. "Jean tell you the end of that little story?" she said.

"Only up to where the worm turned and ate the bird. I filled in the rest."

"I doubt it. Around sun-up, they found that grease-monkey in a ditch—and not with a bar of soap, either, on account of the bastard didn't have much left to wash."

The soldier studied her. She had spoken on a plane where violence, like the time and place at which it occurred, was merely a ticker-tape fact. A region between his spine and navel felt coked, and it was spreading up into his chest and down toward his groin. "You don't talk like anything born," he said. "You were made with an ax, only they left the bark on."

The woman laughed. "I take that off for the right party," she said.

"That's anybody with no taste and five dollars."

"I turned down fifty, if you recall."

"What I don't understand is why five buys it, and fifty gets knocked off for it."

"Knocked off?" she said. "Who told you he got knocked off?"

"They found him in a ditch, you said."

"Sure, in a ditch, but that don't mean he was dead," she said. "He jumped in himself—to stop the bleeding." The soldier rose, and she watched him move toward the skirt of the tree. "He's still a damn good auto-fixer," she said. "He only had to give up working on wagons."

The soldier went to the Ford, walking stiff-legged and on the muscle, and, stalling off an impulse to sprint the car, he tooled it over the gravel and nosed into a slot in the line-up. The woman was at the counter, and when he called her name, she gave him a brief look and then ignored him, as if he were only a peevish patron; racking up an arm-length of dishes, she scudded away to one of the other cars at her station. The soldier summoned her again, this time by winking the lamps, but she made two more round-trips before strolling over to him.

He started to speak, but she stashed him with, "What's your hurry, sonny?" and then, close by, she lowered her voice to say, "You cracked, or what?"

"That bum who waited on me last night—Charlsie," he said. "I think I gave the show away to her."

"It's a cinch you didn't give it with your left hand. You must be wearing half of the cotton crop."

"Funny as a bird shot in the ass," he said. "I only talked to that piece of snatch for ten minutes, but I have the feeling she has me taped."

"She's dumber than dirt. All she knows is how to lay down."

"She's worse than dumb: she's smart. Why didn't you tell me the rest of that story about the gas-guy?"

"I didn't shove you in her lap. Why blame me?"

"Let's not talk about blame," he said. "Let's just for Christ's sake get the hell out of here."

"This is a job. I don't own the dive."

"God damn it, *phrig* the job!"

The woman kept her voice low. "In about a minute," she said, "I'm going to walk off and make out you're stewed. You're getting all strove up over nothing. Take yourself by the arm."

"You can't fall if you're on your face."

"Anybody looks orry-eyed, you go all apart. Keep it up, and sooner or later people *will* catch on. It's bad enough you have to wear that clown-bandage, but why wave it like a flag?"

"A *white* flag," he said. "Is that what you mean?"

"What do you want me to say, Stan? You're hipped, but do I have to be hipped too before you stop flogging yourself?"

The sound of a car-horn took the woman away, and she remained away through a series of departures that cleared her station of all cars but the Ford. A few dawdlers were still parked down the line, but the chefs and countermen had begun to clean up, and now a bus-boy was outside, knocking the props from under the window-screens, and service was over for the night. A door opened at the dance-hall end of the roadhouse, and a man in a tuxedo emerged on a wave of wah-wah from the band. He nodded to the waiting car-hops, who tossed their order-pads into a basket and hurried toward the locker-room.

[ . . . *A later summer, and again you were doing the night-trick at the Red Bank garage, this time to square a year's debts and keep*

140

*yourself till your teacher's credential came through. A long summer, it had seemed then, but only a few moments of it were still with your mind.*

*It was raining that night, you remembered, and with trade slack, you had little to do but lounge under the pump-shed and watch drops break on the brick drive. When a car finally drew in for service, it was only, from where you stood, another muddy roadster with the side-curtains up, but as you went toward it, the door opened, and you were seeing her face for the first time in Christ alone knew how long.*

*'Fill me,' she said.*

*A truck passed, kicking up a wake of spray. 'I got your announcement, Ann,' you said. 'I hope you live happily ever after high noon a week from Friday.'*

*'Are you going to send me a gift?' she said.*

*'What would be appropriate—a reading-lamp with a beaded fringe? or would you prefer something more intimate, like a dozen of your Special Deliveries bound with a stocking you forgot one morning, or, say, the elastic from a pair of your drawers? Speak up, Ann. I'll give you whatever your heart desires.'*

*She said, 'My heart desires that you get in here with me and come for a ride.'*

*'Ed Porter wouldn't want his girl to be tooting around like that.'*

*'I was somebody else's girl before I was his, and he'll find that out a week from Friday.'*

*'What's taken him so long?' you said, but she didn't answer, and you rammed it home and twisted it. 'What in the world do you folks do with yourselves? Why hold out on Eddie-boy?'*

*'Because, God damn you, it still doesn't have to be Eddie-boy! It can still be you!'*

*'Do you remember a cheap supper in a cheap room with a cheap townie? Do you remember seventeen violets tied with twine?'*

*'All the way down to Easton that night, I could think of only one thing—being with you. I'd looked forward to it for weeks, and when*

*I saw you at the depot, I was so happy that I could hardly speak. I was in love with you, Steve, and in the way you get it just once. But up in your room, you called me your wife, and suddenly I got frightened. You thought it was anger, but it was fear—because I knew then and there that I'd have to run the risk of telling you the truth about myself, and most people, maybe even you, didn't always thank you for pulling the wings off their dreams: they'd sooner reach for the moon than enjoy the earth. I was afraid, Steve, but there still was the hope that you'd be different. Well, you weren't. Your dream too had to fly or die.'*

*'The one that died was your own. You didn't have to tell me about Collins and the rest: I knew all about you in my bones, but I was glad to welcome you my house. How welcome was I, though, after I told you about Carlo?'*

*'I hated the sight of you,' she said. 'I hated being in the same room with you. When I left your place, I went straight back to the station, but there was no train out at that time of night, so I took a cab. I rode eighty miles in a cab, because I couldn't even stay in the same town with you. Welcome? My God, it was weeks and weeks before I could look at myself without feeling as if I'd been used as a chamber-pot!'*

*'In all the time since,' you said, 'has there been a single moment when you wondered what was happening to the cheap townie?'*

*'The things I felt forced to tell you about, all of them had been done to myself, never to anyone else. That doesn't excuse them or explain them away. I wasn't trying to do that then, and I'm not now: they weighed heavy, and they still do. But after that story about Carlo, I knew you'd have been the last to forgive me, because you'd have been the last to understand.'*

*'The cheap little guy, Ann. The townie with his nosegay of seventeen wop violets for his heart's desire.'*

*'Going back in the cab that night, I remembered this: "Never worry about being rich, but always worry about being poor." But now "poor" had a meaning I'd never thought of before, and it troubled me*

*that maybe I'd been poor as my father really meant it. I knew what I was—fast and loose, highhanded and low-minded, sullen, bored, drunk often, and always wild—but somehow it didn't seem to come to the kind of poverty my father'd had in mind.'*

*'The curled sandwiches, the lukewarm coffee—did they get a nickel's worth of thought on the meter, a quarter of a mile?'*

*'What you'd done to your brother, though, was down-at-heel, soup-stained, and mean in spirit. There was no size to it, no shape, no grace, no style, no arrogance, even. It stank of the flop-house. You'd been the one who didn't feel left out, I remembered. You'd been the one who said, "What's in there that you want so much?" knowing all the while that you wanted it more than I ever did, enough to run your own brother out of your life for it.'*

*'You're beating a live horse, Ann.'*

*'I didn't come here tonight to beat anything but myself. That'll surprise you, considering the things I've said, but it's the truth. I found out that if you were poor, I was poorer. It took me a couple of years to learn that, and how I did I still don't know. Maybe it was the wedding-announcement—the high-class paper, the raised print, and all—but it doesn't matter. I was poorer than you: that's what counted, and that's why I'm here. I'd run away from something I should've stayed to understand—that the reason for the poor is the rich.'*

*'I learned that long ago,' you said. 'It's a pity we couldn't have learned it together. It's a pity we had to pull the house down to find the key.'*

*'I made a mistake, Steve, and it cost us part of our lives. I'm about to make another that'll cost us all the rest. Don't let me.'*

*'I had a high heart for you up to that night in Easton, but if you'd known then what you know now so much too late, you'd have made it soar right off the earth.'*

*'We've got to do something to stop this bleeding!'*

*'Ed'll probably be wondering where you are.'*

*She sagged, but she made a last try, saying, 'Don't punish me any more, Steve. I've been punished enough. I'm a human being now.'*

*'Give my regards to Mr. Porter,' you said, 'and remember—never worry about being rich.'*

*When she spoke, you knew that she was talking to you no longer, but to herself and in an empty room. 'But what am I going to do with Ed?' she said. 'What am I going to do with the big dumb Princeton slob? What am I going to do? Jesus, Jesus, what am I going to do?'*

*She stared out at the vast vacancy of the world, slowly shaking her head, and in the end she shook it once violently, to clear her eyes, and then she drove away. . . . ]*

With his back to the car-park, the man in the tuxedo stood watching the kitcheners finish their shop-shutting routine, and then, setting his jacket with a rotary shrug, he turned and went to the Ford, where he hiked a foot onto the running-board and said, "Soldier, what's on your brain?"

The soldier peered from the window, and, starting with the man's feet, he made a slow survey up to the man's face. "Hair," he said.

The man placed the fingers of one hand on the palm of the other and studied his nails. "A good answer," he said.

"Next question."

The man said, "I didn't come over here to duel you with horse-shit, though." His collar, a soft lay-down, was loose, but he worked his neck against the band as if it bound him. "I just wanted to give you a steer: go home. And I don't mean wherever you're staying in El Centro—I mean where you come from and where you belong."

"You should've been a cop," the soldier said. "You have the voice for it, and the right manner: everybody's guilty."

Except for a dim blue transom over the dance-hall door, the ranch-front was dark now. "Some are even more so," the man said, and he scraped a match on a sunken windowpane, pinking for a moment the Ford's worn wheel and scored dash.

"The cop eye and the cop mind," the soldier said.

"Hair and cops is what you should've answered," the man said. He tamped a cigarette on the horn-button, and after firing it from the match, he killed the flame with a snuffer of smoke. "The Purple Heart," he said. "The lad with the bravery-badge."

"It's better than a blood-donor ribbon."

"You give blood for both. Where's the big distinction?"

The soldier put his bandaged hand on the window-rim, saying, "This is the big distinction."

"A hard one to see with the naked eye," the man said, "and all the harder when you trade on it. Back home, maybe not, but we don't know you in El Centro, and we only pay off on our own— when we pay off." He tilted his chin and shelled a calcimined rock with spit; the elevation was low, and the tumbling charge fell short. 'Well, that's all I had to say," he said, and, dusting no dust from his pants-leg, he walked away.

As he left the soldier's cone of vision, the woman entered it, like another target. "What were you talking to *him* about?" she said.

"The general subject was medals."

"It's the only damn one you know!"

"You'd have been proud of me. I discussed bravery with great authority."

"*He* didn't look like he was discussing—not with a finger in his collar."

"That was high blood-pressure, the cop's disease."

"I hope you said so. That'd make me *real* proud."

"I touched on it. I told him he had the cop eye."

"Stan," the woman said, "you're crazy. I swear to God there's a crazy streak in you."

"Don't tell me I'm wide enough for *two* streaks."

"Ah, shove over and let me drive," the woman said, and the car was southbound toward the distant incandescence of El Centro before she spoke again. "You want out on the Dunes tonight?"

"If you do," the soldier said.

"I never could understand that kind of an answer. You either want something, or you don't. Without regard."

"It was a way of saying I'd neither compel you nor resist you."

"Somehow that makes it a way of saying no," the woman said, "and if you were a nice guy, you'd have let me say it. It would've built me up a little, made me feel good, but I should've remembered. You don't go in for that, making people feel good."

"You make it sound like a simple thing to do," the soldier said. "It's far from that, as even Christ found out."

"Anyway, He tried."

"And died."

"He probably did more good by dying than He ever would've done if He lived."

"I wonder," the soldier said. A man died, he thought: he didn't pass away, give up the ghost, shuffle off this mortal coil, or join the choir invisible. He died, and having done so, he was dead, and what he died of was death, the process unique. No figure of speech went to its essence, neither sleep, nor day and night, nor the cycle of the seasons, and above all no catchwords for the manner of dying—peacefully, bravely, sustained, unfalteringly—made it acceptable. Life, the real lingering illness, was always to be infinitely preferred. "That's one of the things we'll never know," he said. "Which accounts for why so many people believe it."

"Not you, though," the woman said. "You're too wise."

"With the backing Christ had, He should've lived for the world. If His father made it, then He should've repaired it: it was a rush-job. Instead, though, He spent His time on earth getting sore at the people. He didn't bother to save the ship. He was too damn busy shooting the passengers."

"How do *you* feel about the passengers, Stan?"

"I honestly don't know yet. In some ways, they're the nearest thing to human beings I've ever seen. In others, they're like what you find crawling out of a crack under a sink. I'll have to make up my mind about them before I can go around grinning in their faces."

"Is that how you figure to make them feel good?"

"What would you want me to do—give them the secret hand-shake to show I'm physically strong, mentally awake, and morally straight? Like a boy-scout: trustworthy, loyal, helpful, bushwa, and reverent."

"You left out brave."

At the road-edge, a dog stood waiting for the Ford to reach it, and then, barking, it fell in alongside and paced the car until winded; for some way beyond an afterthought of its voice remained. "A little lower, Jean, and you'd have touched the ground," the soldier said. "All of a sudden, my feet feel like walking."

"He puts on his hat, and he goes," the woman said.

"Went," the soldier said.

"Over the hill, over *another* hill. For Christ's sake, how many hills can one guy go over? How many hills do you think there are?"

"Enough."

"Not for what you use them for: to hide behind. You're running away from the sickness with the sickness in your head."

"If you stop the car, I'll promise to walk."

"You're sick in the head. You'd run if a mouse broke wind. Stand still once, and maybe you'll cure yourself—that, or die now instead of after forty years of running. You'd at least have the satisfaction of knowing you stopped of your own free will."

"You had me fooled for a while," the soldier said, "but you're really a coldhearted piece of ginch."

The woman braked the car on the crown of the road, astride the center-line, and reaching across the soldier, she flipped the door-handle. "Run, Stan, or walk, or drop dead," she said. "I don't care which."

Standing on the pavement, the soldier was seized at once, very near manually, by a sense of disorder, as in a dream, but, lacking the dreamer's casual accommodation to disorder, he drew from the unwieldy reality only the coldest abdominal vacuum of fear. It was as if he had turned a familiar corner to find that there the earth came now to a blue and bottomless end. He looked down at the tips of his shoes to see whether they overhung the void, and he heard a voice saying, "A man was crossing a stream on a series of steppingstones. Near the middle, he lost his footing and fell into the water. What he had taken to be one of the stones was the head of a woman." Then there was a pause, filled with the sound of the idling motor, and he said, "Who said that?" and he waited, but the only voice that spoke was his own. "I thought I was thinking," he said. "I don't know what I'm doing any more. I feel as if I came into a room for something and forgot what I was looking for. The room is the world!"

"Get a hold of yourself, Stan, or you're cooked."

"A hold of myself would be like a drowning man grabbing his own foot."

The woman could hardly be heard above the inconsistent motor. "Would a hold of me be better?" she said. "Because you could have that with both hands, if you want."

He sat close to her as she drove. In the limited light from the dash, her bare knees glistened, and her legs seemed to taper away to nothing, as if submerged. Submerged, he thought, and through a bottle-green gloom, he saw sun-slats like far-off rain, and submarine forests leaning with the current, as if eavesdropping; he saw cruising shapes in the deepsea grass, starfish on the pitted stones, and shining shells in flurries of sand. "As if I were seeing it from a glass-bottomed boat," he said, and the woman glanced at him. "Suppose I told you that's what the world is like when I look at it from you."

"I wouldn't know what you meant."

"A compliment," he said, and he put his hand on her breast; through the thin cloth of her dress, he felt her nipple buttoning itself. "A world without people. A world like a beach that no one has ever walked on, white and smooth, with no jelly sandwiches lying about and no jelly families. A world under water, where the grass waves as in a wind, and fish change color as they fan themselves, and the sand turns up odd-shaped shells, some of them like little candy ears."

"You make it pretty," the woman said, "but take the pretty out, and what's left? I'm only a glass-bottom bedpan."

He laughed, saying, "A lot of women would've been taken in by a speech like that. Why weren't you?"

"It didn't feel like real water. It wasn't wet."

"Sometimes I think the only real thing about me is what I dream."

"You come first with yourself too much, that's why. It's no crime, I guess: most people are that way. But somebody else should at least come second, and there's no one comes after you—second, third, or last. It's Stan Clarke all the time. Clarke with an *e*."

"Make it Steve Pierce," he said, and he turned to the velvetine dark outside. "Whoever Clarke may be and wherever he may lie, let him sleep his sleep."

[ . . . *'She came to the store this morning, Steve.'*

*'Who did, Pop?'*

*'It was the first time I've ever seen her since that day I talked to her in the street. She looked better then, not so underweight, higher color in her face, more snap to her voice. Not that she's really changed, though. She still looks like the picture you have upstairs.'*

*'You mean the one I keep hidden under my shirts?'*

*'That's the only one you have, isn't it?'*

*'Never mind, Pop. Get to the point.'*

*'She said she was getting married tomorrow, and she wanted me to do something to stop it.'*

*'What did she think you could do?'*

*'She thought I could speak to you, and that's what I promised,*

*and that's what I'm doing.'*

*'Well, you've spoken, Pop. You've kept your promise.'*

*'The one I made to her, yes, but I made another to myself, and that's why I closed the store and came on home in the middle of the day.'*

*'What was the other promise, Pop?'*

*'That after all these years, I'd bring up the subject of Carlo—because I've got the feeling that somehow Carlo and the girl are all twisted together in your mind.'*

*'A mind can twist anything, Pop—words, people, steel, and history. Please don't go any further.'*

*'I have to, because there's something you don't know, something I've always kept to myself: I've never stopped looking for Carlo. It must be ten years now, and I've tried everything—those agencies that make a specialty, ads in the personal columns, the police, even. I haven't had any luck yet, Steve, but I'm still trying.'*

*'He's nowhere on earth, Pop. He ran clear to the moon.'*

*'I'll find him some day, but not by tomorrow, Steve. You understand? Not before she gets married.'*

*'I understand.'*

*'If you wait for me, you'll lose her.'*

*'I understand that too.'*

*'You'll regret it, Steve.'*

*'I understand, Pop. For God's sake, can't you see that I understand . . . ?'* ]

The street-lamps of El Centro burned in cotton-candy swarms of insects, and here and there light from a bar or an all-night diner slapped a bright quadrilateral on the sidewalk, but store-fronts and second-story windows were dark now, and no neon nimbus hung over the town.

"Could you stand a drink, Steve?" the woman said, and when he nodded, she aimed the car at a pair of diagonal stripes and parked before a blue-glassed cafe.

Within, they found a vacant booth and sat down opposite each other, painted two-faced by the lighting of the room and the glow of a juke-box selector between them on the wall. The soldier indicated the typed-in titles, saying, "Any preference?" and then, taking his hand from his pocket with thumb and forefinger pinched, he let a snuff of tobacco, lint, and dust fall to the table-top.

The woman pushed her purse toward him. "Anything but do-wacka-do," she said. "I hear that all week."

"You can have 'Stardust,'" he said. "Or is that do-wacka-do?"

"What else?"

"'Smoke Gets In Your Eyes.' Or a thing they broke off the front end of the Tchaikovsky Piano Concerto. Or 'Stormy Weather.' Or 'Can-house Boogie.'"

"If I said, 'Smoke,' would my laughing friend deride?"

Dropping a nickel into the mouth of the machine, the soldier listened to its gastric agony: the coin tripped some deepseated release, and an electrical impulse started a series of clicks, thuds, and whirrings that ended in saxophonic sighs. "Deride?" he said.

A waiter came, took their orders, and went away.

"Tell me something, Steve," the woman said. "If things were different, if you weren't in this kind of a fix, would you give me a second look?"

"What do you think?" he said.

"I think that ordinarily you wouldn't slow up long enough to wink."

"A declarative sentence seems to be in order," the soldier said, and when glasses were set before them, he paid the waiter with a bill from the woman's purse and waived the change.

"People like to know where they stand," the woman said. "But never mind. The way you're getting set, I can figure it out for myself. I don't stand at all: I fall."

The soldier spun his beer-glass on its coaster of foam. "When you told me to get out of your car up the road, I thought you meant it," he said. "Whether you did or not, though, I meant to go, but have you any idea what going was like?" He raised his glass as if to drink from it, but instead he stared at the rope-tricks of the rising bubbles. "It was like being torn loose from the earth. I was about to shoot downhill through space, with nothing to stop me till I hit the bottom of infinity after forever falling. *You* fall, you say?" He watched the woman run a finger idly but evenly around the rim of her highball-glass, and he heard an ice-cube jostle its way to the surface. "If I go," he said, "I fall."

A look of pleasure gradually crested over the woman's weariness. "I wish I could tell you what I'm thinking," she said, and she worked her hands as if the words were trapped and tangle-footed in them. "But it's like I was just learning the language, and I'm ashamed even to try. Some people have a good life. They get good out of it while the good is happening—not before or after, but during. Up to now, I never did. The good things didn't come often, and they didn't stay long when they came—like the train that went so fast it took two men to watch it, one to say, 'Here she comes,' and the other to say, 'There she goes.' But this is a good thing right now, Steve, and for once I'm happy while it's happening, like I was on the train instead of trying to watch it come and go."

"If you had that look on your face all the time, you'd be very beautiful," the soldier said. "Beautiful as only plain can become beautiful."

"People can't make themselves beautiful. It takes somebody else. Talk like that, and you'll see. Even only once in a while, Steve, because a little of it lasts a long time."

"Would it last till we got back to the house?"

"If we started now, you wouldn't have to say another word."

The soldier followed the woman toward the door. As she passed the end booth, she was flagged by the man in the tuxedo, and, say-ing, "Hi, Arnie," she continued on her way.

The man caught her arm. "Who's the guy with the Purple

Heart?" he said.

She said, "Stan Clarke, Arnie Brewer."

Ignoring the soldier, the man said to the woman, "I didn't say what's his name. He would've told me that himself, or I could've found out. I said who *is* he."

"A friend of mine," the woman said. "Is that what you want to know?"

"Not exactly. A stand-up friend or a lay-down friend?"

"You've got a bill like a hummingbird, Arnie, but keep it out of my business."

"This is my business: you work for me."

"Take the job and shove it up your back. Now I *don't* work for you."

"That answers the question, and you're hired again. Sit down and have a drink."

"I just finished one."

"Finish another. Mr. Purple Heart too."

"Mr. Purple Heart needs a breath of fresh air," the soldier said. "Would you direct me to the nearest toilet?"

The woman said, "Let's go, Stan."

"See you tomorrow," the man in the tuxedo said. "Don't oversleep. Don't undersleep, either."

When they reached the car, the woman said, "Anywheres but home, Steve. The look didn't last."

"The Dunes?" the soldier said.

"Chicago would be even better. If we went back to the house now, I'd feel like he was sitting on the bed with us and picking his nose."

"He didn't spoil anything for me."

"You're good to say it."

[ . . . *You remembered the faces, rows and files of them, some in the sun, some in the shade, and some dappled by a vivacious poplar in the schoolyard; and you remembered the shoe-scuffle on the floor, the complaint of paint-stiff seats, the whispered words and the spoken, and the afternoon bell; and you remembered watching from the window as the children fled, and then the door was opened behind you, and you turned to find entering the classroom a man you'd never seen before.*

*He came to a stop near the desk, saying, 'Are you Steve Pierce?'*

*You said, 'Yes.'*

*'I'm Ed Porter,' he said, 'and I want you to believe it would give me pleasure to write "Steve Pierce is a son of a bitch" all over Red Bank with a mop dipped in your own blood. It would help me to do that, it would give me peace of mind, but it wouldn't help my wife, and that's why I'm here. For six months now, ever since we were married, she's been doing her best to drink herself to death. In every way known—cures, talk, travel, drugs, and religion—I've tried to prevent that, but I'm the wrong man, I've always been the wrong man, and in the end, unless you help her, she'll die. I care more for her than I'd like to admit to someone like you, but she happens to be far gone on you, further gone than she is on living, and I'd sooner you had her than the grave. So what I came to find out is this: if I give Ann a divorce, will you marry her?'*

*'Yes!' you said. 'Yes!' And you went around the desk to him, and you clutched two handfuls of his suit, and you shook him, saying, 'Yes! Yes! You big dumb Princeton slob, yes!' And long after the door had closed behind him, your mind (or was it your mouth?) repeated your answer. . . . ]*

Miles east of the town, on a side-road in a chasm of kilted palms, the car crossed an irrigation-ditch that made a cold spring of air in the air. Tire-tracks angled off along one of the embankments, and the soldier followed them to a broad shoulder near a sluice-gate. There he stopped the car and turned out the lights, and the motor ticked a little, as if cracking its knuckles. A strip of reflected sky, white stars on a blue ground, rippled like a union jack.

"Pryor came to the house again tonight," the soldier said. "I forgot to mention it before."

"What reminded you?" the woman said.

"Nothing special."

"If you want to know about him and me, I'll tell you."

"You don't have to. It's no mystery."

"I'll tell you anyway, just so you'll be sure: he stayed with me a few times."

"Only a few?" the soldier said: "The Hundred Days have a hundred nights."

"I couldn't take that much praying," the woman said. "The thing was a sin to the guy, and he wanted it to be a sin to me too. He'd try to get me to pray with him, but always it was *after* the thing, like if we prayed in advance, the thing mightn't get done."

"His prayers are heavier than air," the soldier said. "They wouldn't reach the ceiling if he stood on a chair."

"I didn't mind him praying, if he wanted: praying's his lick. But the way he talked, you'd think he just climbed out of a sewer. The minute after he did the thing, he'd be kneeling naked next to the bed, spouting that dirty dumjohn of his. 'Lord God and Jesus Christ,' he'd say, 'visit the lightnings of Thy wrath upon this sink of iniquity and abomination!' If I'd have been God, I'd have said, 'While you're in it, Jake, or after you get out of it?' But Pryor was crass, and you'd think it was only bad to *be* a sewer, not to *fill* it. 'My feet slipped in the slime of the slime-pit,' he'd say. If he only said, 'our feet,' I maybe wouldn't have cared, because hell knows I'm no green hand: I wasn't green for Paul, and I'm even less so for you. But I guess that's no mystery, either."

"One guy fewer, and you might've come out wrong," the soldier said. "Or one guy more."

"I didn't think you could say a thing like that."

"Why not? I'm God's only misbegotten son."

"You said a good thing, Steve. Don't try to take away from it."

The soldier went to the edge of the embankment. For a moment, he stood looking down at the deep slow run, and then he stooped to let his fingers comb the current, saying, "If I left you, would you take up with Pryor again?"

The woman joined him. Picking up some pebbles, she spun them at the stream, and they made faint china-chimes as they struck the water. "There's no 'again,'" she said. "Not in this life or the next."

"Pryor thinks otherwise—for both places."

"One of these days, he'll learn that when I'm through, I'm through, and the way he's built, he'll cut his throat and dive in a ditch. It might even be this one. If we wait here long enough, he'll likely come by, all swole up like a toad. I'll feel sorry, but the hell I'll do the same."

"What if the toad's name was Pierce?"

"You'll never kill yourself, Steve," the woman said. "You wouldn't have anything left to stick pins in." She walked out of her shoes, and as she went away along the path, she opened her dress and tossed it at a spray of cane. "If I don't come up, it's a suicide," she said. "If I do, it's only a bath." She descended the bank, crumbling its crust underfoot, and when she let herself into the water, a spill of sand rained upon the starched and arching reeds.

The soldier looked at the empty shoes. A pace apart and feebly highlighted at the heels, they were pointed away from him, giving him the impression that at any time they might wander off of themselves. Almost as a precaution, he gathered them into a pair, and when he set them down again, they stood primly touching each other, and both were headed in his direction.

Drifting down to him, the woman caught a clump of grass and was slowly warped out of the channel by the current. "Talk to me, Steve," she said. "I don't care what you say, just so it's words."

"When you went in, you hardly made a sound," he said, and he touched her waterlogged and lacquered hair. "And I sat here thinking, 'I'm thinking of nothing.'"

"Were you afraid?" she said.

"I felt lonely," he said. "Not the way I was before, though: a little like Christ, the only dead man alive." He twisted a lock of the woman's hair into a dripping black cord. "I felt like the only living man dead."

"I wish people didn't have to talk so much about death."

"I wish they didn't die."

"Would you want to live forever?" she said.

"Not in a house without windows."

"You're free of me, if that's what you mean—but I don't think you do."

"Did you ever see one of those modernized zoos?" he said. "There's no more of that cage-and-iron-bar stuff. Only rocks, trees, pools, caves—what they call 'natural settings.' But every last animal is surrounded by a pit. That's the way I'm free, like the monkeys. I can bounce around and scratch myself all I want—but I can't beat that pit."

"Stay away from it," she said. "Just bounce and scratch like everybody else."

"A good life. A certain number of bounces and a certain number of scratches, and—clunk!—you're dead."

"That would happen, pit or no pit."

"Not necessarily," he said. "I had it all worked out once: how to beat the cars. It was simple, like a-b-c, and I remember how I went around in wonderment, telling myself, 'You've answered the question that stumped God!'"

"How did you do it?" she said.

"You'll find this hard to believe: it slipped my mind."

"That's been your big trouble—your mind."

"Imagine how I felt," he said. "I had the formula for conquering death, and I couldn't recall it, you might say, for the life of me. I can't even say now whether I dreamed it. There's nothing you can't settle in a dream, you know, including death. It's the one place where every man is Superman. You fly like a bird, swim like a fish, fight like a tiger, and live like a prince. The only thing you never actually do in a dream is die like a dog. You may be in any kind of danger the mind can fancy, but when death overhauls you, you only have to thumb your nose and wake up. I think my scheme had something to do with switching things around, so that people did all their dying in dreams. I wish I could remember how I brought that off. I might get a prize."

"I'm kind of glad you forgot," the woman said. "I maybe wouldn't be if I was sixty-five, but that's a long way away."

"It's long from here to there," the soldier said, "but from there back to here, it's as short as a thought. Time is the one thing that people consume without ash."

The woman said, "What did you used to be, Steve?"

"How's the water?" he said.

"Too thick to drink and too thin to plow," she said. "You don't have to tell me, but I wish you would."

"Well, suppose I said I was a schoolteacher. What difference would it make?"

"I don't know if it'd make any. *Were* you a schoolteacher?"

"Suppose I said yes."

"Suppose you said the yes without the suppose."

"Yes," the soldier said.

The woman climbed the bank, spread her dress on the margin of the road, and sat down on it. "You know, I expected to be surprised," she said. "But I guess I'd only be surprised if you were anything else."

"I'm one of those educated fools you're always getting tangled up with, only I have a license to prove it."

"What did you teach, Steve?"

"The same lies that other liars taught me."

"Well, what *subject* were you a liar in?"

"The easiest and the most fatal: American history," he said. "I lied through ten centuries of it, from Leif Ericsson to yesterday, and what it added up to was this: one American equals twenty foreigners. Christ, for all the good I did, I might just as well have taught palmistry."

"Why didn't you turn around and tell the truth?"

"Softly," the soldier said. "That's treason."

"You might get to that too after a while."

"If you live long enough, I imagine you get to everything. If my belly hadn't bucked, I'd still be telling a pack of little fart-handles that we're the biggest, bravest, strongest, smartest, true-bluest, and most bodacious bastards on earth. We're half man and half snapping-turtle, I'd be saying, half catamount and half sidewinder—the only people God ever made with four halves, and each a bit touched with chain-lightning. We're fitten, faithful, fresh, and special, and we only piss once a year, but when we do, we piss champagne. We're jim-dandies and ring-tailed roarers, slick and natural, swift and pure, and straight-up-and-dicular except when we do it slaunchways in the back seat of a Chevrolet. We're meaner than bumblebees under a derby hat, and when we pass along the street, we walk on both sides at the same time and cut a furrow down the middle. We keep our eyes open and our bowels the same (Use Dr. Lavage's Lavage! Drink it! Sprinkle it on your hair! Squirt it in your eye! Remember the name—Dr. Lavage's Lavage!). We can strut when we're sitting, and we'd run all day and half the night for a snort and a phrig, because our ticklers come in one size only: big. Our women are double-breasted and single-minded, and being banjo-assed, they go twang! when you pick 'em up and twang-twang! when you lay 'em down. We're regular ripstavers, sired by God on a Meddler mare and still a mite wolfish about the head and ears, and, lady, we can out-wrassle, out-stare, out-belch, out-pray, out-guzzle, out-brag, out-hump, and out-finagle our weight in witches, goblins, sperrits, or anything else from the devil's stable of hell-born sons of bitches."

Above the far fine line of the Chocolates, the quilt of night was wearing thin. "In room two hundred and two," the woman said, "the walls keep talking to you." She leaned back and lay staring up at the sky. "It'll be day soon, Steve."

*[ . . . At Ed Porter's place that night, all the signs pointed to another Porter party getting up steam. The lights were on upstairs and down, and music came from the open windows and the open door, and with cars parked anywhichway in the drive, people passing (as you were) might've thought they were witnessing the early stages of the usual shivaree. They'd have had to stop for a while (as you did) to gather that something was wrong, and even then they'd have had little to go on, only the fact that one song was being played on the record-changer, one song over and over, over and over.*

*There was no party at Ed Porter's. The machine had been playing without let-up for two days and two nights, but not for a party. Four doctors, one from Red Bank and three from New York, were sitting around a bed, watching Ann die with a bottleful of bichloride of mercury tablets eating on her intestines. She was dying to a little old tin tune that you'd danced to in your first summer with her, danced to and so made your own, and you knew that she was hoping you were outside now to hear it and remember it, and you did remember it, sharply enough to relive it, but the fragrance you were breathing as if you needed it to stay alive was dwindling, and the warmth was leaving your arms, and your blood had age beyond the stage of wine.*

*It was close to dawn when the song was played for the last time, and not long afterward, you saw the local doctor come from the house and set out afoot along the road to Red Bank. You stood where you were, waiting for him to reach you, and when he did, he stopped, saying, 'What brings you out this way, Steve—the morning air?'*

*'Is it over, Doc?' you said.*

*He lit a cigarette before answering, and you watched him blow a wad of smoke into the rising mist. 'It was over about half an hour ago,' he said, 'and I hope the same thing happens to her enemies.'*

*'Half an hour,' you said, as if it were vital to fix the exact time.*

*'About half an hour.'*

*He said, 'You used to knew her pretty well, didn't you, Steve?'*

*'A long way back,' you said.*

*'You know what she said just before she died? She said, "I didn't want any son of a bitch to pity me." I don't know what she meant, and I don't know whether Ed did, either, although after she was gone, he played the song all the way through again before ripping up the turntable and throwing it across the room. "I didn't want any son of a bitch to pity me." Who do you suppose she could've had in mind, Mr. Pierce?' And then he shot his cigarette away and walked on.*

*(Her grave was between two elms. You went to see it once, on a spring morning when the leaves were opening, and you remembered thinking that some day her ashes would run with the ascending sap, and the chemicals of her powdered blood would lodge in heartwood, and then the carving on her stone—the words 'ANN PORTER'—would serve as a name for the elms too, and then you kneeled, you remembered, and you put your hands on the mound, saying, 'What did I do to you, Ann? My God, Ann, what did I do to you . . . ?')* ]

"IT HAS BEEN A SPLENDID LITTLE WAR"

It was splendid for the ones tapped for Bones.
It came between semesters, a bother, you know,
For it did me out of a final whirl at end-rush
And a rather sporting girl that I had in view,
But by and large, it was a bit of high-jinks,
A lark I wouldn't have given up for 'varsity
Or a soubrette's bloomers in the chandelier.
Ran into Dick and Reggie on the dock at Tampa
(By Gad, you'd have thought it was Mouquin's!),
Both in blue, of course, and both so *sans peur*
You simply couldn't dream one marked for death,
But a Mauser dumdum had Dick's number on it,
And he'd sung his last rousing "Boola-Boola":
He fell a hero, with spic blood on his blade.
As for me, a nick or two, a touch of the fever,
A scout behind enemy lines (cited in dispatches),
And there you have the long and short of it—
Something to make nothing of if Pater makes much.
Tell him it was a perfectly splendid little war.

It was splendid too for the Hearst circulation.
"DOES OUR FLAG PROTECT WOMEN?" the *Journal* cried,
And it ordered a pen-and-ink from Mr. Remington
To show Spaniards stripping them to the buff:
Three days later, by an uncommon coincidence,
The Maine went up in a puff of Havana smoke.
The *Journal* offered a reward of fifty thousand,
Crying, "THE WARSHIP 'MAINE' WAS SPLIT IN TWO BY
AN ENEMY'S SECRET INFERNAL MACHINE" (diagrams)!
It knew a splendid little war when it saw one.

It was equally splendid for Theodore, who wrote,
"The clamor of the peace-faction convinces me
That this country [read Teddy] needs a war,"
And using his drag with Mr. Lodge, he got one
Made to order, and he fought it singlehanded.
He landed at Daiquiri, ate lead at Las Guásimas,
And with the foe in front and the press behind,
He ran all the way to the top of San Juan Hill,
And then he faced about and ran all the way down,
And when he reached bottom, he ran some more
And faster: he was headed for the White House.
Czolgosz took three years to evict Mr. McKinley,
But Mr. Lodge was patient, and so was Theodore:
It'd been a splendid, a really bully, little war.

And lastly, the Cubans thought it splendid also.
In God's wisdom, they continued to die of t.b.
At the rate of three or four dozen per hundred,
But it consoled them that their hacked-up blood
Was now for the kind *hacendados* of Wall Street:
They died practically free, thanks be to Jesus,
Rarely owing more to the Church and Sr. Morgan
Than their grandchildren would be able to repay.

# "IT WON'T SCOUR, LAMON"

[ . . . *A night, one of many, when going to bed was like being buried alive. The covering, the silence, the thoughts that came to you in the dark, all of them seemed to have bone-breaking and inevitable weight, and soon the air staled and soured and failed to sustain, and your breath quickened, and your mouth dried, and your heart ran away, and you knew that if you lay there longer, you would imagine death and die.*

*It was one of many nights when you sat for hours on the porch, rocking yourself in the light-and-shade shuttle of a street-lamp among the trees. People passing spoke softly, voluntarily muted by the privacy of the hour, and cars, when they came, throbbed slowly into earshot and slowly out, and there were intervals when you heard no sound except the retching rockerarms and the distant call of a bird.*

*It was the first of the nights, though, that he joined you, and you remembered how he clacked downstairs in his worn leather slippers, and how he took a chair alongside you and rekindled a long-dead cigar, and how he sat for a time filling the air with cheap but familiar smoke, and you remembered too the first words that he spoke. 'It won't do any good, Steve,' he said. 'What's past is past.'*

*'But it didn't have to be, Pop,' you said. 'I suppose that's why I keep trying to change it.'*

*'It's a stone wall. I know what I'm talking about, because I broke my head on it.'*

*'I'm harder,' you said. 'If the past is stone, I made it that way. I did all this, and now I want to do it differently, and it's too late by a million years. You warned me. You told me that people were only human, but I wouldn't listen to you. I wanted her to be more than human. I wanted her to be what I've never been myself—and now she's dead, and I'm worse than dead. I'm alive in a stone world, Pop, and it's cold.'*

*'You won't make it warm again with tears,' he said. 'Maybe you won't make it warm again with anything else. It's up to you. You've made your share of mistakes, but you're young yet, and you can still*

*learn something from them. You can still have a dignified life.'*

*'There may have been one last chance after Carlo,' you said. 'There's none after Ann.'*

*'Even after Ann,' he said. 'If you only learn your lesson on the day you die, you still can have dignity.'*

*'She said, "I don't want any son of a bitch to have pity on me"— but she didn't understand. It wasn't pity, Pop. For God's sake, believe me when I say it wasn't pity!'*

*'If you believe it, son, I believe it. . . .'* ]

It was seven o'clock in the morning when the woman brought the Ford to a stop at the end of the blue-gum lane. For almost an hour, the sun had been bombarding the Sink, and it was exploding now on tin roofs and glaring back from the squares of windowpanes, and it found so many faces in prisms of sand that the land glittered like cut crystal; the air seemed to shake, and road-oil made far-away oases. In the iron hive of the radiator, boiling water droned.

The Reverend Earl Pryor was waiting on the stoop, and as the woman and the soldier approached him, he rose, saying, "Good morning, Eugenia."

The woman said, "What do you want? What're you hanging around here for?"

"I want to see you."

"You're seeing me."

"I came to inquire about your health."

The soldier said, "You're a card, Earl."

"I'm addressing Mrs. Bell," Pryor said.

"Go home and address Mrs. Pryor."

"Butt out, Stan," the woman said, and then she turned again to the preacher. "I told you it was all off. I meant it."

"I'm afraid I don't understand, Eugenia. This is purely a pastoral call."

"I let Stan in on your pastoral calls."

Pryor studied the woman for a moment, and then he said, "Our sin was private. It should've been kept private."

The woman said, "The way you drop in at all hours, in the dead of night or at the crack of dawn, who the hell's going to believe you come here account of the church?"

"Let people believe what they believe. The minds of men are evil."

"Not if they're right," the woman said.

"I think now we might pray."

"Let's all pray," the soldier said. "Or is it still a two-handed game?"

"You're rotten in the mouth," Pryor said. "Which means you're rotten in the heart as well."

The soldier laughed, saying, "When you die, friend, you'll baffle the embalmers."

The woman touched Pryor's sleeve. "I want you to go," she said.

"You make a poor choice," he said. "You choose death over life."

"And I want you never to come back."

"As you say," he said. "But apart from your lust for this carrion here, tell me why you refuse to let yourself be saved. I can save you. Why do you stand between yourself and the sun?"

"Because the sun is too God damn hot!" the woman said. "I like it in the shade!"

The sun sanctified a telegraph-pole. Blazing behind the cross-bar, it stoked the insulators up to giant jewels, and Pryor stared at them, saying, "I too like it in the shade, but I see now that there is no shade for the sinner, none in this world and none in the next," and then he went away.

The soldier followed the woman into the house and along the hall. The sudden shift from glint to gloom blacked his eyes, and in the brief darkness, he heard her say, "I think he's crazy, Steve."

"If he was in here, and I was out there, I'd be crazier."

"I like to hear that."

"I like to say it."

"Only this is the wrong time and the wrong place. That guy gives me the flit-flats."

"Forget him. He's psalm-happy. His knees itch."

"You're a mixture, Steve, y'know? You're never what I expect you to be, never the same twice."

"In regard to what?"

"Anything. Me, for instance, or yourself, or, right now, Pryor."

"Did you think he'd give me the flit-flats too?"

"Sometimes you shy at nothing, and other times you eat fire. You're an odd one, Steve."

"All that's odd is I fool you with smoke. Any fire I eat is out."

"Drunks, toughs, wiseacres," the woman said, "those kind of people I can handle. But let somebody be touched, and he's poison to me. I'm done."

"Half the world is touched," the soldier said, "and the other half is half-touched."

"There was a loony in Bakersfield when I was a kid. A big gink, he was, but harmless, always poking about town, always gabbling some jabberwock, and always working his neck like it needed oiling. People were good to him, I remember, and they gave him toys, candy, clothes, and I guess they made him happy, because so far as I know he never done a wrong thing in his life. All the same, for me just to have to pass him on the street was the most terrible agony, like going through all the pain of dying and then living. I knew it was a mean feeling, and I tried my best to get over it, but I never did, and I never will. I can stand the sight of blood, my own or anybody's, and I'm not ascared of the dark or snakes or even death, but a guy like Pryor's gotten to be makes me cold all over and clear through."

"Forget him, I tell you. He's home by now and taking his wife by force."

"He frightens me, Steve. He really does."

"In ten minutes, he'll be normal again—eating two soft-boiled eggs with buttered toast."

"He frightens me most, though, for *you*."

The soldier went past the woman and entered the kitchen. In the sink, a drinking-glass had been filled to the brim with drip-drop from one of the taps, and he watched another globe of water form in the faucet, grow obconic, and break away. "The sinister minister," he said.

"You've talked back to one and all ever since you hit El Centro," the woman said. "I told you not to, but you did it anyhow, and up to now it might could've amounted to nothing, because mostly you were up against nobodies. But Pryor would've been bad for us even in his *right* mind."

"What makes him worse than Arnie Brewer?"

"I don't happen to appeal to Arnie Brewer."

"What do you want me to do—tell Pryor he can have every other night?"

"I've got some money saved up," the woman said. "Not much, but enough so we could get out of here."

"And go where?"

"Mexico."

"The land of Juarez and Zapata," the soldier said. "They'd welcome me there like another Cortez."

"Nobody has to welcome us. The less of that, the better."

"How would I get in—just walk in?"

"I say 'us,'" the woman said. "You say 'I.'"

The soldier sat down at the card-table, near the refrigerator. On the linoleum, a few drops of dried cream were beige scabs, and, scraping them free with the flat of a knife, he said, "I say 'I' because I don't mean 'us.'"

"I wouldn't be in your way, Steve."

"Start running once, and there's no end to it."

"What's so wonderful about standing still? There's no end to that, either. If I never met you, it might be different. Maybe I'd think that what I had was something to stick around for—my fine job, my fine house, my fine life. If I took and ran, I'd be leaving all that, but whoever wants it can have it, because all of a sudden it's nothing."

The soldier chilled his hand on the frosted ice-trays, and then he held the hand against his face until the cold was gone. "We talk about everything under the sun but the sunlight," he said. "Where to go, when to go, how to go—stuff we could settle in a minute once we settled *whether* to go. All the rest depends on that. All the rest is only action."

"I say we should act first and think up a reason afterwards. That way, they won't be catching us by the ass just as we start."

"If you act without a reason, the only reason you ever find is the act itself: you're running because you're running. That's not enough."

"It's enough for other things: you live because you're living. What more of a reason do you need?"

"One that'll justify me," the soldier said.

"You think maybe history is going to judge you some day?"

"I can't wait to find out. I have to judge myself."

"The answer to that could only be this: give yourself up."

"I've considered it."

"Christ, you're as crazy as Pryor!"

"We're neither of us crazy," the soldier said. "We're sick, that's all, and we both have the same incurable disease: we're sinners."

"It's too God damn late to worry about being a sinner," the woman said. "All your life so far, you've been a prize son of a bitch, if I'm any judge, and suddenly you have to justify yourself, suddenly you need a reason. For thirty-odd years, you got along fine without, but now, right away quick, you need a reason. Well, I'll give you a reason, if it's so important: keep on running for me! It's the least you can do after so much running for yourself."

The soldier prodded the discs of cream into size-place. "All you're asking for is the rest of my life," he said.

"You make it sound like it's studded with diamonds."

"It's the only one I have."

"We ought to get one to waste and one to use, and then we'd all be happy."

The soldier said, "The one we get, we get too easily: all we have to do is get born. We ought to be made to qualify, the way we do to carry a gun. A life is much more dangerous. I'm going to take that up with God some time."

"Meanwhile, let's attend to such odds and ends as you and me."

The soldier swept his hand across the table, brushing the arrangement of cream-spots to the floor. "Pack," he said.

[ . . . *The Picnic-man came out to the school one afternoon. A few minutes were left of the closing hour, and he went to one of the rear-row seats and stuffed himself behind the desk-flap. Continuing with the recitations, you glanced at him once or twice, and from the look on his face you guessed that his thoughts had gone counterclockwise. You knew you were right when the bell rang: he seemed to hear nothing, neither the banged-on brass, nor the readying of many shoes, nor the finally running feet. He sat where he was, staring at the artifacts of long-buried memories.*

*You said, 'What were the main provisions of the Kansas-Nebraska Bill,' and he smiled at you over the vacant desks. 'What was the cause of the War of 1812?'*

*He shook his head, saying, 'It's good they didn't ask me when I went for my citizen-papers. I wouldn't have got to be an American.'*

*'You can't be an American unless you know exactly what Jackson said to Calhoun about Nullification.'*

*'Here in this country,' he said, 'they make every little snotnose go to school, and they pack the little heads with all the fine language of history, so that by the time the snotnoses reach twenty-one, they're smart like fortune-tellers. The only trouble is, the smartness don't last: there's no grown-up fortune-tellers walking around. Something*

*must be radically wrong.'*

*You laughed, saying, 'Radically is right, not wrong.'*

*He looked at you for a moment, and then he said, 'You didn't get that from the principal or the Board of Education—and I don't think you got it from the books.'*

*'I got it from living,' you said.*

*His eyes roamed the room, pausing now and then at some picture or some dust-mantled bust, and in the end they returned to you. 'It's what I told you, Steve,' he said. 'There was dignity even after Ann.'*

*'Let's walk home, Pop,' you said. 'I enjoy your company. . . .'* ]

On the couch in the parlor, the soldier lay asleep. The blinds were down, but here and there a ray struck sweat on his almost naked body, and the wet patches shone as if the skin were cellophane. It was near noon, and the sun bore down on the lifeless town until it seemed to hover on the shimmering instant before catching fire; the air, burdened with grit, had the ponderable quality of air in the lung of a vacuum-cleaner. A green fly landed on the soldier's chest, drank its fill, and flew away, and not for several seconds did he move a hand to dab at the itching after-imprint.

He opened his eyes. From the tangle of sleep, the end-word of a censored sequence dangled: Gettysburg. He sought to draw the entire dream into the clear with it, but the snarl seemed only to tighten. Gettysburg, he thought, and old scenes and green-gold vistas filled his mind: the sun was low, but it still reached the Peach Orchard and the massed bayonets of wheat in the Wheatfield, it still flashed on a Rebel button and a whitened chip of Union bone, it still brightened Round Top and shed light on the Angle. Gettysburg, he thought. Why had the name remained, but not the meaning of the name?

He thought of brain-spangled rock and blood on broken grain. He thought of nine thousand dead, of the filial dread of the dying ("Tell Father that I died with my face toward the enemy."), and of such anguished prophecies as, "The world will little note nor long remember"—and it was with some fraction of the same grief that the soldier now recited each word of the brief but invulnerable speech that the prophet had thought so meager ("Lamon," he had said, "it won't scour," and to the last he had felt that the honors of the day belonged to Everett, the man who had spoken two hours by the clock.).

Edward Everett, the soldier thought, and suddenly he sensed that the dream was about to unravel and unreel. Edward Everett, he thought, and a few slow-moving deep-sea diver phrases came back to him ("Overlooking these broad fields now reposing from the labors of the waning year"), but it was the man's name, he knew, not the man's periods, that held the key, and he waited, tense and wondering, while symbols and substitutions dwindled, and the actuality began to loom. Edward Everett Hale, he thought, and now tension and wonderment went, and the dream-sequence stood revealed—Gettysburg: Lincoln: Everett: Hale: *Philip Nolan!*—and the soldier shook his head in bone-deep despair as he tried hopelessly to deny that soon he too would be a man without a country.

There were shoes on sand outside, and then there were footsteps on the stoop, the porch, and the floorboards of the hall, and the woman stopped in the parlor doorway. Shields of sweat, wet crescents, were in the armpits of her dress. "You were dead to the world when I left," she said. "I didn't have the heart to wake you."

"Where did you go?" the soldier said.

She tossed him her purse. "I needed a couple of things," she said.

"What do I do with this?"

"My last stop was the bank. I drew all but the small change."

"Did they want to know why?"

"No, but I let it fall that my car was about shot."

"Clever," the soldier said, and, hooking a finger under its strap, he offered the purse back to the woman. "All yours."

"That don't mean it won't get spent."

"I'm glad you don't say it's ours."

"Why should I? I'm the one worked for it. But what if I *had* said it?"

"It would've been an error. I'm thin-skinned."

"I noticed."

"Also refined. I'm above such things as money. I hold a Master's degree. I'm a Master Bastard."

"Build it up," the woman said. "I'm going to have me a shower."

The soldier caused the purse to swing a little. "Aren't you afraid I might light out with this?" he said. "I'm the right guy for it."

"What guy isn't?" the woman said, and she walked away along the hall.

Despite his recent sleep, the sound of water falling on water drowsed the soldier, and he had to force himself to rise from the couch. He found that he still held the purse, and he was staring down at it when the porch-door opened, and Brewer entered the house.

"Maybe I should've knocked," the man said.

"Not unless you did it with your skull."

"Kind of a queer costume, Mr. Purple Heart. Shorts and a poke. What're you made up as?"

"Think hard, and you'll muff it."

"You look like a man got paid off for a day's work."

Using the strap as a sling, the soldier shocked the purse against a wing of Brewer's jaw. "You're colder than a gravedigger's ass," he said. "Guess again."

Brewer worked his mouth, and a film of red spit appeared between his lips. "You could just be a guy in drawers with a pocket-book," he said.

"Perfect," the soldier said, and as he put the purse on the table, he became aware of the absence of the shower-sound. "State the nature of your business," he said, and he listened to the woman's silk-on-silk approach.

Brewer blotted his mouth, and without turning, he said to the soldier, "Man name of Pryor came to see me this morning." The woman stopped behind him. Her maple-leaf wrapper clung to her in places, transparent where her body was still wet. "Man name of Pryor. Wanted to know if I knew you were staying here. Guess he thought I look after the morals of my help."

"A good employer would."

"I'm not a good employer."

"There *is* no good employer."

"That kind of stuff is what I mean when I tell you to go home," Brewer said. "But I'm back where I started. It's the kind of thing happens when I talk to guys like you: I go round and round."

"Say something with your mouth for a change. You might stop spinning."

"You're asking for reasons now. Would you go if you got them?"

"No," the soldier said, "but at least you'd stop looking like a plaster copy of the Great Stone Face. The land of the mask, this is, and the mask is the same for cop and gangster, banker and sucker, priest and pool-player. Our national hero is any square-jawed monosyllabic cluck with hair, and our highest crime is a show of emotion. We exterminated the Indian only to bow down in the end before the Indian ideal. Me no squaw; me no talk."

"Everybody you meet," Brewer said, "you give them an argument like an organizer, only you do it down the nose, like that Purple Heart of yours was worth a mint of money. You could be purple all over, though, and not bring a nickel at a loan-office. You're no hero in El Centro, and except I'm far wrong, you're no hero anywheres else. But, like I say, I only go round and round." Turning away, he spoke to the woman in passing, saying, "You're too thin these days." After a moment, a car-door slammed, and a starter nagged at a motor.

The woman said, "I better just look at you, Steve. If I say anything, I'll likely regret it."

The soldier said, "I don't think you're thin."

"I wouldn't care if I weighed forty pounds! I want to know how Brewer got that bloody mouth!"

"He made a remark about you."

"A *remark!* What do we care about remarks at this stage of the game?"

"We care at any stage."

The woman began to speak, but, shaking her head, she abandoned the thought as futile, saying instead, "You know something, Steve? I think there's times when you want to get in trouble."

"A man has to test himself once in a while."

"For what—for how brave he is?"

"For whether he's dead or alive."

"You're alive," the woman said. "I'm only trying to keep you that way." She reached for a box standing on end against the door. "That's why I bought you this suit."

The soldier mock-saluted. "The uniform of the United States Army is good enough for me," he said.

"It's just the thing for crossing a border."

"What kind of suit did you get? I'm a nifty dresser."

"One of those cotton jobs. You'll be sweating."

"You're God damn right I will!" he said. "I'll sweat my brains out when that salesman starts asking himself what a widow wanted with a man's suit! Why didn't you let me in on your dumb little scheme?"

"I didn't buy it in El Centro," the woman said. "I bought it in Brawley. They don't know me there."

The soldier tried to look at her face, but he felt as if he had chosen the one direction in which sight seemed to curve, like a thrown ball spent. "You drove twenty miles in this heat to get me a suit on the q.t.," he said, "and I pay you back by calling you dumb." The look was on the floor now, at the woman's feet. "It's a sample of what to expect."

"Get off yourself and stand up," the woman said. "You just didn't know."

"When are you going to get tired of my not knowing? When do I wreck myself with you?"

"Well, you damn near did it last night."

"I'll damn near do it all my life."

"It won't be because you want to."

"It's about time you stopped finding excuses for me," the soldier said. "'He didn't mean it.' 'He didn't understand.' 'Why, he wouldn't hurt a fly.' Phrig that. Where's the man that wouldn't hurt a man?"

"I don't find excuses," the woman said. "I just overlook a lot of reasons for starting a fight. Nobody being perfect, you have to make do with people."

"The old allagazam: live and let live. Some people ought to die, at least two out of every five."

"Why didn't you stay in the Army and do some of the killing?"

"They were training me to stand with my back to the Stock Exchange and fire at my friends."

"Brewer said you talked like an organizer. It was no lie."

"How else can you talk if you want to make sense?"

"Every time we get onto the subject, you come up with a new reason for chucking away your rifle. Not that I care, but why don't you pick out a good one and stick to it?"

"I want the one that'll open the door—and the door stays closed."

"There's plenty of doors don't open in this great big beautiful world."

"It's always only one special door that counts, and till you swing it, you're locked out of life."

"A million soldiers did the same thing as you—except they only had the nerve to dream about it."

"Your reasoning bucks me up. It makes me the bravest man that ever fouled his pants, and the millions of guys that stayed are the yellowest that ever jumped inside a red-hot stove and pushed out all the dents."

"Talking to you is like riding behind you on a merry-go-round. No matter how fast I go, I'll never catch up."

"I could fall off," the soldier said. "Otherwise it's a good figure of speech."

"I'm no good at figure of speeches, or figures of speech, or however you professors say it, and when it comes to reasoning, I lay no claim to that, either. It's a good thing for you that I don't, because that's the last thing you want, is reasoning: it'll only get you in deeper. What you're really after is somebody to wave a wand over you and clean off your messed-up life, like magic. You want a miracle, but, mister, there ain't no such a thing."

"Did you ever do anything that was unforgivable?" the soldier said. "Think back. Did you ever feel that from a certain word or act onward, there was only guilt without absolution?"

"Yes," the woman said. "It won't seem like much to you, maybe, but it bowed me down when I did it, and I'm bowed down still. My father was a holding-out sort of man, what you might call cold. He never said a great deal, and it seemed like he just couldn't bring himself to make the kind of a to-do over my mother that she always wanted him to. She was the softer type, easy to hurt, and she took his quietness—his reserve, if that's the word—to mean that he didn't care for her. He did, though, and more than she ever knew, but he couldn't show it, and she died thinking he'd just as soon she got the dying over with. I did too, and in a hot fit one day I told him so. 'You killed my mother,' I said, and he said, 'Is that what you think?' I said, 'You're God damn right I do! You froze her to death!' He didn't say any more. He simply got up and walked out of the room. But all of a sudden I got to know my father like my mother never did, and I knew something else: that I'd have to live a long life to find out how to hurt a man worse than I'd done already."

"You felt remorse—is that what you're saying?"

"I'll always feel it."

"In other words, you have a conscience."

"Sure, I have. What did you think?"

"All right," the soldier said. "Then what's so miraculous about *my* having one?"

"I've got to watch out for that mind of yours," the woman said. "It's crooked, and words get a kink coming out of it. I never told you it was miraculous, you having a conscience. I only said you expected it to work wonders for you, which it won't."

"You're talking about some skinny little conscience that casts a shadow like a hair."

"I wouldn't care if you had one wide enough to fold over and wear double. It still wouldn't wipe out the things that fret it."

"Why have a conscience at all, then?"

"Because it's a good thing for people to feel badly once in a while," the woman said. "They learn a lesson, maybe, and they stop being such sons of bitches for a week. That's all a conscience can do—give you a chance to change. You want more from it, though. You want it to change the past, and it never will."

"What becomes of all the son-of-a-bitchery I'm responsible for?"

"It stands," the woman said.

"It stands on the place where I'm supposed to live."

"I put a rock through my father's heart. That stands on me, *à la mode*."

"We'll make a fine pair of fugitives," the soldier said. "Overloaded with sin and banking on a bum spare."

"Just so we get to where we're going."

"You can still back out, Jean."

"For Christ's sake, say one good thing!"

"This is as good a thing as I know: quit me."

"But I'm all wound up with you," the woman said. "Don't you understand that? If I tried to get loose, I'd tear."

"Then I'll say another thing, not quite so good: I wouldn't know what in hell to do without you."

The woman reached for his hand and absently wiped away its gloss of sweat. "I hope you never have to find out," she said, and she let the hand fall.

[ . . . *The morning was a bright one late in the spring term, a morning after a night of rain, and as you walked toward the school through a world of clear-cut objects—people, trees, stock in the fields, and houses near and far—you felt that only its curve prevented you from seeing all there was on earth. So lucid was the air, you remembered, that sight seemed to have the stereoscopic power of separation, and, like books on a shelf, no two things, however distant, merged. Your mind too was a muster of items proximate but distinct, but this separation gave you no pleasure, for here what you desired was the reverse: the many books must be made into one.*

*Seated at your desk, you watched boys drift in from the court-yard. The commotion outside—the calls, the cries, the blurts of sound that the young made as if to let off excess life—was dying down, and within there were whispers and the soft speech of feet and the same but now muffled explosions. The bell rang, and you opened your roster, waiting for a few stragglers to reach their seats. You wondered what you would say when there was silence.*

*You heard yourself speak. 'The history final is a week away,' you were saying. 'As you know, it will cover the period from the adoption of the Constitution to the end of the Civil War (You thought: The reason for the poor is the rich). Ordinarily, we'd spend these last few days brushing up on the term's work in preparation for the exam (You thought: Radically is right, not wrong). Ordinarily, I say, but what if I told you I was tired of lying to you, that very little you've learned from me will help you to lead a dignified life (You thought: The way things are is not the way they always have to be)?' You rose now, searching dozens of fresh faces fine-framed in down, eyes as good as new, and thirty-odd beginnings not yet condemned to a common and useless end, and you said, 'Wouldn't it be wonderful to know the truth?' The eyes looked up at you from the round little faces, but what you were aiming at was the round little lives. 'I've taught you that this country belongs to you,' you said, 'but it doesn't. It'll be yours some day—nothing on earth can stop it from being—but right now it belongs to scoundrels who pretend to be patriots, to sinners who pretend to be saints, to hangmen who pretend to be judges, and to the rich, only to the rich (You thought: You expect too much from people) . . . !'* ]

When the woman finished work at the Rancho, it was almost one o'clock in the morning, and for some time the soldier had been waiting for her in the Ford at the edge of the car-park. "Put this with the rest," she said, and, handing him a thin fold of bills, she slid herself onto the seat. "I feel like school was out for life."

At the highway, the soldier let a Diesel pass and then headed southward behind it, lighting the red and yellow buttons of its placket until it drew away and dimmed them. "You should've walked off in the uniform," he said. "Then we'd have been related."

"I did hate to leave the boots."

"I hate to leave Brewer. A man after my own heart—and all the blood in it too." A car approached with cauterizing brights, and the soldier signaled for relief. Getting none, he switched on a pistol-grip spotlight and aimed it at the oncoming eyes. They died down and passed, and the silver-plated Sink returned. "I use the last dozen miles of my own my native land to engage in a duel over nothing with a man I can't see and don't know but despise. I ought to be trying to soak up enough of what I'm leaving behind to do me for the rest of my life. At the border, remind me to put a pinch or two of American earth in a pillbox, so that no matter where I go, I'll bear with me always a small part of the Union, and when I die, if you're still with me, I want you to pry open my jaws and pour it into my mouth and then bury me in a five-and-dime flag. I foretell that in time a shrub will burgeon from my grave in the shape of a dollar-sign."

"You love this country, don't you, Steve?"

He answered in a low voice that the woman almost missed under the piston-churn of the motor. "So much that I dream about it," he said. "I dream about it all the time."

"What do you dream?" she said. "Do you remember?"

"I heard a story somewhere once," he said. "It's probably told of every big nation, probably almost a folk-tale, but the way it came to me, it was about Russia. It goes like this. A peddler put up for the night with a peasant, and in the morning, the peasant asked him to interpret a dream. 'There was a road crossing a vast steppe,' the peasant said, 'and on the road a pair of boots were walking.' The peddler said, 'Was there no more to the dream than this: the road and the walking boots? Were there no people in the dream?' The peasant said, 'The earth was empty and silent, and save for the boots endlessly walking, there was nothing. I fear I have had a bad dream.' The peddler said, 'Not so, my brother. What you dreamed of was our Russia.' The peasant was astonished, saying, 'I have lived all my life in the place where we now stand. How can a man dream of a thing he has never seen?' The peddler said, 'I have seen it all, my brother, but I have yet to dream of it so well as you. I envy you that dream.'" The soldier paused for a moment, and then he said, "In the dreams I had of America once, there were great clean thunderheads in a topless sky, and water turned and tumbled over mountain rock, and the trees were all women in the wind—but what I dream of now is filth."

"Would you want to tell me about it, Steve?"

"Would you want to listen?"

"Anything you say, I'll listen."

"I had this dream for the first time the year I began to teach," the soldier said. "Every so often, it comes back, and I dream it all over again in the same way. I dream of waking up and sensing that something very valuable is missing. What it is, I never learn, but I know that I must get it back, and I begin to hunt for it. I look everywhere, in my pockets, in the cupboards, in corners, under rugs, and between the pages of books, but I feel all along that the thing, whatever it is, is gone. I give up finally, and, going to a window, I see a rubbish-truck parked in the street—and it comes to me suddenly, with the certainty you have only in dreams, that what I'm seeking is on that truck and among that junk. I rush outside, but the truck is moving away now (does anything stop when you chase it in a dream?), and I have to run for it. After a hard try, I manage to hook on and climb up over a mound of trash, and I fall to tearing it apart piece by piece, certain that I'll recognize the object when it comes to hand: a burnt cross, with spikes still embedded in the charcoal; a mattress punctured by its own spiral bones; a cracked toilet-seat; a stack of old funny-sheets; a stuffed eagle, moth-eaten and lacking an eye; a paper hat and a paper serpent; a cigar-store Indian holding nothing in a clenched hand; a false face to fit a hooked nose; a rubber sitting-ring; a sign reading "KEEP OUT—THIS MEANS YOU"; an Erie timetable for the summer of 1909; a papier-maché bust of P. G. T. Beauregard; a toy bank; a jar of formaldehyde containing a thumb; a pair of manacles; a canceled stock-certificate; a strand of barbed wire; and an empty cornucopia. All that and much more, none of it do I identify as the treasure, but the feeling persists that I'm near it, and I keep on digging. By now, though, the heap of refuse—all but the pickled thumb—is decomposing, and wood, metal, paper, and paint are a rancid slime, a cold and cartilaginous rarebit, and it clings to me in stinking shreds and strings, a mucilage, an inescapable spider-spun gum, and the more I root in it, the more I'm stuck with, and soon my hands are catcher's-mitts of almost immalleable decay. I'm about to quit when, far down in a pus-filled pit, I touch a substance that I know at once I haven't touched before. I lay hold of it, and very carefully I begin to bring it forth. At that instant, the dream always ends."

The woman said, "The thing you're looking for—you say you never know what it is in the dream. Do you know what it is when you're awake?"

"Yes," the soldier said. "Do you?"

"What you lost was America."

The soldier looked at her briefly and turned back to the road. "Right," he said. "Right as rain."

"You're always so surprised when I know something. It's like all you expected was 'Huh?'"

"If you know so much, tell me why the dream ends where it does—just as I put my hands on its heart."

"Because if it went further," the woman said, "you'd find out if the heart was beating."

"Nothing could live under that load of crap."

"If you're so sure of that, how come you don't dream it in the dream?"

"In West Virginia," the soldier said, "there are little company coal-towns strung out one after another along the Kanawha River. Towns of three-four hundred, mostly, and all unincorporated— meaning they're private property, and if you don't like it there, move on, brother, and move fast. A peculiar feature of those dumps is that the only level ground in them is the road. On either side of it, the slope is sheer, running down to the river and up to a timbered ridge. The downside is where the pitmen live, in shacks made of gas-oline-tins and old railway-ties; all that touches the earth is the stoop in front and two stilts behind, and they look as if they're hanging onto the world by their teeth. The upside is something else again. It's all grass and groves, and that's where you find the Legion Hall, the company store, all the churches the poor bohunks can support, and, no matter how small the town, two or three funeral-parlors. The upside is always green (you get perpetual care only after you're dead), and in the evenings, the living from the shacks come to sit in the cemeteries, six feet above where they'll some day lie—unless they're caught in a cave-in first. Church, Legion Post, and grave-yard: the cloth, the uniform, and the shroud. The good life."

The woman said, "I asked you something, Steve, and you didn't answer. Why isn't the heart dead in the dream?"

"I was bumming through the South once," the soldier said. "Hopping freights, riding blind, thumbing hitches, but this particular thing happened while I was hoofing it across a long narrow bridge. There was quite a bit of travel, and it was pretty steady in both directions, so I had to watch my step and stick close to the guard-rail. Along about the middle of the bridge, though, I noticed that it'd been some while since any cars had come up behind me, and I looked back to see why. The lane was blocked by a creeping-Jesus of a wagon, and lined up after it there must've been a good two dozen cars. The driver of the wagon was sitting sideways on the seat, his head down near his knees and his bare heels almost touching a wheel-tire, and he was sleeping hard enough for two. The sight was odd, but what made it all the odder was that the driver was black, and the people he had tied up were white. Oddest of all, however, was that not one of them made a move to get by, neither a move nor a sound. It was as if they were thinking ahead to the day when someone blew a horn, and fifteen million Negroes woke up on a narrow bridge."

"I'm still asking about the dream," the woman said.

"This country is heavy-laden with its own ruination," the soldier said. "It's sick and sore all over, it's dead in some spots and dying in the rest, and it ought to be wheezing its last in some ditch instead of bellowing about a liberty it gives only to the rich and the son of a bitch. Is that what you're waiting to hear?"

"That and the thing you always leave out," the woman said. "That if this country ever dies, you'll die with it. It's in you like a disease. You know it, only it shames you to say it."

"Why did I run, then?" the soldier said. "Why did I do the one thing that all people everywhere condemn?"

"It's sometimes a long way from the heart to the mind."

"It's even longer on your hands and knees."

"You're only a guy, Steve, but that don't mean you have to crawl."

"I'm only a guy, and I ran. Other guys are only guys too, and they stayed. They care less about America than I care about Peru— but they stayed, and I ran. Explain that, and you explain all."

"Different guys do different things," the woman said. "Or is that too simple for you? Being what's-the-word complicated, maybe you need some abbadabba, which you'll never get from me."

The soldier said, "For a couple of people throwing in with each other, we're pretty far apart, wouldn't you say?"

"In some ways," the woman said. "We don't always see the same-shape rock, I guess, or the same-color sky. But we can talk and understand most of the words, and every so often we can even *not* talk. That's enough to start with. Damn few have as much. Maybe by the time we finish, we'll know a lot more—for instance, why you ran away."

"A lifetime is a long while to be on the gaff."

The woman said, "You think you'd be off if you knew the answer now? You're the kind that never gets off. If it wasn't one thing, it'd be another."

"The more you say, the less I understand why you don't get rid of me—and don't tell me your skin would go too."

"What would I get if I packed you in—the perfect guy?"

"Some day you might meet this Mr. Right I hear so much about," the soldier said. "You need a meal. Why settle for a toothpick?"

The woman looked away through the side window, and, speaking to a blue-serge panel of night, she said, "If things were the other way round, if you were hard up for me once instead of me all the time for you, that's the question *I'd* ask."

"But things being what they are . . . ?"

"I'm getting all I ever hoped for and more than I deserve."

"You ought to face me when you say a thing like that."

"It isn't the kind of thing you want to be seen saying."

"How does it save you to say it to all that sand?"

"It doesn't, really," the woman said, and she turned back, her features enlightened by the glow on the road. "I'll say it to you, if you want. I settled for the toothpick when I married Paul; I never dreamed I'd get the meal as well."

The soldier laughed, saying, "A guy was giving an order in some Greasy Spoon. He said to the waitress, 'Beef stew and a kind word.' The waitress brought him the stuff and started back to the kitchen. The customer said, 'How about the kind word?' and the waitress said, 'Don't eat.'"

Above a rise in the pavement ahead, the sky was rouged by the neon radiance of Calexico and Mexicali. The woman stared at the low-flying cloud of light, and after a moment she repeated the last words the soldier had spoken. "Don't eat," she said, and then she shook her head a few times, as if to free her mind of their meaning. "You get born with nothing," she said, "and you grow up so damn empty-handed it's pitiful. The only big things you can remember are a stuffed dog that spoiled you for dolls and a little red pair of shoes your old man brought home when he was drunk—big events. And then one day comes a happening that frightens you, and you run to your mother about it, and she tells you it's nothing, it only means you're a woman, and as time goes on and you look around at what other women have to show for their lives, you realize that your mother told you the truth: it's nothing, nothing but bleeding once a month from here and all day long from the heart. And you wonder, where are the good things that everybody talks about and nobody seems to have, and are you going to live and die on rumors or will you some day get your hands on a fact? And then all of a sudden you're grown up enough to have it come to you that maybe the good things aren't things at all, that maybe you can't handle them like fruit or furniture, that maybe they're only *feelings* about things, without color or form and never to be touched or seen, and maybe you can have all you want of them, you or anybody, no matter if your ass is out and your belly hollow. So you think, let me be hollow now, and when the right time comes, I'll be filled. You build your life on that, and finally you know that the time is today, this very minute, and your whole mind and heart and body feel like a mouth opening . . . and then you hear some sour joker laugh and say, 'Don't eat.' That's the kind word he gives you for a lifetime of hunger. 'Don't eat,' he says!"

The soldier saw lids of tears quiver on the woman's eyes, and within him a fist seemed to unfold into a cold and empty hand. "Forgive me, Jean," he said. "Please forgive me."

[ . . . *Sun-inclines invaded the principal's office to varnish the carpet and revarnish the golden-oak chairs. The rays penetrated the glass cube of a paperweight on the desk, and rainbows rippled on the dead-white walls, enlivening a sepia print of the first Thanksgiving and a steel engraving of Alexander Hamilton. On a pedestal near the window stood the plaster bust of an anonymous patriot. It wore an expression of defiance and disdain, as if called on to relinquish a point of honor. It wore dust in its ears.*

*'Sit down, Pierce,' the principal said, and, taking up a pencil, for a moment he drummed an idle measure on the desk-edge. 'I sent for you to say that you're under suspension.'*

*You stood up, saying, 'Under suspension! What for?'*

*The principal's eyes wandered off to the picture of Hamilton, and he said, 'Come, now, Pierce.'*

*'Come yourself!' you said. 'I'm asking what for, and I want the answer without any help from that Federalist bastard on the wall!'*

*'Is that a sample of what you teach your class?' he said. . . .* ]

CHAMPAGNE FOR OUR REAL FRIENDS

What they desired him to say was a simple thing,
And, to make it simpler, it'd been said before:
"This country needs a war"—that's all they wanted,
Nothing to burden the mind, nothing to be invented,
A plain statement of fact, a declarative sentence,
But it was worth as much to them as an army corps,
And they'd have cut his profile on a mile-high rock
And made him a collector's-item with a stamp-issue
If he'd sold them a small speech from his big mouth.

He had that, this Debs, a big broad sweet mouth,
But it was no showcase for price-tagged words,
And you couldn't point and pull out your wallet:
You took what you got, and you got it for free,
So when he leapt up on that barrel (or wagon-tail,
Or flatcar, or bandstand, whatever was handy),
He gave away some not-for-sale language, to wit—
"The master-class has always declared the wars;
The subject-class has always fought the battles."

They didn't like that, didn't like any part of it:
It cost them the army corps, worse, cost them cash,
And that hit them where they lived, loved, and died,
And made it a crime of the black heart, treason,
For which the traitor won ten penitentiary years
And lost the lasting memory of coins for his face.

He was a sick old man when they sent him to the jug,
And he grew a good deal sicker and somewhat older
While his appeal was being drug up to Mr. Wilson,
A prissy gent, too proud to fight before he was ready,

But only too downright willing when he was able:
Mr. Wilson, got by a preacher on a preacher's miss
And therefore closely inbred to God Almighty, said,
'They will say I am cold-blooded and indifferent,
But it will make no impression on me, none at all.
This man was a traitor to his flag and his country,
And he will not be pardoned in my administration."
Mr. Wilson kept his promise *verbatim et literatim*—
He was a tried Christian and a true Princeton man.

When the time came, nine hundred thousand people
(Subject-class, other traitors, etc.) named Gene
For the chair that Mr. Wilson sat paralyzed in,
But this show of hands cut no Presbyterian ice,
And Mr. Wilson inched along and finished his term
As cold of blood as before and equally indifferent.
It took a more distant relative of God and Jesus
To sign a pardon for Convict Ninety-six-fifty-three.
It took a man with spots on his vest (oil, they say),
A man with a sprig of nigra on his family tree
("We understand each other perfectly," Gene said),
A brandy-soak, a poker-player, and a womanizer,
A smoke-filled President from a smoke-filled room,
But all the same a candidate for the Marble Halls,
A man with his one good hat in the ring of heaven,
And he'd have made it if Woodrow hadn't vetoed the Lord.

Gene never filled out an application for admission:
He wanted to stay where he belonged,
With the subject-class,
With other traitors,
With the people.

# REAL PAIN
# FOR
# OUR SHAM
# FRIENDS

*[ . . . You sat on a chair near the head of the bed, and you watched him sleep. His breathing was rapid and shallow, but deep enough to reach the level of pain, and each exhale was a sigh. His face was pale, with a bluish cast, as if he needed a shave. He didn't, though, because you had shaved him yourself earlier in the day. The blueing showed in his fingernails too: cyanosis, the doctor had called it. You took up a bottle from the bedside table, and idly you read the directions for taking on the label.*

*'Candy,' he said. 'Sugar-coated nonsense.'*

*'I thought you were asleep,' you said.*

*'Pills. Pills to fool the Angel of Death.'*

*'Pop, you'll outlive Pike's Peak.'*

*'My father told me a story about a friend of his in the old country. A great comedian, he was, even on his deathbed.'*

*'You're not supposed to talk so much.'*

*'If I shut up, will I live forever?'*

*'I don't know, but I'd like you to.'*

*'This man, this comedian, he was dying, and the doctor told the wife that he wouldn't last till morning unless a miracle happened. Along about the middle of the night, the sick man told the wife to put on her best dress and all her jewelry, rings, pins, everything, and then come and sit down next to him on the bed. The woman began to cry bitterly, but he insisted, and to humor him she did as he wanted. She sat there for a while, crying all the time, but finally she noticed that he was smiling, and in spite of her grief, she had to ask him why. He said, "When the Angel of Death comes for me tonight, he will find an old man, gray and tired and sick, and he will reach out his arms to take me, but then he will see you, all decked out in your finery, with powder on your face and earrings in your ears—and maybe he will take you instead of me. . . ."' ]*

At two o'clock in the morning, the main street of Calexico was still bright-lit and thronged. Everywhere pulsed tubes and sinews of neon, like a medical-chart come to life, and livid in the glow under the arcades, slow counterflows of walkers passed between rows of livid loungers at the curb and the building-wall. The cross-streets, into one of which the woman directed the soldier to turn, quickly petered out to huddles of light-squares, to stranded singles and chinks, and then to black-and-blue night.

"Straight ahead a couple of miles," the woman said, "we'll come to a packing-shed on the south side of the road. You'll know it when you see it. It's as long as a pier."

In the headlamps, a line of power-poles leaned back from the black-top as if simultaneously astounded. Beyond these, the few trees sailing the flat Sink threw little shadow: a vaguely darker dark lay below their skirts, like undergarments slipped. A road and a spur of track curved away toward the loading-platform of a shed shaped like an ark, an unbroken pentagonal block against the sky. Glossed by the stars, the crinkles of its iron roof seemed to be in motion.

The soldier stopped the car, and the woman said, "Around back, there's a footpath through a grove of manzanita. Take that and follow it to the end. It leads to the bank of the All-American Canal. The far side is Mexico, and I hope you can swim." A wind-broom swept the plain, water gurgled in the entrails of the car, and metal ticked as it shrank: there was no other sound. The woman grasped the soldier's arm, saying, "I'm asking for Christ's sake can you swim! God damn you, you bastard, don't tell me we come all this way for nothing!"

"I swim like a snake," the soldier said.

It took the woman a moment to quell herself and compel her hand to yield. "You're sure the kind that don't take prisoners," she said. "When you get locked in that dome of yours, the rest of the world can just go die. What do you think about that's so stinken important?"

"Pick a letter from A to Z," the soldier said. "Starting with A, I think about an ant in Africa known as the Anomma. Its food is meat, all cuts and all kinds: meat on the wing or on the hoof; meat that swims, crawls, or burrows in the ground; live meat or dead meat. The Anomma hunts in mile-wide sheets of death and devastation, a hundred billion at a time, and whatever living thing is in its way either flees or dies."

"The only ants I ever met were piss-ants."

"The coming of an army of Anomma is heralded by panic-stricken flights of birds, as if from a volcanic eruption or a forest-fire."

"And that's your important thought under A?"

"I'm a deep thinker, don't you think?"

"I don't believe you could tell a hind tit from a horned toad."

"Consider my subtle symbol of the ants."

"Balls, it's subtle. If I get it, it's on the nose. The ants are you—in other words, grief."

"She's a smart one, Steve," the soldier said.

"A horse would've understood. A lousy waitress, even."

"What can I say to make you leave me? I've tried everything I know."

"You could use the word 'love,'" the woman said. "That'd turn the trick, I imagine."

"It would? Why?"

"It'd be like you left two bucks under the Lysol bottle."

"Is that what the word would mean in my mouth?" the soldier said. "I must be venomous."

"No more so than the next one. It's just that the word would be in your mouth and no place else. You live your whole life with your mouth. It's never what you *do* that counts; it's only what you *say*. You've got a faceful of words for everything under the sun. You can do the most terrible things and talk them away, and you can do good things and talk those away too. For you, it's like only thinking was real, and food and houses and shoes, and people were just imaginary."

The soldier reached behind him for the box containing the suit, and a time or two he plucked the string, snapping it against the cardboard. "Can this be talked away?" he said. "If you think so, you believe in words far more than I ever did." He opened the door and stood down from the car, and the woman took his place behind the wheel. He bowed slightly, saying, "Pardon me, madam, but can you direct me to hell?"

"You're standing in it. The way people say, 'Go to hell,' you'd imagine it was some place else."

"I should've said that under H. I'm the deep thinker."

"Yes," the woman said. "But pay attention, now, because once we split, you'll only know what you don't forget. When you make the other side of the canal, switch to the civvies and drown the uniform with a rock. Then head for Mexicali—that's the Mexican side of Calexico, the town we just left—but keep away from the ditch. Stay well south and try to hit Mexicali from below, like you belonged there and only went for a walk in the tules. Meet me at a beer-joint called El Nacional. You ought to make it easy in an hour, but I'll give you two just to be sure. If you don't show up by then, I'll know something went sour, and I'll double back to the California side and wait for you at Perry's Grill in Calexico. What else can I tell you?"

"One thing. Who gave you the directions that you're giving me?"

"A chap I stopped in the street. He didn't say his name."

"El Nacional or Perry's Grill—one or the other, then."

"You'll be careful, won't you, Steve?"

"Very," he said. "As if I had but one life to lose for my country."

The woman U-turned the Ford and drove back toward Calexico, and the soldier, holding to the shadows, headed for the area behind the packing-house. Ice-chutes overhung a string of refrigerator-cars running the length of the siding, and from the far side of the tracks, the manzanita grove ranged southward. The shrubbery was dense and the path through it winding and overgrown, with snares of root underfoot and mendicant branches to be shrugged off, some of them twice, from fore and aft. Between the grove and the canal, a slant of sand had been shirred by the wind, the pattern broken only by a single saunter of footprints that looked like black stones in the starlight. The soldier broke it again as he went down the slope to the flume, and, kneeling at the edge, he let the water run against his hand.

This was the dreaded verge of the world, he thought, and here the flat ancient earth ended, and the flight, the fall through space, began. Beyond his hand, he thought, lay the void, lay dark and infinite nothing, barren, eternal, and, like time, one-way. This was the furthest fringe, he thought, and if he chose to pass it, the choice and the passage would be the last voluntary acts of his life. He rose, holding his hand before him and watching it drip [ . . . *It's American water, mister, a private blend of oxygen and hydrogen for white men only. If you know what's good for you, you'll speak softly about such impurities as sodium-cyanide, carbolic, gunoil, and Indian blood— we were after gold, mister, and gold don't fall from trees. And while you're about it, you'll speak softly of all the rest: of the promises that we never meant to keep, the rights that were only equal on paper, the justice that's just ice, and the freedom that's only for me. Speak softly, mister. . . .* ], and he thought that behind him too lay the void, no less dark and no less barren: there was no choice between nothing and nothing.

He lowered himself into the water and shoved off from the steep chamfer of the ditch. The current took hold and waltzed him once around before he could settle into stroke, a one-armed sidling tow, like a tug. The box, drawn by its string, floated for a while, and then, waterlogged, it sank and sea-anchored him, and he made little head-way across the flow and much down it, and not until he hooked the string on his teeth and overswam the box like a dog on retrieve did he begin to shorten the distance to the far embankment. There were no handholds where he reached it, and he let himself drift from eddy to eddy until the run beached him among some reeds.

It was done, he thought. The course begun a month before (a month? why not a year, seventeen years, a lifetime?) was now complete. This was where the blind tangle of time had led him, he thought: knotted, twisted, crisscrossed, and snarled, it uncoiled itself here. There were no more scrolls and involutions to follow—the rest of the way was straight. Straight, he thought, but straight to where and to what if not to death? He had broken into the clear at last, only to see clearly the destination he had been thrashing toward—the grave. The boots were walking the plain, he thought, but the plain was no longer endless.

[ *'. . . You'll be careful, won't you, Steve. . . . ?'* ]

Water seeped from his hair and overran his face. He felt it flowing down him everywhere, falling from his finger-tips and draining from his feet into the sand, and he endured for a moment a sense of hemorrhage, as if he were being bled of all that his body was burdened with. Expelling its substance, a shell of skin remained, and he seemed to have no more weight than his name, no home, no history, neither obligation nor memory, and no allegiance except to his mouth, his nose, and the vestiges of his balls. He picked up the sodden shapeless bundle of cardboard, twine, and puckered cotton (his lifesavings, he thought) and stared away along the canal toward the west. The sky above the twin towns was tangerine.

[ *'. . . Meet me at a beer-joint called El Nacional. . . .'* ]

It would be a one-room dirt-floored hole, he thought. Three of its walls would be painted peach and pistache, and on the fourth a crude *goyesca* would frame the mirror of the bar. The beer-soaked air would bear as well the flavors of peso perfume, sheep-dip, and tobacco, and through smoke rising and falling as if on a sigh would come high quick talk and a *paso doble*. The faces would be waxwork faces, arranged beyond any expression that he would easily understand, but all of them, he thought, from the silk young to the canvas old, would be beautiful. None would stare when he entered and sat down, nor when he ordered, nor while he drank and waited, and he would sit revolving his emptied glass, and he would feel alone there, but alone in company, like one of many strangers sheltered somewhere from a rain. He would feel both near and far, soothed by contact yet secure from invasion, and he would look once for luck at the doorway, but, seeing no white brassards on the dark, he would slide a little lower in his chair, safe, and safely light a cigarette.

[ *'. . . You'll be careful, won't you, Steve . . . ?'* ]

But careful of what? The danger would be past and fast fading, he thought, like the dangers of his Gettysburg dream: here no brains and blue bowels would garland oxidized rock, no blood would seep into springs, no wrecked men would crawl over a vast dump, sprung and dismantled, and no speech would be spoken off an old envelope and failed with ("It won't scour, Lamon."). There would be no peril for him in the causes of a now foreign country: finished or unfinished, the episodes of its chronicle would never again be his concern.

[ *'. . . You'll be careful, won't you, Steve . . . ?'* ]

He would be without concern of any kind, he thought, and feeling as volatile as the levitant smoke, he would glance about at the self-vizored faces, at the unknowns to whom he was close but alien, and he would see little that long arrested the eye—an odd-shaped bottle on the bar, a bull-fight poster, a gesture, a good color here and there against the rash pistache—and not until his gaze was fixed on nothing would he realize that certain words, absorbed from the poster, were playing themselves again and again on his mind: "*Plaza Monumental Barcelona Plaza Monumental Barcelona Plaza Monumental. . . .*"

[ *'. . . You'll be careful. . . .'* ]

At that instant, he would become aware of a break in his breathing, like a missing step in a flight of stairs, and then for a while he would breathe consciously, as though his lungs would cease to function if he forgot to make them fill and expel, and, still looking at nothing, still sitting still, he would wonder why the remembered and repeated words had so disturbed him: "*Plaza Monumental Barcelona.*" He would turn to the poster.

[ '... *Won't you, Steve* ... ?' ]

Printed in primaries and pasted to the plaster, the lithograph, he would find, had lost little of its boldness since *2 de Octubre de 1930*, on which day it had been promised that *Bienvenida y Solorzano, mano a mano* would kill 6 *Hermosísimos Ejemplares* 6. There would be no response in him to any of this special but trivial information, yet he would be unable to look away, and, puzzled, he would seek further for the fact or token that first had made him skip a breath. Would it be the raw red and green lettering, or the violet and indigo *sombra?* Would it be the blue sky, the yellow embroidery, or the orange *barrera?* Or would it be the stud, *la prestigiosa ganadería*, that had bred the bulls, or would it be the breeder, the *Excmo. Sr. Conde de la Corte* of Badajoz? Or would it be the scale of prices, or the small-print names of the *cuadras?* Or would it be . . . ? And all at once, the lighter-than-air machine that was his body would crumple and plunge toward the earth. Badajoz! Jesus Christ, the bull-ring at Badajoz!

[ '... *You'll be careful, won't you, Steve* ... ?' ]

He would try desperately to stop thinking, but the thought, the dangerous thought, would be in the open and running free. The bull-ring at Badajoz, soaked not with the blood of bulls reared by the Excmo. Sr., nor of Solorzano, nor of Apañao his picador, nor of Manuel Aguilar his banderillero, nor even of hundred-peseta bone-bag nags: soaked, yes, soaked into a round red swamp, but the pigment had been drawn from every man caught in the act of wearing a callus, every man with a bruise from a rifle-recoil, every man who had forgotten to rinse powder-scorch from his hands with his piss! Four thousand such had been racked up against the gored *barreras* and chopped down dead in the sand—not with darts, lances, *verónicas*, and the sword, but with lead!

[ *'. . . You'll be careful, won't you, Steve . . . ?'* ]

"Yes," he said.

And then, he thought, he would move his head to scan the faces in the room.

The image of El Nacional waned like a whisper on a windowpane, and the union-blue night returned, cross-stitched with stars. In his hand, the soldier still held the saturated box, and near his feet the flowing water rustled the reeds. He raised his eyes to the far shoulder of the canal and to all that lay beyond it, and he knew then what he had so long sought to leave unknown—that the harpoons of history were in him to stay. No place on earth, neither here nor at a distance, offered escape, and to seek it further, by a mile or by miles in the thousands, would be to flee fire only to freeze. Neither the far-away nor a head in the sand nor the diminutions of age would change the knowledge that no countries were foreign and no men strange. The single division was everywhere, the division of the rich from the rest—that was the fire, and, running from it all his life, he found it still at his heels.

[ *'. . . You'll be careful, won't you, Steve . . . ?'* ]

"Yes," he said, "I'll only risk my life," and, sliding down the embankment, he swam back across the canal. When he reached the other slope, he climbed it to level ground, and there he paused for a moment to watch the sand drink from his shoes, but now his sense of being drained (because nothing remained, was it?) was gone. He made his way through the brake of manzanita and headed for the meeting-place in Calexico.

[ *. . . An afternoon in the fall, overcast and still, and the smoke of burning brush rose straight before flattening out to haze and sweeten the air. From the porch, you watched the always mobile maples that lined the street, and now and then you saw a loose leaf lurch to the ground and lie warped and five-fingered in rigor mortis.*

*'A day to give you the blues,' he said.*

*Wrapped in a blanket, he sat near you in a wheel-chair. 'I've always liked this time of year,' you said. 'I've always looked forward to it.'*

*'So did I—when I knew I'd still be here in the spring.'*

*'I tell you and tell you . . . ,' you said.*

*'You tell me and tell me lies. What am I, Steve—a child?'*

*'I tell you what the doctor tells me,' you said, and you went to the end of the porch and stood there for a moment with your arm around the corner-post, picking at flakes of paint in the fluting, and then you came back and stopped before him, saying, 'Pop, there's something on my mind, and I've got to talk to you about it. It may hurt your feelings, but I have to say it all the same.'*

*'Say it, son.'*

*'I don't want you to leave me anything. Whatever you own—the house, the furniture, any money you still have in the bank—please, Pop, leave it to the Home, not to me.'*

*'What I've got isn't much, Steve. You could stick it in your ear.'*

*'No matter how much or how little, I couldn't take a dollar of it. It doesn't belong to me.'*

*'I guess nothing ever belonged to you,' he said. 'All these years, and you never really felt like you owned anything here.'*

*'Only you,' you said.*

*He looked away downstreet, saying, 'What more could a man ask?'*

*'He could ask whether he had all my love,' you said, 'and if he did, the answer would be yes.'*

*He turned to you, and you remembered what he had told you once: that among his people, it was the old men who were beautiful. 'You're a good boy, Steve,' he said, 'and I'll do what you want about the Home.'*

*You took his hand and held it for a moment before saying, in a very low voice, 'Will you do it soon, Pop?'*

*He nodded. 'Tomorrow, son,' he said, 'and now I finally know all the things I wanted to know. You're a good boy, Steve.'*

*'I'm not,' you said, and you went down the steps to the walk. 'I'm not,' you said, and, reaching for a fallen leaf, you spun it till the crying stopped.*

*An afternoon in the fall, it was. . . . ]*

Calexico was a long march through an upcast of heat that dried the outer layers of the soldier's uniform, but a flux of sweat kept the armpits and the waistband dank. The string-tied lump dangling from his hand slowly stiffened under its buckled crust of cardboard, and after a while it left no transient trail of drops on the pavement. Fine dust rose from the roadside in a wind that harped as well on the overhead wires.

On the main street of the town, the soldier went toward the on-and-off of a self-spelling and self-expunging sign: P-E-R-R-Y. He stopped in the doorway, and peering at booths lightened only by the cathedral of the bar, he discerned faces suspended like fish in tanks. A hand on his arm drew him back to the sidewalk.

"I waited at the Nacional till four o'clock," the woman said, but the soldier was watching the electric-sign once more eat the word P-E-R-R-Y out of the sky, and he made no response. "What happened? Was somebody around?"

"Around where?"

"Where you tried to cross."

"I did cross," the soldier said.

The woman stared at him, studying his face in the five-letter glow and the no-letter gloom. "You got over?" she said. "You actually were in Mexico?"

"Yes."

She said, "Steve . . . ," and then she withdrew her voice from the thought and shook her head. "I was going to ask you something, but what's the use? I wouldn't understand the answer. It's no good listening to Greek."

"What you want to know is why I came back," he said. "I can tell you that in English."

"There's times when your English gets so fancy it sounds like a foreign language. This'd be one of those times, so let's just go home and make believe we were only out for a drive."

The woman drove. To the right of the road, over the far Chocolates, the night showed a faint melt and fade, a belt of sky a shade less deeply dyed than the rest.

"For all your talk of being simple," the soldier said, "you understand whatever I understand, fancy or plain. This happens to be plain: I didn't really come back at all; I never went away."

"That's the kind of bull I've been leery of from the start," the woman said. "You *did* go away: you quit the Army, you ran for the border, and you got across. You were out, all the way out, and now you're back all the way in—but I'm supposed to make yes like a dummy when you say you were right here all along. That's bull in any language."

"I was never able to desert Steve Pierce."

"More bull. You deserted Steve Pierce so long ago that you wouldn't know yourself if you woke up in the same bed. Steve Pierce! Who the hell is Steve Pierce? Anybody in the world but you. You're Stan Clarke."

"If it were only a matter of names!" the soldier said. "But Clarke or Pierce or anything else, I was still in chains."

"Why didn't you find that out up here? Why did you only get smart when you were safe?"

"Some people kill themselves to learn whether death is better than life."

"Bull," the woman said. "All bull."

"That word has you by the ear."

"Look who for Christ's sake is talking! An egg-yellow son of a bitch that all his life was only working his way up to running out on his country in cold blood! My God, if anybody has anything by the ear, it's you—scared stiff of death, and twice as scared of living! What a way to be built! To go from fright to fright—Jesus, if I was like that, I'd sooner been drowned in a douche!"

"It could be that just for once I was brave," the soldier said.

"I can't argue with you," the woman said. "I told you I wouldn't understand, and I don't. Other people might, but all I can get from this shenanigan of yours is a gall-bladder attack. Up to now, you've been shot with luck, but sooner or later some MP is going to ask for your papers, or your pass, or whatever it is the bastards ask for, and you'll be queered—and if not with him, then with the next one. Or if your luck holds there, it'll give some place else. It's bound to, with Brewer, maybe, or Pryor, or whoever you pick on to come it over, and that could be anybody, because who *don't* you come it over? In Mexico, you were safe, from guys like that and even from yourself, but that was bad, being safe: you wouldn't have been able to prove what you're trying to prove. Christ only knows what it is, and nobody knows to who, but here you are again, you deep-thinking fool, ready for a pat on the head and a 'Good for you.' Well, maybe it is good for you. Maybe you'd only be getting what you want if they caught you. I don't know. You're an odd guy." Far ahead, the hidden lights of an oncoming car fantailed up from a rise in the road. "But tell me this. While you were swimming back and forth like a phriggen frog, did you ever once wonder if it'd be good for *me?*"

The approaching lights spilled over and ran down the highway toward the Ford. "For the few minutes that I was in Mexico," the soldier said, "you were out of sight and out of mind. If I'd stayed longer, you'd have been out once and for all, for good and forever."

"If you say you came back account of me, I hope you die."

"I came back because I couldn't drag myself forward. I couldn't pull the load another yard."

"The load didn't stop you deserting. You ran away from the Army like a striped-ass ape. Why did it stop you in Mexico?"

"Up to that moment, I'd coked myself into believing in the possibility of escape. I'd thought I could shuck the United States like a dirty shirt. But so far from that, I put a second one on right over it, the dirty shirt of Franco Spain—and I knew that wherever I went, I'd put on more, a third, a fourth, a fifth, a tenth, and some day I'd smother to death in filth. Every country has a dirty-shirt history, and no man ever got clean by running away from his own."

"Why didn't you do something when you had the chance, Steve? Why did you have to go that far to get lost?"

"To get lost?" the soldier said. "I didn't get lost—I got found." He paused, and the pause was filled with motorpound and the rip of rolling rubber. "I got found, and I can't understand why I think the finder was you."

"You're saying one of your good things now. You better spoil it before I get to like it. Say something rotten."

"Suppose I say another good thing instead."

"I wish I didn't have to suppose so much," the woman said, and she moved her hand in a gesture that embraced, for all its vagueness and restraint, the world. "Why does all that have to be one big suppose? Why won't it come true?"

"The other good thing . . . ," the soldier said, but the rest hung. "The other good thing . . . It's hard to say."

"If it's really so good," the woman said, "its socks don't have to match." In the dawn-worn sky over the Chocolates, a hackle of fire was rising. "Let it say itself," she said, but the soldier was silent, and once more the piston-stroke was heard, and the insistent tires spoke.

In the tree-lined lane leading to the woman's house, the car made medicine of the blue-gum pods and the blue-gum leaves, and the tinctured air, flaked with dust, boiled in the flat sunlight and flashed. Heat climbed weaving from the shut-off motor, and the windshield seemed to writhe, as if molten, distorting all beyond it—the shrubbery in the yard, the parched grass, the stoop, even the man waiting in the shade of the porch. On his faded blue shirt, the man wore a six-pointed silver star.

As the woman neared him, the man touched the peak of his

cap, revealing a hammock of sweat slung underarm. "Morning, Mrs. Bell," he said.

"Morning, Jeff," she said. "Anything special?"

The man dipped his head at the soldier, saying, "Clarke, here— if he's Clarke."

"Stan Clarke, Jeff Rand," the woman said.

"What can I do for you?" the soldier said.

"I'm supposed to, like the papers say, quiz you."

"Wouldn't that make you kind of inquisitive?"

The policeman reached behind him and plucked his stuck shirt loose from his back. "Far's I'm concerned, you don't have to answer," he said. "I'm supposed to ask, though, and I'm asking."

"He'll answer," the woman said, and she looked at the soldier. "Jeff's a friend of mine."

"Who isn't?"

"His wife's a friend too."

"I apologize," the soldier said to Rand. "The uniform threw me."

"It shouldn't of," Rand said. "You got a uniform yourself."

"I didn't pick it out. Personally, I prefer something in tweed."

"I never could figure why a cop was an animal to make people hold their nose. It's okay to be a plasterer or a trombone-player, but let a man join the force, and it's like he quit bathing."

"It's the word 'force,' I think."

Rand studied the soldier for a moment, and then he nodded, saying, "That's a way of putting it I never heard before, but there's truth in it, and I'm going to remember it. All the same, I happen to never wrang a guy's arm for fun, so it don't cover me."

The woman said, "Does it cover your fat slob of a boss?"

Rand looked down at his shoes, tipping up the toes as if to make certain that they still contained his feet. "Buell's the one sent me, Jean," he said.

"And who put him up to it?"

"Arnie Brewer."

"The bastard."

The soldier said, "What did they tell you to find out, Jeff?"

"Who you are, where you from, and all like that."

The soldier took out his wallet and handed it to Rand. The policeman flipped it open and withdrew the contents of one of the slots—a packet of folded papers and a few cards. He tried to spread them, but, damp, they clung to each other. "You sure do sweat," he said. "You sweat like a nigger at election."

"Negro," the soldier said.

"God damn it!" the woman said. "What're you doing—answering questions or running for office?"

"I stopped running—remember?" the soldier said, and he returned to Rand. "Negro—capital N-e-g-r-o."

"It was only an expression," Rand said. "No need to paw the ground."

Indicating the papers in Rand's hand, the soldier said, "And that isn't sweat on those. I jumped into a ditch."

"God damn it!" the woman said.

Watching Rand, the soldier said, "How many times are you going to say that?"

The woman let a moment pass, and then she said, "Stick around if you want some coffee, Jeff," and, climbing the stoop, she went into the house.

The policeman seated himself on the steps. He fumbled with the limp memoranda as if baffled by his possession of them, and after a brief inspection, hardly more than a glance at a paper and a few of the cards, he returned the wallet to the soldier, saying, "Sit, kid. It's too hot to struggle standing up." The soldier joined him, and he stared away across the yard. "Life is full of broken glass."

"Negro," the soldier said.

"Negro," Rand said. "You feel better now?"

"Braver," the soldier said.

"A good way to be. People don't like people that're yellow, even if they're yellow too. That's the big trouble in this world. It isn't so much people hating each other; it's people hating themselves. They can't stand being like they are, so they try and change somebody else."

"What you're saying is, all people are cops at heart."

"I didn't realize it," Rand said, "but it finally tells me what I'm doing in this rig. I never knew before."

"We could write a book, Jeff," the soldier said.

"Anybody could write a book. There ain't a pissing man that ain't a book right now, a book walking around on end."

"Over broken glass."

"Life is lousy with it."

"That makes one full turn, Jeff. When do we get down to business?"

"There's no hurry," the policeman said. "Matter of fact; there's no business. I know all I want to know about you."

"I must be a pretty short book."

"In a couple of minutes, I'm going to write up my report for Chief Buell. It'll go something like this. First off, the date: July 11. That's important. Two hundred years from now, it'll be even more important. The date first, then something about being informed there was a suspicious character loitering around premises 6a Rincon Lane, City of El Centro. I proceeded to said premises, I'll say (a cop proceeds—he never just goes), and I found Mrs. Eugenia Bell, tenant, and one Stan Clarke, the character under suspicion. I requested this Clarke to identify himself, and he shown me Honorable Discharge papers from the U. S. Army, the same being in good order. Signed—Jeffery Rand, Shield Number 17."

[ *'. . . The papers are forgeries,' you'd say. 'I bought them in San Francisco for a hundred and fifty dollars.'*

*What would he say? 'You got took,' maybe. 'They seen you coming.'*

*'There's no such person as Stanley Clarke,' you'd say, 'and there's no such town as Port Quincy, Delaware. My name is Stephen Pierce, and I come from Red Bank, New Jersey. I was born there on May 7, 1913, at Creek Road, corner of Wayne. I went to Molly Pitcher High School for four years, and then, for four more, to Lafayette College, in Easton, Pennsylvania.'*

*What would he say? 'I always wanted to go to college,' probably. 'I would've took up agriculture.'*

*'By profession, I'm a teacher,' you'd say, 'and I taught history till I got the urge to teach the truth. They kicked me out for that.'*

*What would he say? 'They couldn't of had a better reason.'*

*'A roomful of kids,' you'd say. 'A roomful of kids, and I looked down at them, thinking, "This is the earth, where, according to how you use it, the dead are buried or the living grow. It's one or the other, a great common grave or a vast vineyard: it can't be both." I wanted it to be the vineyard. I wanted the stones to flower and the sand to bloom, and I wanted the air to be filled with birds that sang of life, not death. A roomful of kids, and I could do as I pleased with them—make them flourish or keep them barren. It was another Third Day of another Creation, and, like another God, I could bring forth grass and cause the tree to yield, or I could condemn the seed and suppress the herb. I made my choice, and I was kicked out for it. I wasn't God any more; I was only a bum in a false beard.'*

*What would he say?*

*'And being a bum,' you said, 'I bummed around for a while after that, and wherever I went I saw waste—not a roomful now, but a nation, not twenty or thirty, but millions, a country of six-foot kids with three-foot minds. And then the war came, and I was told to fight for it. Piss on that, I said, and I walked away. There you have it, Jeff. What do you say . . . ?'*]

The policeman rose from the steps. "I ain't hungry this morning," he said.

"Aren't you even going to stay for coffee, Jeff?"

"It's bad for my heartburn. Did you ever have the heartburn? I get it so bad it wakes me up in the night sometimes. I take all kinds of stuff—pills, powders—but there's only one thing'll do me any good, and I can't make it go down. You know what it is, Stan? I could throw away this star and join that God damn Army I hear so much about!"

The soldier looked up at him. "Broken glass for you too, Jeff?" he said.

"It's all over the place," Rand said, and, waving his hand, he turned away and walked off down the lane.

For some time after Rand had gone, the soldier remained seated on the steps, his mind like a vacated house, littered with scraps and shards but all the more barren for them, and his eyes like windows giving on a blank wall. He saw nothing, and he thought of nothing, and he was unaware of the heightening sun. The heat leached his head of sweat, drank from him, and slowly he began to grow a coronet of pain, as if his skull were being inflated against a fillet. Sight came back, but it came warped, and shapes seemed to tremble in the tremblant air. He rose, but, standing, he felt as if held in solution, and with no more effort than the exercise of a will to move, he mounted the stoop to the porch. There, though, and at once, his buoyancy withdrew, and he stopped a fall only by seizing the banister as he foundered. He was still holding it when the woman came to the door. She helped him to reach a chair, and for a space of time its back-rest served as a spine for a body that sagged as if boned. A pulse clog-danced in his inner ear, and all but his hands concealed the caper: they jogged in time with his heart.

As if filtered by the heat, the thin word "Steve" was heard, and stubbornly the soldier's head responded to his endeavor to turn it. "Steve," the woman said.

"I never liked the name," he said, "but I'll always remember the way you say it. You make it sound like a last thought at night."

"I want to talk to you. I don't want to juggle words."

"Watch me, then. I can keep dozens in the air."

"I want to talk to you!" the woman said. "And, God damn you, you've got to answer! This has to stop, do you hear? For days now, you've been acting like you had your whole life to make up your mind, and all the while you've only been an hour ahead of the meat-wagon."

"To make up my mind about what?"

"Sit there digging a hole with your toe, and I swear to Christ I'll stick my finger in your eye! To make up your mind about this—*this!*"

"So in the end," the soldier said, "what my life comes to is a demonstrative pronoun. What distinction! To live thirty-odd years only to wind up as something the curious can prod with an umbrella: 'this.'"

"All lives come to that sooner or later," the woman said. "But there's no rule you have to wait for it in El Centro."

"Where else would I wait? What's the name of the place where I'd be safe from Steve Pierce? My lifelong enemy—and I'm no hour ahead of him, either. He's here. He's looking at you. He's saying this. And some day he's going to kill me!"

"Kill *him!*"

"I've tried all my life."

"But never so it counted," the woman said. "Always in your mind, always too late, always with half a heart, but never for real. Try once like that. I beg you, Steve."

"Give myself up, you mean?" the soldier said, and when the woman nodded, he smiled. "I'd be getting rid of my enemy by doing away with his. A poor victory, especially if there's a hell: I'd be fighting Steve Pierce till it froze over."

"What exactly would happen?" the woman said. "If you gave up, that is."

"You ask a question I'm well qualified to answer. You have before you, in fact, an Army lawyer, and I invite you to test me. I know the Articles of War frontwards, sideways, and ass-end-to."

"I only want to know what applies to you."

"Wherever soldiers bivouac, wherever a campfire burns and arms are stacked, there men will sing of Pierce, the great hairsplitter. Let me recite the rule regarding 'Quarrels, Frays, and Disorders.'"

The woman rocked herself gently for a moment, and then, in a mild voice, she said, "I sit here wondering why I don't go off like a bomb."

"Ask me about 'Subordinates Compelling Commander To Surrender,' 'Improper Use Of Countersign,' and 'Forcing A Safeguard.' You'll be amazed."

Still mildly, the woman said, "Won't you talk to me once like I was human, Steve? Just once?"

[ . . . *You stayed there for a while after the hearse and the one car had gone. It was a cold day, gray and windless, and the bare trees were written like rivers and their tributaries on the sky. Over the filled-in grave at your feet lay a mat of green raffia, and looking down at the imitation grass, you remembered words long withheld but finally spoken.*

*'It wasn't enough to call you Pop,' you had said, 'and it wasn't enough to tell you how much I loved you. You still were sad, and you're sad right now, and I'm the reason for it, because I've never yet been a son. All it would've taken was the saying of one thing, the only thing you've ever wanted to hear from me, but I've made you wait for fifteen years, and now it's too late to do you any good, too late even to be believed. But I can't let you go away sad; I haven't got the heart. No matter what I've said or done to make you think otherwise, I haven't got the heart. So let me say now what I've owed you all along: I never held Carlo against you. Against myself, always, but never against you.'*

*He tried to reach your hand with his, but he was too weak to move, and you leaned closer while he said, 'You're a good boy, Steve, a good son,' and then for the first and last time you kissed him. . . .* ]

When the soldier spoke, his tone too was subdued. "As if *you* were human?" he said. "The trouble's always been with *me; I'm* not. There isn't much humanity in this suit. What you take for a heart is really an ice-bag. You feed me, you work for me, you praise me, you give me the run of your house and the run of you, you even join with me in a crime—but you're doing all that for someone who doesn't exist. When you look at me, and I look in the mirror (some-one said that to me once), we see different things."

"That don't scare me," the woman said. "I'd only be scared if we saw the same."

"I used to think that way," the soldier said, "but not any more. You can't look at the sun and call it anything under the sun, and still less can you look at it and not see it at all. Yet ever since you've known me, that's just what you'd like me to bring off. 'What's all the fuss about—a little old thing like desertion? Pick it out of your teeth and chew on the other side.'"

The woman struck a match on the rocker-arm, and before touching off a cigarette, she stared at the pale straight-up flame. "This is one time you read me wrong," she said. "I'm not telling you to stick your head in the ground and your ass in the air—not after Mexico and Jeff Rand. I say, go back to the Army and take your beating. Whatever it is, it can't be worse than you're giving yourself. The Army couldn't be that cruel."

The soldier looked at her, but she was fanning the coal of her cigarette with a thin skein of smoke. "Articles of War 58," he said. "'Any person subject to military law who deserts or attempts to desert the service of the United States shall, if the offense be com-mitted in time of war, suffer death or such other punishment as a court-martial may direct.'"

The slow rocking of the woman's chair ceased, and a remnant of smoke drifted from her mouth and vanished, and it seemed to the soldier as if her life had paused at some station in time. "Death," she said, "or such other punishment."

"Go back and take your beating, you said."

"What would that mean—'such other punishment'?"

"Oh, some officer would take me aside and give me a talking-to, a reprimand. He'd urge me to spend a little more time on the post and a little less on the road. Fatherly advice against falling in with bad company."

The woman clubfooted her cigarette on the sole of her shoe, briefly inspected the bent and charred tube, and shot it away over the porch rail. "Seriously," she said.

"Forfeiture of pay and allowances," the soldier said. "Am I serious enough, or should I mention a possible item of twenty years at hard labor?"

The woman was rocking herself again, and so barely perceptible was the motion that it seemed to be powered by her heartbeat. "You harp on the most you could get," she said. "What's the least?"

"With the Stan Clarke papers, the Purple Heart fraud, and the bandage," he said, "how could I get the least? What fact would I offer to melt their minds?"

"The fact that you went back knowing what would happen to you. The fact that in the end you put the Service ahead of yourself."

"You can't clean yourself with a dirty hand."

"The fact that deep down the country counts for so much with you."

"Yet if I said what I think, I'd convict myself out of my own mouth. The country does count, but only as all countries do—for what it could be, not for what it is."

"Is it really so bad, Steve?"

"When a thing was great once, what is it when it's less? Is it simply less than great, or does the shrinkage, however slight, make it little? Can you write 'God' with a small *g* and still bow down? The wonder of the world, they called us, the blazing blinding wonder, but are we the wonder now or only a photograph of the sun? No square mile we began with is missing, no river, no plain, no inch of coast-line, no fine word we spoke kneeling alone or standing before all, and what we had was fruitful, and it multiplied—the square miles, the rivers, the words, the riches—and in time we came to own the earth and all that the earth contained, and still hungering, we grew wings to drum up trade in space. But cornering so much, we lost much more, for what are we profited if we gain the whole world and lose its people? Vaster now than ever, stronger, flashier, louder, even so we've dwindled in their eyes, and they say, 'Beware of those who started with slogans and ended with ads. Beware of those conceived in liberty and dedicated to dividends. Beware of Christers bearing merchandise.'"

"Why did you come back, then?"

"Breathes there a man with soul so dead who never to himself hath said: 'This is my own, my native vomit'? I'm a dog without a country."

"You could've had this one. You can have it yet."

"At the price they'd ask, it wouldn't be a bargain."

"There are no bargains in this world!" the woman said. "You want to be a patriot, but it's got to come cheap, and you want a perfect country, but only if the saps and suckers of the past did all the perfecting. The backbreak, the worry, the skimping, the beatings and framings, getting rooked by the rich and dragged down by the poor, that was for a bunch of dead-and-gone slobs named George— and when the struggle is over, when the last shots are fired, and the smoke clears, then, Christ, the deep thinkers come along, the Steves and Stans, ready to heist up the flag and cheer like all hell. Bargains, shit! There's no such thing, and if you still think otherwise, it's damn little history you learned while you taught it. Very few on this earth get what their mouths water for, but nobody would ever have got anything if they all did like you—sit on your ass and stare at your belly-button."

The soldier said, "That bothers you most—the sitting still. If I ran away, you'd be satisfied. If I hid in a hole, you'd be satisfied. If I gave myself up, you'd be satisfied. But what you can't understand is the sitting still. I sit because I'm canceled out. The uniforms worn by soldiers fighting to free the slaves were made by ten-year-old children working from five in the morning till seven at night—and the children and the soldiers died, and the slaves remained slaves. I sit because I'm nullified by the double-cross. My running days are over, I never learned to fly, and I won't crawl, so I sit. What else is there to do?"

"You could stand, you yellow son of a bitch! You could just *stand!*"

A car came to a stop in the lane, its windshield a mirror for the sun, and the figures of Brewer and Pryor loomed as if emerging from fire.

"I asked you to go home," Brewer said. "Now I'm telling you."

The soldier glanced at the minister. "How about a little something from the Book?" he said.

"'Be not wise in thine own eyes,'" Pryor said. "'Fear the Lord, and depart from evil.'"

The soldier laughed. "If Christ died for you," he said, "he sure as hell went for a song."

"'They have sharpened their tongues like a serpent,'" Pryor said. "'Adders' poison is under their lips.'"

"All the stink in this life comes from talk," Brewer said. "Let people talk, and before you know it, you've spoiled them for listening."

"In the next world," the soldier said, "I hope I have no ears."

"You just could lose them in this one," Brewer said. "Somebody is got to give the orders, and somebody else is got to take them. Otherwise, somebody is got to get hurt."

"'What man is he that liveth and shall not see death?'" Pryor said.

"For the same thirty pieces of silver," the soldier said, "I think you'd have betrayed the whole family—Father, Mother, and Son."

"This ain't drawing water or sawing wood," Brewer said. "It's only making you late."

"Is it?" the soldier said. "Late for what?"

"Your train."

"Am I taking a train?"

"It's taking you."

"I don't believe it's going in my direction. I'm headed straight down."

"Pick any train in any direction—for ten dollars' worth."

Pryor said, "For the good of my congregation, I donate that sum from church-funds."

"For the good of your congregation," the soldier said, "buy a pistol and blow your brains out."

"You're staying, then?" Brewer said. "That's final?"

"As final as death," the soldier said. "With all respect to this shit-sack of a preacher."

Brewer nodded and turned away, and Pryor followed him. The woman waited until the car had gone, and then she said, "Knowing you, it's a mistake to tell you this. It'll likely only get your back up all the more. But just in case, do you remember about the gas-station guy?"

"Very clearly," the soldier said.

"When Charlsie Oliver came back from her little ride up the Sink, who do you suppose she went crying to? Think hard, now. And who do you suppose got up the party to go calling on the guy? Don't give the first name that comes to mind: think. And, lastly, who do you suppose dreamed up the guy's come-uppance? Your answer ought to be the same for all three questions." The woman rose and started for the door. "You still think that train is going without you?" With the screen open, she paused. "You're lucky he didn't pick out a freight, a sealed fruit-dispatch, but he still could, and he will, and that'll be final like you said. Final as death." The screen closed, and the soldier was alone.

They would come back, he thought, and take him away.

The moonlit night would be like a negative of day, he thought, light for dark and dark for light, and as their car sped across the Sink, it would raise behind it a feather-duster of dust that would float long in the dormant air, like smoke in a room. In the ditches, roads of water would flow unbroken and asphalt gray, and the shaken reeds would speak in spirant whispers, endlessly saying the same strange single word. Far out on the plain, the car-lamps would find twin arcs of track, and twin gleams would skate the steel converge to brighten the shiplike shape of a packing-shed. Its ramps would be walled in by yellow reefers, their hatches bolted and their drains dripping, rolling-stock waiting stock-still for a head-end, for some not-yet-stoked Mikado, that would come at dawn. The motorcar would be stopped and darkened, and its simmer-down would be followed by a tick or two, as from a spent clock, and for a moment there would be the sound of silence, and then, straight ahead, in the shadow of the train, a hand-torch would wink on and off twice.

They would invite him to go for a short walk.

They would nip the seal on a reefer, he thought, and pry open its narrow double-thickness doors. A faint fog of chilled air would spill down, scented with the aged wine of fruit-soaked wood, a cellar-smell, damp and temperate, and he would try to drown himself drinking it. There would be words now, commanding him, and when he failed to obey, there would be a show of force (would he fight back? would he make this his first and last stand? would he kill to win here, or here die losing? would he act for once, or would he merely think of action to the end?).

Behind him, then, they would close the doors.

Through the zinc-lined walls, he would hear the latch being shot and pliers at work on a fresh seal, and then he would hear muted laughter followed by the sound of ballast mashed underfoot, and then a motor would grind, race a little, and fade away, and for a long time he would stand deaf, dumb, and blind in the cold and fragrant dark. The floor-slats would begin to tremble now, slightly at first but crescent, and the braying of a locomotive, muffled by the closed doors and the distance, would break the quiet. He would brace himself against the stacked-up crates, and the oncoming car-to-car shock of coupling would reach him and pass by, and then, from the right-of-way alongside, he would hear filtered voices (but would he beat on the walls? would he make an outcry? would he pray? would he try in any way to be saved? or would he think it brave to do nothing?).

The locomotive would bray again, two reverberant longs, and then, backing to shake out slack, it would take the highcar haul out of the siding, and wheel-flanges would scream on the sharp curve leading to transcontinental rail, and now, straightened away, the black power ahead would give tongue once more and dig in for points east (would the sky be dark still, he wondered, or would a risen and smoke-screened sun describe his funeral train on the sand? would all eyes be closed in sleep, or would some have opened to see the shape and fitting color of his coffin—a yellow boxcar? would a single head be bared as he passed, even if only for the wiping of a sweatband, or would he be suffered to go without a last and accidental salute?).

Somewhere on this eyeless journey, he would die. Somewhere between Niland and Yuma (set your watch ahead one hour), between Yuma and Tucson (elev. 2386 ft.), between Tucson and El Paso (set your watch ahead one hour), between El Paso and Paisano (flag-stop to entrain or detrain pay passengers)—somewhere east of the Sink, his timetable would become subject to change without notice, and he would die. A perishable among perishables, only he would not survive the trip: somewhere between two switch-towers, two mileposts, two crossings, two creosoted ties, he would ripen beyond ripeness and start to rot (but what part of the record would he live to review? how much of the westbound history of his people would he pass?).

*[ . . . At a roadside in the lower left-hand corner of America, among the trash of traffic (the rubber scabs, the spring-leaves, the glass and tin, the rusting rinds), a blind squaw stands in the land's-end dust, peddling homemade merchandise to the down-East tourist-trade, the people from the upper right-hand corner of heaven—and now, between a knick-knacked devil in a purple skirt and a Christer with a brass collar-button in his open neckband, a final treaty is in the making, not for Long Island, the Adirondacks, or the state of Maine, but a buckskin doll with wampum eyes. . . .*

*. . . In a hollow on the plain of St. Hyacinth, a shepherd kneeled before a swamp-grass fire, and looking up at faces like paper lanterns against the dark sky, he said, 'Me no Alamo! Me no Alamo . . . !' (All day he had heard the sound of guns. It had come up over the savanna with the dawn and with black smoke, and the sun had seemed to be going down where it rose, and all morning long and all afternoon the guns had spoken and stained the prairie air, and then it was evening, and still from near and far the shepherd could hear the carbines talk to each other across the ravines and the bayous of the San Jacinto, and a wind came with the night, and the ewes were restless, and to quiet them the shepherd ran the risk of a fire, a small one, hardly more than a hat would span, and, flaring up, it died quickly down, but it brought the faces, the paper lanterns, and the embers made them glow, and the shepherd was afraid.) One of them said, 'Remember the Alamo, you greaser son of a bitch!' and the shepherd said, 'Me no Alamo! Me no Alamo!' but they shot him. . . .*

*. . . When he saw them coming along the hedgerow, he knew (because he had dreamed his fear too often not to know) that they were coming for him, yet he made himself straight, and, letting his spade fall, he waited for them among the bright green plants, slowly dusting his dry black hands. They halted an aisle away, and for a moment they stood staring at him in silence, and then the Master said, 'Tell me their names, Jerusalem. Tell me their names, and I'll*

*set you free.' The only sound was the rasping of the rubbed hands, as of leaves in an air, and the Master said, 'Tell me their names, Jerusalem, and tell me where their weapons are hidden. Tell me the sign they were going to use, Jerusalem, tell me the time and the place, and I'll give you freedom-papers and a sack of beans.' There was no sound now, none at all, not even the palm-on-palm whisper of the black hard hands, and the Master said, 'Once more, Jerusalem—the names of those who would have risen against me,' but the black man's mouth stayed mute, and the Master, drawing a whip from his boot, said, 'Spread-eagle him, lads. He'll talk for the lash.' They slung him between two saplings, and he hung there sprawled like a nailed-up pelt, but he spoke no word (or none that was heard on earth), and the Master said, 'One last time, Jerusalem—the names!' and now the black man raised his head and smiled at the whole wide world. It was the smile that the Master went for with the whip, but the black man died still wearing it. It never came off: it was still there when the people from heaven lost count of the strokes; it was still there when the black face was gone; it was still in space, still in the Master's mind when his legs buckled, and he sank down into the soft dirt; it was still before his eyes, still the only thing he could see while he fingered the spattered ground. It never came off. . . .*

*. . . He said, 'Here on this beach, where the sun wakes up from sleep wearing morning, the people from heaven hunt for hell on their knees, and in the end, brothers, they will find it—no longer kneeling, but on wheels, and not in the sand, nor among the trees, nor under the waters and the sky-high hills, but in their own small hearts and their own vast greed. With beads, with looking-glasses, with scissors and vermilion, with nine-day wonders and picayunes, they will quiet your title to the earth, leaving you such estates as your fingernails sequester and the cracks of your toes withhold. You know all this, brothers, yet you yearn to run and greet them, to bow down at their feet, to lap their spittle and clutch at the little they will gladly give you for much. Why, while you still have a world to stand on, do you not*

*kill them, brothers . . . ?'* ]

Dressed as before, but carrying a cotton parasol, the woman came from the house and paused near the soldier, saying, "I have to go uptown for something. I won't be long." Without looking at her, and speaking as if the words were sounding themselves, the soldier said, "Their own small hearts and their own vast greed," and then he shook his head in disengagement, and fact subdued fancy. "I spoke in my sleep," he said.

"You do everything in your sleep," the woman said. "Your whole life's been one long unbroken dream. You won't even wake up to die."

"You hold forth on life and death with much fluency," he said. "What's happened to you? Have you caught my sickness?"

The woman descended the steps and went part of the way to the lane before turning to say, "I think I have, Steve," and then, opening her sunshade, she walked through the hangar of eucalyptus to the glaring street.

The soldier watched her until she was gone.

[ *. . . He said, 'While you still have a world, brothers . . . ,' but it was too late, even then at the beginning. The Christers had it, and for the peppercorns that gold would make, for toothpicks and flagpoles, for jackstraws and ping-pong prizes, they lashed it down with iron rail, ligated its arteries with concrete, invaded its flesh with machinery, broke its bones with cannon-balls, and strangled it with chewing-gum. 'While you still have a world . . . ,' he said, but it was gone as he spoke, and gone too were those who had nothing for the rainy day of death and, dead, went not to heaven big with swag. 'While you still have a world, brothers . . . ,' he said, but it belonged to the shark and the shyster now, to the psalm-singer and the crosser of palms, and Dry Monopole poured from slipper-heels as flippin'-jinnies frenched dollar cigars, and because the ginnies had the picks and the idiot-spoons, the bankers whored in the private cars. . . .* ]

The private cars, the soldier thought, the private cars, and this would be his, numbered but nameless, and one of many that were all the same, with no plush, no brass, no double glass or triple trucks, no awninged platform, no regulated air: it would be an icebox on wheels, dark, vinaigretted, and winter-cold, and it would roll him away over the ballast of broken promises that smothered the promised land [ '. . . *All that they say to you, all that they have promised to you, it was a lie, it was an illusion, it was a cheat, it was a fraud, it was a crime. They promised you liberty. Where is liberty? They promised you prosperity. Where is prosperity? They have promised you elevation. Where is the elevation . . . ?'* ].

In the chemistry of the blood, he thought, in the bone-components and the four dimensions of the mind, in the air and the earth, in the spoken language and the written word, in the waterways and the navigable winds, in the buffalo-grass, in the piled stones of the cities, in the tides and the seasons, in the faces, in the names, in the legends, in the Gods and heroes, in the short history of a headlong race. [ . . . *She said, 'You love this country, don't you, Steve . . . ?'* ] In the corn-dance, he thought, in the Beale Street Blues, in the white steeples and the witches, in the buttes and the Palisades, in the soiled canvas of clipper-built clouds, in the open-hearth abbeys and the leafless forests of the oil-fields, in the jigsaw of the Grand Union, in the lumber-rafts and the stern-wheelers, in the strutting 4-4s and the skating Pacifics, in Marse Linkum, in the chain-gangs and the electric-chairs, like you, Vanzetti—in everything, he thought, in everything! [ '. . . *I dream about it,' you said. 'I dream about it all the time. . . .'* ]

And then once more the dream came to him, rearing from the long-familiar filth and cumbered with the same despair and the same inoperable anguish, but on the miscellany of images and emotions, a superimposition appeared, as faint and transient as steam in the open air—great clean thunderheads, and white water, and trees that were women in the wind—and he heard himself say, "Sweetheart, how much I could have loved you!" and now, exiled and estopped, he began to weep.

A voice said, "Show me your papers, Joe."

The soldier raised his eyes. On the walk before him stood a corporal wearing the chalky rigging and crossed-derringers device of the military police. Nearby but looking at something far away, the woman idly bored into the lawn with the ferrule of her parasol.

"Papers," the corporal said.

The soldier rose. "The ones I have would fool you," he said. "I bought them."

"You're under arrest, then, Joe."

"I've always been."

"Let's hit the road," the corporal said.

The woman overtook them as they entered the lane, but the soldier did not stop when she touched his arm, and she stumbled along beside him, saying, "I had to do it, Steve. I couldn't let you sit there any more. I just couldn't." The soldier said nothing. "I only did what you wanted to do yourself, but you never would've, Steve, never in your life, so I went and did it for you. You see that, don't you, Steve?" The soldier said nothing. "The best you ever could've hoped for was living on the run, hiding, eating your heart out, but the way you're made, you wouldn't have lived very long: you'd have killed yourself. So what I did was right, Steve, and I'll always think so, only it would help a lot to hear you say it." The soldier said nothing. "It wasn't easy, Steve. I had to give up something too, more than you'll ever believe, but we'll make it up some day if you'll only understand. Tell me you do, Steve. Please tell me you do." But the soldier remained silent, and the woman drifted to a stop, saying, "Is that how you're going to go, Steve—without a single word?"

The street was only a few yards away. "Jesus Christ, Joe," the corporal said, "tell her something!"

The soldier looked back. "Thanks," he said, and then he walked on.

# ACKNOWLEDGMENTS

Profound thanks are extended to the following for their generous financial support which helped to defray some of this book's production costs:

Adrian Astur Álvarez, Justin A Baldwin-Bonney,
Thomas Young Barmore Jr, Bob Bason,
Brad Bigelow (NeglectedBooks.com), Matthew Boe,
Timothy Bohman, Brian R. Boisvert, Ian Bowater,
Chris Call, Tobias A Carroll, Scott Chiddister,
Chelsea Clifton, madison jack cockrell, Sheri Costa,
Michael Thomas Costello, Randy and Haley Cox,
Jason Crane, Malcolm & Parker Curtis,
Frank Derfield Jr., Brian Dice, Daniel Dion,
James Duncan, Curtis B. Edmundson, Isaac Ehrlich,
Fred Filios, Steve Fuller, Justin Gallant, John M. Gamble,
Dan Giancola, Robin Gillis, GMarkC, Damian Gordon,
Fernando Boxhoorn Goulart, Dave Griesbach,
Everett Haagsma, Denis S. Hakes, Aric Herzog,
Sam Himmelfarb, Mattie Jacobs, William Jarvis,
Erik T Johnson, Haya K., Margaret Fagan Key,
Larry Kerschner, Paul Kuliev, Kyle,
Brian de León Macchiarelli, Kira MC, Jim McElroy,
Donald McGowan, Michael McGrath,
Dr. Melvin "Steve" Mesophagus, William Messing,
Jason Miller, Kirby Miller, Spencer F Montgomery,
Marcia Morrison, Gregory Moses, Scott Murphy,
Matt "Devilboy" Murray, Irwing Nieto,
Michael O'Shaughnessy, Andrew Pearson, Julie Phillips,
Patrick M Regner, Mike Richards, Rebecca S,

Frank V. Saltarelli, Jason Smith, Michael Snead,
Kelly Snyder, Yvonne Solomon, SpongeBama, K.L. Stokes,
Kate Torgerson, Cato Vandrare, C Wendland,
Paulie Wenger, Christopher Wheeling, Isaiah Whisner,
Charles Wilkins, Jeff Wilson, Chris Wolf, T.R. Wolfe,
and The Zemenides Family

www.ingramcontent.com/pod-product-compliance
Lightning Source LLC
Chambersburg PA
CBHW021151110726
47900CB00002B/515